ON SPINE OF DEATH

TAMARA BERRY

Poisoned Pen
PRESS

Published by Poisoned Pen Press, an imprint of Sourcebooks
P.O. Box 4410, Naperville, Illinois 60567-4410
(630) 961-3900
sourcebooks.com

Printed and bound in the United States of America.
KP 10 9 8 7 6 5 4 3 2 1

Chapter One

TESS KNEW THE EXACT MOMENT THE BLOOD started dripping down her hands.

The frigid air of the cellar where she was trapped had long since caused her skin to grow numb. She couldn't feel the sharp slices of the zip ties digging into her wrists or the thick trickle of blood moving down her fingers, but that didn't matter. As soon as her veins opened up, the enormous, mangy rat in the corner would lift his nose, twitch his whiskers, and come in for a taste.

"Rats!" Tess cried. "I'm going to get eaten by rats!"

Since she'd long since slobbered her way out of the duct tape across her lips, her shout came through loud and clear.

"I'm not kidding," she added, her voice wavering frantically. "He's the size of a terrier. Let me out of here!"

The rustle of approaching footsteps was accompanied by a thump as the cellar door above her head swung open. Tess winced at the sudden brightness of the outside world, which didn't abate even when a head popped down through the hole to block most of the light.

"Ohmigod, Mom. People on the street are starting to ask questions. What's wrong with you?"

Tess felt no relief at the sound of her daughter's voice—or at the sight of the pitch-black, chin-length bob hanging down over her head. "What's wrong with me is that I'm about to be attacked by a rabid animal with a taste for my blood."

"How do you know he's rabid?"

"I don't. But that won't matter to the people at the hospital. Unless we manage to catch him and bring him in to be tested, they'll make me get all thirty rabies shots either way. It's protocol."

Gertrude, who was fifteen going on fifty, wasn't moved by this picture. "Then say it."

Tess screwed up her face and did her best to ignore the squeal of her rodential nemesis crawling closer. "No."

"Mom, you made me promise. I can't let you go you unless you say it."

"I won't."

"Fine. Then I'm getting back to work. Herb is letting me use the sledgehammer."

"A sledgehammer?" she echoed. "To do *what*?"

From upside down, Gertrude's grin looked like a grimace. "We're taking out that old brick wall near the back of the store. You never told me that demolition could be so much fun. He says if we can't get the bricks out this way, we'll have to bring out the big guns."

The head started to disappear before Tess could decide whether or not to ask what *big guns* entailed. In the two weeks since renovations on her grandfather's old hardware store had started, she'd learned it was best not to ask too many questions. Questions led to long-winded tales of asbestos, lead, radon, and other construction horrors that would cost—by Herb's estimation—tens of thousands of dollars to repair.

"Make sure you wear a construction hat," Tess warned.

"Yes, Mom."

"And those cute steel-tipped boots we bought you."

"Stop calling them cute. They're not cute. They're *functional*."

"Fine. Wear your ugly and useful boots. And if you get anywhere near a rusty nail—"

"I'm leaving now," Gertrude interrupted with a snort of disgust. "These bricks aren't going to smash themselves."

In a moment of panic—and, she was willing to admit, desperation—Tess called out once more.

"No! Wait. Leave the trapdoor open a crack. It smells damp down here. I think I can taste mold spores starting to take root on my tongue."

This didn't move Tess's daughter any more than

the threat of rat attacks or rabies had. "That's not how mold spores work." Gertrude said and paused. "Well?"

Tess heaved a sigh. "Fine. Go ahead and abandon me. I'll just stay down here to make a meal for the creepy-crawlies of the world."

"Okay," Gertrude said cheerfully. "Let me know if you change your mind, *Magdalene*."

Tess watched as her daughter closed the trapdoor, once again plunging her into a world of darkness and mold. *Magdalene* was Tess's safe word, but there was no way she was saying it. By her estimation, she'd only been down in the cellar below the hardware store for about an hour. To call it quits after such a lackluster attempt at escape would only prove her daughter right. *And* Ivy *and* Sheriff Boyd *and* everyone else who'd said there was no way Tess could do it.

Take one woman, bound at the wrists by zip ties, and attach her to a chair. Duct tape her mouth, leave her without any tools, and shove her into a convenient hole. Mix and let rest.

"But I wasn't counting on rats," Tess muttered as she started to once again saw her wrists against a sharp edge at the back of the chair. "No one said anything about rats."

Even as she spoke, she knew that the woman in her book—code name Magdalene—would be encountering rats inside her prison. Tess Harrow, renowned thriller writer, was something of a legend when it came to using real-life incidents to fuel her fiction. Her last book, *Fury in the Forest*, had been based on her own experience of finding a dead body in the pond behind the rustic cabin she now called home. The book was already in its sixth printing and showed no signs of flagging.

As she continued sawing, more frantically now, the first band of the zip tie gave way. Tess shouted in triumph, even though the action caused the second band to dig deeper into her flesh. She was going to have some serious zip-tie burn after this, and there was still a good chance that rat would take a bite from one of her fingers, but it was worth it. She'd been *sure* it was possible for a fortysomething, slightly overweight divorcée to escape from the deep underbelly of the criminal world. Not *quickly*, obviously, and not with anything approaching finesse, but those things could be glossed over in the retelling.

"That'll show my editor," Tess said as she began sawing at her hands anew. "You don't have to be Keanu Reeves to escape from a tight spot. With a little persistence, anyone can—"

BOOM!

At the sudden rattling of her prison walls, Tess gave a start of surprise, but she refused to let it derail her. If she knew her daughter—and she did—Gertrude was taking to the sledgehammer like a teenager to, well, a sledgehammer. The steady trickle of dirt from above her head was vaguely alarming, but no more so than any of the other horrors down here.

Tess had no idea what her grandfather had used this cellar for, but there was no denying the creep factor. When they'd first uncovered it from below the ancient linoleum floor they'd peeled up, Tess had half expected it to contain the bodies of her grandfather's enemies. Instead, she'd found a burst of inspiration.

Which, when you thought about it, was just as good.

"Keep it quiet up there!" she called, but without any expectation of being answered. Her shoulders were starting to burn, and the trickle of dirt was starting to turn into a torrent, but she could feel the last of the plastic giving way.

Or rather, she *would* have, if the world hadn't suddenly started shaking around her.

BOOM! BOOM!

"Seriously, you guys! If you're not careful, I'm going to be—"

Her next words died—and were buried—on her lips. So was the rest of her. Amid the avalanche of debris, rocks, and dirt that opened up on top of her, Tess lost her ability to do anything but scream.

And even that was taken away from her before too long.

Being buried alive would do that to a woman. Especially once she realized that dirt wasn't the only thing falling from the ceiling. With a last, desperate gasp of air, Tess found herself being showered with what looked—and felt—like human bones.

She didn't know whether it worse to die of a femur to the head or a lungful of damp, loamy soil, but it didn't matter. As her chair tipped and fell—with her arms still strapped to it—she lost all track of everything except how it felt to be six feet under.

Chapter Two

"I THINK WE SHOULD LEAVE HER TIED UP."

Tess glared from her position on the ground, her hands still bound behind her and the taste of earthworms in her mouth. "Very funny, Sheriff Boyd. If you don't get me out of this cellar right now—"

"You're right." The tall, well-built frame of the sheriff's head deputy, Ivy Bell, crouched next to Tess. "We need to photograph and catalog this evidence before we move her. Hold still, Tess. It'll only take half an hour."

"*Half an hour?*" Tess echoed, but she might as well have not spoken for all the attention the two officers paid her. They were loving this, she knew—she could tell from the slow, methodical way they moved through the rubble that used to be the cellar. *And* from the way Ivy kept telling Tess to smile and say cheese for the camera.

"Relax. These bones are at least thirty years old," Sheriff Boyd drawled. "They can't hurt you."

From her angle on the ground, Tess could only make out the sheriff's scuffed cowboy boots and jeans-clad lower legs, but that didn't matter. She knew down to the dark, silken strands of his hair and the quirk of a cleft palate scar above his lip how he looked. And *not*, as some people might think, because she was particularly interested in him as a person. It was just that he happened to be the spitting image of the fictional detective who'd gotten Magdalene trapped in a cellar in the first place.

Detective Gonzales, who only existed inside the imagination of Tess Harrow and the several million people who'd read her books, would never leave a woman tied up so he could collect evidence. He might be a hard-boiled man of the law, but he was also a *gentleman*.

"They're human, that's for sure," Ivy said as the camera flashed. "I'm guessing they were buried underneath the floorboards, but all that sledge-hammering must have dislodged them."

"You say that like I wanted this to happen," Tess said. She tried to wriggle her way out from under-neath a humerus, but Ivy commanded her to lie still. Tess continued, "It might surprise the two of you to discover that I don't *like* finding dead bodies every-where I turn. Nor do I enjoy having several feet of dirt fall on top of me. I could have suffocated."

Since she'd been nowhere near suffocation—and since both Ivy and Sheriff Boyd knew it—her protests were largely ignored.

"I told you it was too dangerous to start construction on the hardware store without first checking the foundation," Sheriff Boyd said. "My exact words were, and I quote, 'You're likely to bring the whole roof down.'"

"The roof is fine. It's the floor that didn't make it," said Tess.

Ivy released a low whistle as she dropped the last of her evidence markers and snapped a few shots. "And a good thing, too, or we might never have found this poor sap." She paused. "Check out the marks on this rib, Victor. That's a hatchet job if I ever saw one."

Tess called on the last of her strength and thrust her bound wrists against the splintered edge of her chair. To her surprise—and relief—it worked. The plastic, already strained and ground down, gave way. With a cry of thanks, she yanked her hands out of their bonds and twisted her body to examine the bones in question.

Since the bones were literally on top of her, it didn't take long for Tess to see what the sheriff and Ivy were talking about. The bones had been entombed in the floor of her grandfather's hardware store for so long that they no longer held any horror—or any flesh. Tess reached for a scapula only to have her hand smacked away.

"Don't you dare." Ivy spoke with a sharp reprimand

that reminded Tess of a schoolteacher. "Those aren't for you."

"I wasn't going to stick it in my pocket and take it home," Tess protested, but she was careful to give Ivy a wide berth as she flexed her fingers to get the circulation flowing back to them. As she'd suspected, her wrists were raw, and there was dried blood crusted on her fingernails like nail polish. Those were small considerations when compared to the fact that she was standing in the scattered remains of an actual human being. "Who do you think it is? And why was he buried in the floor?"

When neither Sheriff Boyd nor Ivy answered right away, Tess held up both hands.

"Nuh uh. I know what you're thinking, but my grandfather didn't do this. He was a curmudgeonly hermit, but he wasn't a *murderer*." Since it seemed important to point out, she added, "And even if he was, he'd know better than to bury his victim in his own hardware store. That's the fastest way to a jail sentence that I've ever heard of."

"Who's going to jail, and how often can I come visit?" a voice called from above.

All of Tess's interest in the mortal remains of their mystery skeleton vanished at once. Gertrude had been through enough murder and intrigue to last a lifetime; the last thing Tess wanted to do was provide more fodder for her therapist.

"Sheriff Boyd and Ivy are just being dramatic," she called up. "No one is going to jail."

"Not yet, anyway," Ivy murmured. Tess glared so hard that Ivy had to cover whatever else she planned to say with a cough.

"Don't come down, Gertie. I'm heading up." Tess reached for the cellar ladder and was surprised to find Sheriff Boyd waiting to help her. He held the wooden frame with one hand, his other extended to give her a boost.

"Get her out of here, if you can," he said, his voice low. "Even with bones this old, we'll have to call the coroner in."

Tess felt her chest grow tight. No one knew better than Sheriff Boyd how a discovery like this could impact an impressionable teenager. There was a good chance Gertrude would treat it with the cavalier disdain she showed for pretty much anything that revolved around adults, but there was also a chance she'd take it deeply to heart.

"I'll do my best," Tess promised. When the sheriff didn't let go of her hand right away, she hesitated. In the eight months she'd lived in the small, remote town of Winthrop—population of 466—she'd only touched this man a handful of times. They'd solved a murder together and faced immediate peril in each other's arms, but Sheriff Victor Boyd was a man who did things by the book.

In this case, the book said that a recently divorced thriller writer with a penchant for getting herself in trouble was not to be touched—or trusted—lightly.

"What is it?" she asked. "What's wrong?"

His glance fixed on the raw patch of skin around her wrists. "The next time you want to research kidnapping escape methods, I'd appreciate it if you didn't do it underneath a construction site."

Her heart gave a small stutter. "Why, Victor. Are you worried about me?"

He released her hand as quickly as he'd taken it. "Don't be ridiculous. I just don't want to have to deal with the media outcry. The last time you were involved in attempted murder, it took me six weeks to get rid of the reporters."

Getting Gertrude to leave an active crime scene turned out to be an impossible task.

"Are you kidding?" the teenager demanded as the coroner's van rolled up and a pair of blue-uniformed officials stepped out. They had a stretcher behind them, though Tess doubted they'd use it. A dusty collection of bones didn't need a stretcher; a plastic bag would suffice.

"The sheriff doesn't want you here. You'll contaminate the scene."

Gertrude snorted and rolled her eyes. When they'd first moved to Winthrop, Tess's daughter had sported a bright pink head of hair. The midnight-black bob, long on one side and shorn on the other, suited her much better, especially when paired with her ripped black jeans, oversized sweater, and newly pierced septum. If teenage angst had a poster child, Gertrude Harrow was it. Tess thought she was adorable, even if her refusal to leave an active crime scene was not.

"I think the scene is already contaminated," Gertrude pointed out. "Did you see the size of the hole I made in the floor? I didn't even do it on purpose. Herb said there's probably been termites working away at that wood for years."

Tess sighed and glanced at the front of her grandfather's hardware store. The windows had been removed and replaced with temporary plywood, the door pried off its hinges and patched over with the same. As ugly as it looked on the outside, the inside was worse. Apparently, her grandfather had neglected to update any of the infrastructure in his forty years of tenure selling rakes and hoes.

"All old buildings have their problems," Tess said. "You'll see. By the time we're done renovating it, you won't remember what it was like before."

Gertrude's look of disbelief spoke volumes. At this rate, renovations would continue long after

Gertrude graduated from high school. They'd managed to tap into the electricity and water grids out at their cabin easily enough, but transforming a decrepit hardware store into a modern, cozy bookshop was no small undertaking.

Especially if they were going to uncover decades-old bones in the process.

"Please can we stay and watch?" Gertrude clasped her hands in front of her and batted her big, green eyes. "We have to pick a job to shadow for school, and I was thinking about doing mine at the morgue. This is a good way for me to test it out."

"Gertie!"

Those big, green eyes grew even bigger. "What? We're supposed to pick something we're interested in. I'm interested in dead things."

Tess bit back a groan. Of course she was. Gertrude had never taken the easy path. Even as a young child, she'd forged her own way. Why crawl when you could walk? Why walk when you could run? Why run when you could wear your poor mother down until she got you your own bus pass?

"Wouldn't you rather job shadow me?" Tess ventured. "I could teach you all about being a writer."

"Ugh. I already know that. You pretend you need to be tied up and stuffed into a cellar for 'research purposes,' but really you just don't want to work."

This was taking things too far. "What are you

talking about? I work all the time. I wrote a thousand words just this morning."

"You wrote a Yelp review for that new takeout place in Twisp. That doesn't count."

Tess couldn't help but laugh. Lord save her from a too-bright, too-observant teenager with nothing but time on her hands. The school here wasn't very academic. "It was a good review. I have twelve likes already."

"Ohmigod, Mom. They're not called likes, and no one cares about Yelp." Gertrude paused as the two officials from the coroner's office banged and jangled the stretcher through the temporary front door. "So can we stay? I know you worry about me, but I really am interested in this kind of stuff. I either want to job shadow at the morgue or at that taxidermist shop just outside town. Mildred said she'd be happy to have me."

Since the only thing worse than taxidermy was a child who was sure to throw herself wholeheartedly into the arts and crafts of it, Tess gave in. The last time she'd talked to Gertrude's therapist, she'd been informed that it was important to let her daughter decide if and when she was ready to put her past trauma behind her.

Clearly, Gertrude was ready.

"Fine, but we have to stay back. Sheriff Boyd warned us not to get in the way."

"You mean Sheriff Boyd warned *you* not to get in the way," Gertrude said, but she walked with Tess across the street so they could view the events from a safe distance.

Tess wasn't sure how interesting the spectacle was considering they couldn't see inside the building, but Gertrude seemed content enough. Especially once a familiar blue truck pulled up, and their favorite bookmobile librarian popped her head out.

"Are my eyes deceiving me, or is that the coroner's van parked outside your store?"

"Nicki!" Gertrude ran to greet the librarian, her grin wide. "You're just in time. Mom found a skeleton. A dead one."

Nicki Nickerson, a tall woman with skin like gleaming walnut and the kind of looks that belonged in a perfume ad, found nothing strange in this remark. Considering how much of a role she'd played in the last murder Tess had stumbled upon, this was no surprise. There was much more to Nicki than her charmingly eccentric librarian facade let on.

A mind as sharp as a box of tacks, for one thing.

An undercover FBI badge, for another.

Nicki's eyes, hidden behind a pair of cat-eye glasses, met Tess's over the top of Gertrude's head. Even from this distance, Tess could see them dance. "A dead skeleton, huh?" she said. "That sounds exciting."

Tess pulled a face. "The man I hired to demo

the store let Gertie be in charge of the sledgehammer, so of course the first thing she did was bash through the floor. Apparently, the bones have been buried under there for quite some time." As Nicki opened her mouth to respond, Tess rushed on. "And no, my grandfather wasn't a crazed psychotic killer who hid people underneath his place of business. Sheriff Boyd and I have already decided that no one would be that stupid."

Gertrude cleared her throat. "Actually, Sheriff Boyd didn't say that. *You* did."

"That doesn't make it any less true," Tess retorted. "You'll see. It'll probably end up being someone who was there long before Grandpa moved in. The building was first built in the 1800s as a saloon. For all we know, it's some old-timey cowboy the owner shot in a duel."

Gertrude accepted this story with a shout of delight and a plea for her mother to let her cross the street so she could get a better look at the bones. Tess gave in with a sigh and waited only until her daughter was out of earshot before speaking.

"Yes, I know the town's first saloon burned down a hundred years ago," she said, not mincing matters. "And that my grandfather's store was built in the 1970s. Please don't tell Gertrude I lied. The last thing I want is for her to start imagining dead bodies interred underneath every wooden slat."

"*Are* there dead bodies interred underneath every wooden slat?"

Tess sighed. That bit about the hatchet mark on the rib was starting to worry her. "Let's hope not. I'm already in trouble for not having an expert come in to inspect the foundation before I started demolition. I can't imagine the red tape if it turns out I'm sitting on top of a serial killer's trophy room."

Nicki's laughter went a long way to dispel any fears Tess might have harbored on that score. Not only was Nicki an expert on all things Winthrop—the natural outcome of having served as the county's mobile librarian for the past year and a half—but she was an expert on all things murder. Technically, her expertise fell more along the lines of money laundering and other white-collar crimes, but an FBI agent was an FBI agent. Tess was willing to accept her at her word.

"How's our little friend doing today?" Tess asked with a nod in a northward direction. The man Nicki was currently investigating, Mason Peabody, ran a logging operation close to the Canadian border. The company had questionable ties and even more questionable business practices, but building a case against it took time.

"I have no idea what you're talking about," Nicki said with a toss of her head that sent a pair of long, turquoise-studded earrings flying. One of the hallmarks of her undercover persona was to always appear in earrings that would give any other woman a headache. In real life, Nicki dressed much more utilitarian.

Tess was about to apologize for nosing in on official business, but Nicki stopped her with a heavy sigh. "Actually, it's not going well. Ever since the bird flew the coop, I've been struggling to find a foothold."

Tess knew all about that, too. Around the time of the last murder that had rocked this town, Nicki had been close to flipping Mason's brother Zach and getting him to testify against the family business. Mason was one of a set of triplets—Adam, Mason, and Zach—all of whom had inside information on how the money-laundering business was run. Unfortunately, the heightened police activity—not to mention all the reporters nosing around—had spooked Zach into backing down. Nicki had basically been forced to start from square one.

"I'm sorry." Tess winced with ready sympathy. Since she was in large part responsible for all the publicity, she was likewise responsible for Nicki's setback. "If you need my help, let me know. I can do just about anything, even if it's only to spitball ideas."

Nicki cast a shrewd glance at her. "Actually, that's not half bad."

Tess immediately perked. As much as she

enjoyed planning and solving fake crimes, the real thing was a lot more exciting. "Really? Because I have some thoughts about how you might—"

Nicki held up a hand and laughed. "Oh, no you don't. You forget that I've read all your books. Your way of solving crimes is to have your detective hero commit twelve more felonies in the process."

"Nicki!" Tess protested, stung. "I thought we were friends."

"We *are* friends. Which is precisely why I'm asking you to keep your spitballing on the page where it belongs." She paused. "There might be something else you can do for me, though."

Sounds of commotion across the street prevented Tess from asking what that something was. Instead of rolling the stretcher out the door, the medics had folded it up and were carrying it lengthwise. Sheriff Boyd followed behind them with a black body bag slung over one shoulder.

"Aw, man." They could hear Gertrude's shout of disappointment from across the street. "You already picked him up."

"Sorry, kid. Biohazard." The sheriff grinned at the teen in a way that released a surge of conflicting emotions in Tess's breast. She appreciated that the sheriff took a paternal interest in her daughter—especially now that her ex was out of the picture—but in all their time together, he'd never smiled at *her* like that. "I thought I told your mom to clear you out of here."

"You did." Gertrude skipped along the sidewalk next to him. "But she's easy to wrap around my finger. Mom guilt is a powerful thing."

"I can hear you, you know," Tess called.

Both Gertrude and Sheriff Boyd ignored her, so Tess had no qualms about dashing across the street and ducking inside her store. The scene that awaited her was one of extreme disorder. The walls and floors, already stripped bare to make way for the renovations, were further upset by a huge, splintered hole where Tess planned to put in a gourmet coffee bar.

Even at this stage in the construction process, she wasn't sure what had prompted her to transform her grandfather's old hardware store into a small-town bookshop. She didn't have time to run a store on her own, and the local tourist trade was more interested in exploring the great outdoors than spending sleepy afternoons looking for something to read, but neither of those had stopped her from throwing everything she had into the project.

"Staying busy is a healthy way to get through a rough patch," her therapist had said. "You can slow down and reflect once you're more emotionally detached from what happened."

"You just want to put my poor library bookmobile out of business," Nicki teased.

"She's procrastinating," Gertrude refuted them both.

Of all of them, Tess suspected Gertrude was the most accurate. It wasn't that she *needed* to be embroiled in a crime in order to write a book, but there was no denying it helped. Her last book had been a struggle to put on the page until real life had intervened with a plot, a twist, and a handy villain all in one package. Now that life was settling down and spring was turning the entire forest into something out of a fairy tale, the words were drying up—as the five frantic emails from her editor demanding to know how far she was on the next Detective Gonzales book could attest.

"It ain't my fault." A tall, angular man who was at least seventy years old emerged from the wreckage, a scowl on his face and a tool belt hanging heavily from his hips. Herb looked every inch of what he was—a local handyman who charged exorbitant rates and worked at a snail's pace. "I didn't know the whole floor was gonna cave. You didn't tell me the whole floor was gonna cave."

Tess could hear Ivy snort in derision underneath her feet.

"I didn't *know* the whole floor was going to cave," Tess pointed out. "I wouldn't have tied myself to a chair in the cellar if that had been the case."

Herb shook his head and clucked a disapproving

tongue. "That's just it. I don't hold with women being kidnapped and held in the cellar. Even if they do enjoy that kind of nonsense."

Ivy snorted louder.

"I don't enjoy it," Tess tried explaining. "It's for realism. Unless I know the heart-stopping fear of being trapped in a dark, confined space with my hands bound to a chair, how can I accurately describe it?"

"That's another thing I don't hold with."

"What? Hands-on research? Realism in fiction?"

Herb shook his wizened head. "Ladies writing about murder. It ain't right."

Tess didn't have to defend herself. Ivy was more than ready to do it for her. The deputy's head, complete with the tight knot of her hair at the base of her skull and a look of disapproval lighting her steely gray eyes, popped up through the floorboards. "Herb, you're a small-minded old fool, and you always have been. Why can't a woman write about murder? Or anything else she wants to, for that matter?"

Since Ivy had recently sold her own sci-fi novel at an auction that put several of Tess's early advances to shame, her rage was understandable. Especially since someone died on just about every other page of her manuscript.

"I never had a floor cave underneath me before," Herb said.

"What does that have to do with the price of eggs?" Ivy demanded.

"Well, now." Herb rubbed a slow hand along his jawline. "The way I see it, this lady here is cursed. First, she came into town and dragged a whole lot of murderers with her."

"One," Tess interrupted, nettled. She wasn't cursed; she was unlucky. It was different. "I dragged *one* murderer, and it was hardly my fault."

Herb didn't pay her the least heed. "Then she starts tearing this old building down, and what happens? She locks herself up in a basement and rains bones down upon her head."

"Technically, you were the one who rained them down on me. The floor was perfectly intact when I went down there."

Herb began unbuckling his tool belt in a way that sent a spasm of alarm through Tess. She'd never worked with anyone as slow as him, and he had yet to haul away even one scrap of the wood, drywall, and brick that was starting to build an alarming pile out behind the store, but she needed him. Manual labor had never been her strong suit, and she could hardly leave the building exposed like this for long. There was a tarp covering the back door, for crying out loud.

"I can't work under these conditions," Herb said, his lips thin and his voice flat.

"Wait. I'm sorry, Herb. I promise not to tie myself

up while you're here. Or to write about murder until you're done. I'll focus only on the transition scenes for now."

It was too late. She could have promised to pen a quirky beach read and deck herself out in four-leaf clovers, but it wouldn't have done the least bit of good. Tess knew a determined curmudgeon when she was looking at one. This town was practically teeming with them.

"I quit," Herb said as he dropped the tool belt to the floor.

The weight of it—hammers and screwdrivers and the half-eaten tuna sandwich that had served as Herb's lunch—thumped onto the boards with so much force that Tess could hear the floor give way long before she saw it happen.

To the best of her knowledge, there was nothing underneath that part of the store except dirt and concrete, but that was more than enough to send a rattling cloud of debris into the air. Much to her dismay, she screamed out loud, but not before she caught sight of where the tool belt landed.

There, underneath the remains of Herb's lunch, sat another pile of bones.

And this time, they looked a heck of a lot fresher.

Chapter Three

"LADY, YOU MUST BE OUT OF YOUR MIND IF YOU think I'm going anywhere near that project."

"Are you kidding? *That* murder palace?"

"Aren't you the author who kills people and then writes books about it? Thanks but no thanks. I like my head where it is."

"Tess, I'm your agent, not your personal assistant. If you want me to go to battle with your publisher, I'm more than happy to pick up the phone and get to work. But finding you a handyman isn't part of our arrangement."

Of all the phone calls Tess made in a fruitless attempt to find a contractor—*any* contractor— willing to repair the damage wrought by a team of deputies tearing up every single floorboard in every single square inch of her grandfather's hardware store, the last one stung the most.

"But Nancy, I'm desperate." Tess paused at the threshold to the store, her heart sinking deeper the longer she stood staring at it. After the second body had been recovered, Sheriff Boyd had ordered his whole team to search the place from top to bottom. It had taken three days, and although they didn't uncover any more human remains, they *did* find a family of opossums in the rafters. That was enough to fuel Tess's nightmares for weeks. "No one will touch the place. Not only is it a disaster zone, but everyone is afraid to come near me. They think I'm a murderer."

"*Are* you a murderer?" Nancy inquired politely.

"No, but it's starting to look as though dear old Grandpa might have been." Tess sighed and shifted her cell phone to the other ear. "The good news is, I'm writing again. Detective Gonzales just found the bones of a long-dead corpse underneath his father's ice-cream shop. He suspects someone planted it there to frame him."

That perked her agent right up.

"Good. Use that. Dig deep. If you can promise me another headline to tie in like the last one, I might even be able to bump the advance."

"But I don't want more money," Tess protested. "I want someone to clean this mess up. Tell the publisher to send me a young, strapping handyman who isn't afraid of a few crusty old bones, and I'll write whatever they want."

"Look on Craigslist like a normal person, Tess. There's nothing I can do from three thousand miles away."

Tess sighed as she hung up the phone. It had been a long shot, but desperate times called for desperate measures. And these times were desperate, there was no doubt about it. Although she hadn't been allowed to stay in the shop while Ivy and Sheriff Boyd had pulled out the second body, she'd seen the hatchet marks all the same. That was bad news no matter which way you spun it.

"I swear, the next time someone unloads dead bodies on a property of mine, I'm going to…" She trailed off as a vision appeared before her. A vision—or a miracle. She was having a hard time deciding which.

Against all odds and Nancy's refusal to help, Tess found herself facing a handyman. And not just any handyman, either. This was one was young and— there was no use denying it—*strapping*.

"I couldn't help overhearing your phone call," the man said, grinning so deeply that dimples appeared in both his cheeks. "Does this mean the contractor position is still available?"

Tess cast a swift glance up and down the bare, dusty main street, sure this must be part of an elaborate prank. Everywhere she looked, Wild West kitsch greeted her eyes. The area surrounding Winthrop, Washington, was known for its mountain biking and cross-country skiing opportunities, but the town itself leaned hard into its reputation as a cowboy outpost.

The handyman obviously subscribed to the same aesthetic. Tess had never come face-to-face with a real cowboy before, but this man had the look locked down. His jeans were worn and faded, held up by a belt buckle the size of a salad plate. His boots were dusty and spurred, his shirt a tight-fitting flannel open one too many buttons at the top. Tess knew that for a fact because she couldn't look away from the wide vee of skin and hair peeking up at her. She hadn't even known is was possible for a human being to have muscles there.

Dragging her eyes up to meet his gaze, she only grew more flustered. The man, his ethereal blue eyes glinting, knew *exactly* what she was thinking.

"You're here for the contractor job?" she managed.

He tipped his cowboy hat to reveal a crop of curls that would have done a golden retriever proud. "If you'll have me. This is the address, right? 122 Main Street? Soon-to-be home of the Paper Trail?"

Tess was instantly on her guard. She hadn't told many people the name she'd chosen for her once and future bookstore, for the same reason that parents-to-be jealously hoarded baby names. She didn't want anyone to steal it. A writer-owned bookstore in a Wild West–themed town *had* to be called the Paper Trail. It was just plain common sense.

"What did you say your name was?" she asked, taking a wary step back. Considering the number of bodies that had been uncovered in this town recently, she wasn't about to lower her guard. She didn't *see* a hatchet, but that didn't mean he wasn't carrying one on the sly.

"Oops. My bad." The man held out a hand. "I'm Jared. Jared Wright. It's nice to meet you."

Instead of taking the man's hand, Tess stared at it. One of her greatest skills in life—and, if you asked Gertrude, one of her most annoying traits—was her ability to note every detail about a person and commit it to memory. The man's outward appearance was convincing, it was true. His clothes looked well-worn and -washed. His boots had obviously tread through many a byre, and there was a convincing scruff of a beard along his jaw.

But if those hands had ever touched so much as a hammer, Tess would eat the hat off his head. She'd never seen such soft skin on a grown man before.

"I'm sorry, but the position has been filled." She cast another quick glance around the street to find it just as deserted as before. Too late, she remembered that Gertrude had mentioned a high school basketball game today. With a shortage of other entertainments in the offing, the whole town had a tendency to show up in full Mountain Lion green to enjoy the spectacle. "I already hired someone. He's inside."

Jared's face fell to a comical degree. "Really? That's not what I was told. When did you hire him?"

"This morning," Tess lied, backing up even more. If she could make it inside the building, she might be able to push over the pile of rubble to block the door. She could escape out the tarp in the back, or maybe even reach her cell phone and get a call for help out before he attacked. "I couldn't say no. He's very tall and strong. *And* he carries a gun."

"If that's something you require, then I've got it covered." Jared leaned down and yanked up the leg of his jeans. They fit tightly, but not so tightly he couldn't flash the piece strapped to his ankle in a black holster. "I always carry heat on the job."

That did it. A gun might not be as much of a clincher as a hatchet, but Tess wasn't taking any chances. Before the man had a chance to pull the gun out and shoot her—or worse—she turned on her heel and fled. She might have gotten away, too, only she hadn't accounted for the man's agility. In one flying tackle, he dashed across the space between them. Hitting the back of her thighs with a thump, he landed his whole body on top of her, pinning her to the dirt.

"There's nothing to worry about," he growled, his mouth pressed hard against her ear. "I've got you now."

———

It took Tess exactly six-point-six seconds to reverse their positions.

One of the perks of being a writer of crime thrillers was that Tess had spent many an afternoon learning the details of self-defense. She knew—and had practiced—getting out of almost every offensive attack that existed. Standing strangles, leg chokes, a knife at the throat...you name it, and Tess knew the moves to escape it. Being trapped underneath a two-hundred-pound man wasn't the easiest position to get out of, but she had the element of surprise on her side.

With a twist of her body, she wriggled until she was supine underneath Jared. His hips bore down on hers as he struggled to figure out what she was doing. That was when she struck. Wrapping her legs tightly around his waist, she rolled her body with every ounce of strength she possessed. Caught off guard, he had no choice but to roll with her.

Now Jared Wright was the one pinned underneath *her*—and she intended to keep things that way. Lifting her arms without a care for what she was doing, she came at him. Hands, nails, and fists flew as she rained them down on his face.

"You picked the wrong person," she said as she struck a particularly hard blow to his cheek. "Tess Harrow doesn't go down without a fight."

"Wait! Stop!" Jared's arms came up to cover his face.

"Not so fun to attack a defenseless woman now, is it?" she said. Instinct warned her to get up and run away, but she couldn't help thinking about his gun. The last thing she wanted was to leave him free to shoot her in the back as she fled. "Maybe you'll think twice next time."

"I give!" he cried. "I surrender! Someone help!"

Tess barely had time to register these remarks before she was being lifted bodily from Jared's chest. She was panting and half-feral by this point, but that didn't stop this newcomer from wrapping his arms tight around her torso and holding her tight. Matters weren't helped any when she recognized the familiar scent of evergreen and peppermint, accompanied by the drawling, semi-sarcastic voice of Sheriff Boyd.

"Okay, Tess. That's enough. Leave the poor man alone."

"Poor man?" she echoed, her whole body wriggling as she tried to get free. It didn't work. Whatever else she might say about Sheriff Boyd, the man was *strong*. "He's the one who came after me—and in the broad light of day. I was defending myself."

To her surprise, the sheriff chuckled—and in such a way that her whole body shook with his. That, more than anything else, caused the fight to drain out of her.

"And I think you succeeded. Look."

He set Tess gently on the ground and gestured at her attacker. Blood trickled from the man's nose and welled up in bright dots from a scratch along the side of his face. He panted heavily as he struggled to get his breath, his whole body covered in dust. Already, Tess could make out the faint outline of a bruise forming along his jaw.

"He has a gun," Tess informed the sheriff. "Right ankle holster. It looked like 9mm handgun, but I can't be sure. He claims his name is Jared Wright, but it could be an alias. You might want to check his driver's license."

The sheriff paused and glanced down at the man. "Any of that true?"

"Yes, but I have a permit for the weapon, and all my identification is back at the hotel." Jared struggled to a seated position. Instead of taking offense at having been beaten by a woman half his size, he put a hand up to shield his eyes and grinned at Tess. "Those were some moves, lady. Where did you learn all that? An MMA octagon?"

Tess wanted to hold on to her anger, but she couldn't help feeling flattered. No one had ever accused her of having martial arts training before. "Don't be absurd," she said, flustered. "I took a few self-defense courses, that's all."

Jared accepted the handkerchief the sheriff held out to him and pressed it to his nose. He shook his head when it came away bloodstained. "You've got an arm, I'll give you that." He nodded at Sheriff Boyd. "Thanks for coming to my rescue. For a minute there, I was afraid she planned on killing me."

"She did," the sheriff said dryly. He helped Jared to his feet. "You're lucky I showed up in time to stop her. What'd you do to set her off?"

"Nothing. One minute, we were standing here chatting about my job application, and the next, she was running away like she'd just seen a bear. I thought she was in trouble, so I threw myself on top of her to protect her."

Tess could only stare at the man.

"That was when she turned on me," Jared said as one making a rueful confession.

"A bear?" Tess demanded. "Turned on you? Sheriff, if you don't arrest this man at once, I'm calling Ivy and making her do it for me. He knew the name of my bookstore even though I haven't told it to anyone, and then he flashed his gun at me in a menacing way. Plus, his hands are as untouched as a baby's backside. What was I supposed to think?"

The sheriff rubbed a slow hand along his jaw. "You're calling it the Paper Trail. People are constantly flashing their guns at you—usually in self-defense—and what the *devil* do his hands have to do with anything?"

"Wait—what?" Tess felt a ping of disappointment. "How'd you know the name of my bookstore?"

"Because you mention it every time I come within a ten-foot radius of you, that's how. Look, Mr. Wright— I'm sorry about this. I understand if you want to press charges, but I don't recommend it. This woman has more lawyers than a Harvard class reunion."

"I do not. I have a Stanford amount, at the very most."

Jared choked on a laugh. The sound encouraged Sheriff Boyd to continue along these lines. "She'll also have bail posted within the hour, so it's not like it'll be any use," he said. "You're better off making peace with it—and with her. Tess is known as a bit of an oddity around here."

"I beg your pardon," Tess protested, but it was no use. The two men had already moved on.

"Oh, I know all about Ms. Harrow. Nicki put in a full report." Jared handed the blood-spattered handkerchief back to the sheriff. "She *did* tell you I'd be coming, right? Is it too late for me to replace the other guy you hired?"

"Nicki?" Tess echoed. "What does she have to do with anything?"

Jared cast a quick look around before stepping close. Tess might have felt alarmed at the proximity if not for the way Sheriff Boyd stiffened next to her. An oddity she might be, but she knew she was safe as long as he was around.

As soon as Jared decided that the coast was clear, he lowered his voice to a near-whisper.

"I'm the agent they sent to help her nail Mason Peabody," he said as he stuck out his bloodied, baby-soft hand. "And from what I understand, you—and your contractor position—are going to be my cover."

Chapter Four

"Jared?" Nicki stared at Tess from across the hand-hewn wood table that sat in the middle of the main room of her cabin.

When Tess and Gertrude had first moved out here, this cabin had been a rustic outpost, free of anything approaching modernity. Now that they'd been living here for eight months, it felt more like a home—mostly because Gertrude's belongings were scattered about. Nothing updated a space like baskets overflowing with replacement chargers and biology textbooks scattered at random. Even the highly polished shotgun above the door seemed more cheerful after Gertrude had draped a pride flag over the top.

"Are you kidding me?" Nicki continued. Her face was starting to show serious signs of strain, a vein that Tess had never noticed before pulsing in her forehead. "*That's* who they sent? *That's* the hot-shot agent they promised me?"

"So he wasn't making it up?" Tess asked. "Jeez, Nicki. I thought he was here to murder me. A heads-up would've been nice."

Nicki yanked herself out of the chair and began pacing the length of the room. "I should have seen this coming. I know how they operate. I know what their priorities are."

Tess didn't respond. She knew a rant when it was shaking the floorboards underneath her.

"Do they have any idea how difficult it is to build a case against a man like Mason Peabody?" Nicki continued. "He was almost elected sheriff of this county, for crying out loud. That's how entrenched he is in the community around here."

Tess knew. The election had taken place last November, the race a close one until Sheriff Boyd had solved the murder case that Tess had practically dumped in his lap. The fame it carried had done wonders for voter turnout. Sheriff Boyd might not be willing to admit it, but he had a lot to thank her for.

"Which is why I asked them to send me Krueger. Or Imani. Or even Francis, though he'd have stood out around here even worse than I do." Nicki turned on her heel and continued stomping. She made so much noise that even Gertrude, buried deep in the recesses of her headphones, popped a head out of her room to see what was happening. "But, no. They send me Jared Wilson. Jared Wilson!"

Tess waved Gertrude back into her room and attempted to calm her friend down. "He seemed nice enough to me. I mean, I didn't love being tackled for no reason, and there's something seriously wrong with his hands, but he took everything in good humor. Even Sheriff Boyd says he didn't seem so bad."

Nicki turned to glare at her. It wasn't often that Tess saw the other woman in anything but a state of easy-going good humor, so she felt a quaver of fear. The Nicki who worked for the FBI—the one who was single-handedly tracking a millionaire logger and his empire of corruption—was someone to be feared.

"Jared Wilson—Wright, Wrong, whatever it is he's calling himself for this cover—is no more equipped to handle a man like Mason Peabody than you are."

"Hey!" Tess felt compelled to protest, but it was no use.

"The only reason he's even in the FBI is because his daddy pulled some strings. He got kicked out of Quantico two times. *Two times*, Tess. Think about that. They decided more than once that he wasn't fit for duty. Yet he keeps getting promoted, keeps getting placed on high-profile cases where nine-tenths of the work has already been done for him. Do you know what we call that?"

Tess did. Privilege, nepotism, gross negligence—Nicki had her pick.

"So what do you want me to do?" Tess asked. "I can refuse to hire him, but he already started moving the bricks out of the alleyway. I think he might actually end up coming in handy."

Nicki's only response was to fall back into her chair. Tess knew that her position as best friend to an undercover FBI agent was to take Nicki's side and promise to do anything in the name of justice, but she was in a fix here.

"No one else will come near the store," Tess begged. "You know how people are. One murder scandal, and they think you're interesting. Two, and all of a sudden you're the town pariah. Maybe I can just keep him long enough to get the rubble cleared out."

Nicki dropped her head to the table, but Tess wasn't fooled. That thump was the sound of capitulation.

"He's not a puppy," Nicki muttered. "You don't get to adopt him for a few months before taking him back to the pound."

"Nicki, how dare you? I'd never take a puppy back to the pound."

Nicki's low chuckle shook the table. "Don't say I didn't warn you. When I suggested to my superiors that you might be able to provide a cover story for another agent to come up here, I thought I was doing you a favor. I was wrong. Jared isn't a favor; he's an idiot."

"An idiot who can carry heavy things is okay by me," Tess said. She paused. "If we're being honest, he's not so bad on the eyes, either."

Nicki's head shot up. "Don't you dare, Tess. I absolutely forbid it."

"And when he was pinned between my legs, I could almost swear—"

"Ohmigod, Mom. If you say one more word about a strange man between your legs, I'm going to move into the hardware store and live with the skeletons." Gertrude, who'd come into the room without making a sound, rolled her eyes as far as they could go. "Adults are so gross."

"And skeletons aren't?"

"Ask me that question again tomorrow." Gertrude moved toward the kitchen with two empty mugs in her hand. Tess swore that no matter how many times she cleared out the teenager's room, the empty plates and cups multiplied by the dozens. It was like living with a feral-rat child.

"What happens tomorrow?" Nicki asked.

Tess cleared her throat. "School, I hope."

"Yes, Mommie Dearest." Even though Gertrude spoke with heavy sarcasm, there was a light in her eyes that was impossible to ignore. "But my job shadowing starts at three, so don't expect me home until after dinner."

"Wait. That's starting already?"

"Technically, we don't have to go until next month, but I don't want to miss any of the good parts. Tommy beat me to the taxidermy shop, but when I told the coroner who I was, she jumped at the chance to have me. Ms. Sylvie is great. Did you know you don't have to be a doctor to cut dead people open? You only have to have a certificate. It's not like you can kill someone when they're already dead."

Tess knew it behooved her, as an involved and loving parent who only wanted what was best for her daughter, to put up a fight. There were too many potential horrors in a place like the morgue, too many ways for Gertrude's life to be irrevocably altered.

But when she spoke, it wasn't to berate the girl.

"Gertie, do you have any idea what this means?"

Gertrude grinned. When she smiled like that, the sunshine radiating as if out of her soul, Tess knew that nothing in the world could be as bad as it seemed. "It means you have an inside man at the morgue. Don't worry, Mom. I'll take lots of notes. We'll figure out who killed those people in no time."

"That bit about the hatchet has been bothering me."

Tess breezed into the sheriff's office without bothering to stop at the reception desk. These days, she was such a familiar sight that none of the deputies tried to stop her.

"Tess, how many times do we need to have this discussion? You are not now, nor have you ever been, a member of my force."

Tess waved the sheriff off and threw herself into

the chair on the opposite side of his desk. She wasn't fooled by Sheriff Boyd's scowl or demeanor—both of which threatened a mood of melodramatic proportions. How could she when a bowl of stale caramel candies sat within reach? As they happened to be her favorite thing—the staler, the better—she knew she'd been expected.

"I can't quite put my finger on why, but I'm working on it." Tess took one of the candies and popped it into her mouth. "And before you say anything, I'm talking about something big. I don't mean any of the usual implications."

The sheriff fell for the bait...just like she knew he would.

"And what, if you don't mind my asking, are the usual implications?"

"Oh, you know." Tess waved an airy hand. "That for a hatchet to dig that deep into the bone, there needs to be an excessive amount of force—a *male* amount of force. Or that it's virtually impossible to match the microscopic striations of a particular hatchet to the markings on the bone, so your chances of finding the murder weapon are slim."

The sheriff heaved a sigh and set aside the paper he'd been filling out. Pulling off the glasses that had been perched on the end of his nose, he fixed his gaze on Tess. "Have you been reading forensic textbooks again?"

Tess grinned. "Nicki hooked me up with a slew of them. You have no idea how handy it is to have a librarian as a best friend."

"The sooner that woman finishes what she came here to do and leaves, the better," Sheriff Boyd muttered.

Of all the possible things he could have said to Tess, that one hurt the most. She lived in constant dread of the day Nicki nailed Mason Peabody and returned to her office in Seattle—not because Mason deserved to go free, but because Tess's life was all the richer for having a close female friend in it. Ivy made an acceptable alternate, but life in Winthrop wouldn't be the same without the cheerful rattle of the blue bookmobile.

"That's not the point," Tess said, doing her best to push her feelings deep down. The arrival on the scene of Undercover Jared didn't bode well for the chances of this case dragging out much longer, but a woman could hope. Maybe all that nepotism would end up making things worse.

"And what is the point?"

Tess shook her head. "There's something off about this case. The first body—the old one— had thirty-seven hatchet marks. That's a crime of passion if I ever saw one. But the second body only had three. Either the killer got a heck of a lot better at murder, or it's a totally different crime."

The sheriff glanced sharply at her. She reached for another caramel, but he tugged the bowl out of her reach.

"How do you know how many hatchet marks they found?" he demanded.

"I have insider information," Tess said, breezing casually over the truth. The reality—that an excited series of texts from Gertrude demonstrated her daughter's deep and disturbing enthusiasm for her new job at the morgue—would only make him take away her caramels for good. She sneaked one while he was distracted. "Have you made any headway on identifying who the bodies belong to?"

"Why would I tell you that?"

"Because if you do, I'll put you in contact with my hatchet expert. If anyone can tell you something about the marks, he can."

The sheriff did a double take. He didn't *want* to ask a follow-up question, but some things were more important than pride. Curiosity was one of them.

"Why the devil do you have a hatchet expert?"

"Well, he's not technically mine. I haven't needed one—that's one of the few types of murder that Detective Gonzales hasn't come across. *Yet.*"

The sheriff pinched the bridge of his nose. "Yet?"

"I'm calling my new book *Fury under the Floorboards.* It's got a real Edgar Allan Poe edge to it. I'm thinking about taking things a little darker than I usually do."

His only response was a groan.

Tess ignored it. "Which is what I'm trying to tell you. My hatchet expert is a writer friend of mine. He does *real* horror—buckets of blood, talking cars, the whole deal. I know he's done quite a bit with hatchets in the past. I could give you his info, if you want."

Sheriff Boyd stood up with a start. "I've heard enough."

"But you'll like him!" Tess also got up, but not before first taking a few more of the caramels for the road. "He's not like me at all. He's exceptionally meticulous with his research."

"More meticulous than tying himself up in a physically unstable cellar while construction takes place overhead? Thanks but no thanks."

Tess flushed. She really wished people would stop harping on that. It wasn't like she'd *wanted* to have the floor cave in on her. "I mean he personally took several different kinds of tools to a dead cow that he bought for the sole purpose of hacking to pieces. The bone saw was particularly interesting. You might have read some of his work. He's published in *Forensic Magazine*."

The sheriff swiveled his head to stare at her. "You're friends with Peter Oblonsky?"

Tess beamed. "So you *have* heard of him."

"Of course I've heard of him. I don't live under a rock."

"I'll call him as soon as I get home. You two will have lots to talk about."

"Tess, don't—" the sheriff began, but his voice faltered about halfway. Something almost like a boyish smile touched his lips. "You don't think he'd mind? Talking to me, I mean?"

Tess had thought, when she'd first met Sheriff Boyd, that nothing could have been more delightful than finding out he'd read all her books—and that, however unwilling he was to admit it—he liked them. She'd been wrong.

"You're blushing," she said.

"I am not."

"You love him."

"Stop being ridiculous."

"You *respect* him."

The sheriff cleared his throat in a way that fooled neither of them. "His research on the effect of atmospheric pressure on ballistic trajectories is groundbreaking. Of course I respect him."

"So you'll tell me who the victims are?" Tess asked. If she was going to start flashing her author friends around like a security badge, she might as well get something out of the deal. "It's only fair."

"Why do you want to know so much?" the sheriff asked, faltering.

"Because my grandfather's reputation is on the line. Because the taint of murder will doom my bookstore before it opens its doors." She thought, but didn't add, *because I need to know what Detective Gonzales is going to do next.*

He heaved a sigh before reaching for a manila folder on his desk. "It wasn't difficult to identify them. The dental records were a quick match."

Tess tried not to appear too eager as she flipped the file open and scanned the pages. She wasn't surprised to find that the first victim—she of the thirty-seven hatchet wounds—had been young and pretty. Crimes of passion often focused on those two particular attributes above all else. Annabelle Charles, twenty-three, had been a missing person since 1988. Too long ago to be front-page news, but not long ago enough for the pain of her loss to have been fully eradicated.

The second body, however, gave her a shock.

"Lucretia Gregory?" she asked. "Wait. Isn't that the name of the hiker who—?"

The sheriff nodded. Any of the enthusiasm he'd felt at being introduced to Peter Oblonsky had disappeared, leaving only the grim face of a man who'd seen more than his share of death in this life.

"The hiker who went missing from these woods five years ago?" His voice was curt. "Bingo."

Tess swallowed heavily. She didn't know a lot about that particular story, but a missing hiker was the sort of thing that lingered in a small town like this one. From what she understood, Lucretia had been trying to re-create the Reese Witherspoon *Wild* experience right here in the Methow Valley backwoods. Only instead of getting great legs and a six-figure book deal out of it, Lucretia had vanished and never been heard from again.

"She didn't get lost," Tess said, more to herself than to the sheriff. "She was killed and buried in my grandfather's hardware store."

"Looks that way."

"He didn't do it," Tess said, though she had no basis for such a claim. With the exception of dear Grandpa's reclusive curmudgeon ways and his lack of real estate upkeep, she hadn't known him very well. For all she knew, he was a werewolf who stalked those woods under the light of the full moon. "What possible reason could he have for doing such a thing?"

"The same reason anyone has. Pride, greed, lust, envy, gluttony, wrath, or sloth. Take your pick."

Tess wished she had a snappy comeback, but the sheriff wasn't wrong. Every thriller writer worth her salt knew that in order to make a plot convincing, there had to be a reasonable motivation for murder. With the possible exception of psychopaths—or werewolves—very few crimes strayed from the norm.

And as much as she hated to admit it, two dead

women buried under her grandfather's floor were about as *norm* as you could get.

"I'll call Peter as soon as I have a free moment," Tess promised as she heaved her bag over her shoulder and turned to leave. All of a sudden, the excitement of the chase had grown uncomfortably flat. "And you'll keep me posted about the rest? I hate to ask too much of my contact at the morgue."

"It's Gertie, isn't it?" the sheriff asked with a shake of his head. "No, don't try to lie. I should have known better. If I was half the detective I pretend to be, I'd have put two and two together the moment I handed over a reference letter."

Tess couldn't help but laugh. "She asked you for a reference?"

He grunted in irritation but a smile played about the corners of his mouth. "When has anyone in your family *asked* for anything? She demanded, Tess, and I, like a fool, gave it to her."

Chapter Five

"Isn't an undercover agent supposed to be more...undercover?"

Tess sat on a lawn chair in front of the boarded-up window of her grandfather's hardware store, a pen and a pad of paper in hand. She was ostensibly plotting out the next few chapters of her novel, but she mostly wanted to be on hand in case any new bodies turned up. Even though the deputies had been over this place with UV lights and tweezers, she wasn't taking any chances. Any minute now, she expected Jared to uncover a bloody hatchet lodged in a beam.

Jared paused in the middle of lifting a stack of lumber that weighed as much as she did, a comical frown crossing the handsome—and slightly bruised—lines of his face. "You don't think this is cutting it?" He glanced down at himself. "I asked the guy at the feed store, and he said these pants are all the rage in the construction world. They have loops and pockets for everything. Look how many hammers I'm carrying."

Tess had to fight a giggle. He was, in fact,

carrying a total of three hammers, all of which swung perilously near his…hammer. Not that he seemed the least bit worried about a workplace injury—or about anything, really. He'd been here since six o'clock in the morning with a whistle on his lips and showed no signs of flagging. Tess defied anyone to find a more cheerful and dedicated contractor.

"No, you look good," she said. Honesty and all those rippling muscles compelled her to add, "Great, actually. No one would think to question your authenticity."

It was true. Nicki might have a problem with this man's ways and means of operating within the confines of the FBI, but there was no denying his commitment to his wardrobe. Like the cowboy clothes he'd donned that first day, his thick work pants and sweat-stained T-shirt looked as though they'd been worn—and worn hard—for months. Tess knew enough about forgery to recognize a master. With those kinds of skills, she was pretty sure Jared could whip up an authentic-looking Declaration of Independence overnight.

"Then what's wrong?" Jared asked. "Is it my accent? My work ethic? Please don't say it's my hands again. I've been rubbing them with sandpaper every night, but you can't build calluses overnight."

There was no stopping the giggle this time. It

felt light and airy, especially when Jared joined in. Tess couldn't remember the last time she'd giggled with *anyone*, let alone a man who was fifteen years her junior.

"It's not your hands," she assured him. "I just meant in terms of me knowing your real identity. And Sheriff Boyd, now that I think about it. Aren't you supposed to be more discreet? Slip so deeply undercover so that only your superiors know who you are? I never guessed about Nicki until—"

"Until all other avenues had been explored." Nicki's voice, hard with warning, sounded from the doorway. "I took Tess into my confidence when—and only when—I had no other choice."

"Nicki!" The expression on Jared's face changed in an instant. Remembering his cover, he colored and coughed. "I mean…Nicki, right? The one who drives the bookmobile?"

"Too late, boy wonder. Anyone who planted a listening device in here would already know everything." Nicki gave a derisive snort and came the rest of the way into the store, a heavy cardboard box in her arms. Tess rose to take it from her, but Jared beat her to it. "Lucky for you, I did a full electronic sweep this morning. You're all clear, Tess, in case you were wondering."

Tess had no idea that Nicki had such cool technology at her fingertips, but she liked it. "Was it

Mason you suspected of planting bugs, or the sheriff's department?" Tess asked.

"Mason, of course," Nicki replied. "Sheriff Boyd wouldn't place surveillance without just cause and a warrant first."

It was true. Getting Sheriff Boyd to break a rule was as easy as getting Tess to follow one.

"This box has books in it," Jared announced flatly.

"Does it? Someone alert Scotland Yard. Now that Sherlock Holmes is on the case, we'll have all the answers in no time."

Jared flushed to the roots of his hair. "I only meant that I'm not sure what you want me to do with them. There aren't any bookshelves in the store yet."

As there weren't even walls yet, this went without saying. Jared, however, seemed determined to say it anyway.

"I could probably have some fitted up by this weekend, but—"

"Oh, for the love of Pete." Nicki waved for him to put the box in the back room, a generous term for the four studded walls surrounding a dry sink and a rusted toilet on a raised platform. "They're my excuse for stopping by so we can work on the case together. I'm a librarian. We sometimes have extra books. No one will think it's weird if I drop off a box of them every now and then for Tess's used book section."

"But I'm not going to have a used book section,"

Tess said. "I want to carefully cultivate my stock to represent a diverse array of—"

"You don't have to *literally* sell them, Tess." Nicki's voice was starting to sound dangerous. "I just need an excuse to meet with Jared from time to time. Why do you think I suggested the contractor position in the first place? You and I have such a well-established relationship that no one would think to question my stopping by every day."

"Couldn't you just pretend to date each other?" Tess suggested. "That seems a lot easier to me."

From the way Nicki reared back—as though jumping to escape an oncoming train—Tess could tell the idea didn't appeal. And not just because Nicki had zero interest in dating partners of the male variety.

"You wouldn't have to actually *be* together," Tess said, laughing. "Haven't you ever seen a romantic comedy?"

"No, and I'm not about to start now. Give me a movie with explosions, or give me death." Nicki made a face at Tess. "Why don't you pretend to date him and save me the trouble? That would work as a cover story, too."

Tess pretended to be shocked. "What? Sleep with an employee? I'm a woman of *morals*, Nicki. What would the townspeople think?"

They both glanced over to find that Jared was no

longer blushing up to the roots of his hair—he was blushing *everywhere*. In Tess's opinion, it didn't make him appear any less attractive; if anything, it rendered his boyish good looks even more authentic.

"Oh, relax," Nicki said irritably. "No one is going to make you date anyone—fake or otherwise. Let's just stick to the plan for now."

"And what, exactly, is the plan?" Tess asked. "As an integral part of this undercover operation, I feel like I should know."

Nicki shook her head in a silent warning, but Jared either didn't notice or didn't care. He cleared his throat. "Well, that's where you come in, Tess. Er, Ms. Harrow. Or...wait. *Mrs.* Harrow?"

Tess fought a grin. "Tess is fine."

Jared shot her a grateful smile. "Ideally, I'd like to get hired on as part of Mason Peabody's logging crew."

"Unfortunately, Mason has cracked down on his hiring practices ever since one of his employees wound up dead and in Tess's pond," Nicki said with the clipped tones Tess recognized as her federal agent voice. "He can't afford that kind of scrutiny again, so he's only hiring people he's worked with in the past. We tried, but we can't get a foot in the door."

Tess nodded as though this made perfect sense—which, in all fairness, it did. This was exactly the kind of convoluted plan she liked to put in her books. The more elaborate the setup, the more satisfying the payout.

She said, "You want Jared to work for me for a few months so I can put in a good word with Mason."

Nick nodded. "Mason likes you. He'll listen to you."

To be perfectly honest, Mason Peabody only liked that Tess had written a puff piece about him for the *Seattle Times*. It had been an investigative ploy, and she hadn't actually expected it to go to print, but the day it landed in her editor friend's email box must have been a slow news day. The slander she'd written about Sheriff Boyd had been enough to turn the poor man apoplectic for a month.

With a sigh, Nicki added, "Tess, I was hoping we could keep your part in this quiet, and that it might all work out organically, but Jared doesn't do anything organic."

Jared hooked a thumb in one of his many pant loops and grinned. "It's true. I'm a cowboy, born and bred."

Tess laughed. She hadn't yet decided whether Jared was one of the smartest men she'd ever met or one of the stupidest. She didn't think it was possible for anyone, even someone as good-natured as he was, to be impervious to the insults Nicki leveled on his head, but nothing she said or did seemed to shake him.

"Does this make me an honorary FBI agent?" Tess asked.

"Absolutely not," Nicki said. "And I'm leaving

before you ask me to issue you a gun. But see if you can get Mason to the bookstore to take a look around and meet Jared. You said he's still interested in buying the building to turn it into condos, right?"

Tess nodded. Mason had made the offer last summer, but dreams of the Paper Trail had pushed all thoughts of a quick sale aside. Now that there were dead bodies and piles of bricks everywhere, however...

"Wait a minute." Tess swiveled her head to stare at Nicki. "You don't think Mason wanted to buy this place because he knew there were bodies buried here, do you? Like...as a preempt? So he could move the skeletons before anyone asked questions?"

Nicki shrugged before heading out the door. "Maybe. The sooner I have that bastard nailed, the sooner we'll find out for sure."

─────────

Tess was careful to pick Gertrude up from the morgue that evening.

Not—as the girl was quick to point out— because she wanted to launch herself at Sylvia Nerudo, coroner extraordinaire, but because it was important for her daughter to feel supported in her chosen career path.

"How was it?" Tess asked as soon as Gertrude

stepped outside, shrugging herself into her ubiqui-
tous hoodie. Tess was glad they made her change into
official scrubs while inside the building. She didn't
want any dead bits coming home with her. "Did you
learn a lot about the act of processing evidence?"

"You mean, did I encounter any intriguing clues
while I was in there?" Gertrude asked, but with a
grin to take the edge off. "Not really. Old bones are
kind of boring. Everything has to be sent off to a lab,
and then you just sit around waiting for someone
else to tell you what they found. If I want to get into
the really good stuff, we need a fresh body."

"And by needing 'a fresh body,' we hope she's not
committing to a murder spree of her own," said an
older, petite woman in a nondescript pantsuit as she
stepped out of the building to join them. Her salt-
and-pepper hair was almost as curly as Tess's, though
it was contained in a ponytail that kept the strands in
place—and, Tess imagined, from contaminating any
bodies she was working on. "You must be Gertie's
mom. Tess, right? You should be proud to have a
daughter like her."

As she spoke, Sylvia put a hand on Gertrude's
shoulder and squeezed. Something that felt an
awful lot like jealousy flooded Tess's stomach.

"She's quite a child, I'll say that much," Tess allowed.
And, because it seemed like the more pressing of her
concerns, she asked, "What do you mean, 'a murder

spree of her own'? Are you saying that the two bodies you found are officially linked? Two missing women, two deaths, more than two decades apart?"

Sylvia gave a start of surprise. "How do you know all that?"

"I warned you, Ms. Sylvie," Gertrude said with a shake of her head. "She's obsessed. She probably knows more about this case by now than you do."

Tess knew Gertrude's voice was heavy with sarcasm—they could probably tell that from the moon—but she couldn't help noticing a touch of pride in there. Gertrude would never admit it, but she enjoyed having a mother who knew this much about murder, even if it was usually confined to the page. In fact, if Tess didn't come up with a good fictional suspect soon, she'd need to sit down with the girl and pick her brain for ideas. She'd already put a thinly veiled facsimile of Mason Peabody in her last book. She could hardly keep dragging out the same red herring every time.

"Is that so?" Sylvia asked. She tilted her head at an inquisitive angle. "What have you gathered so far?"

Tess knew when she was being tested. "Not much," she admitted. "The first victim is a missing persons case from the eighties. The second is that hiker who went missing back in 2017. Their ages are too far apart to make for a solid tie—Annabelle was twenty-three to Lucretia's thirty-eight—and the number of hatchet marks seem to indicate two separate jobs, but the fact that the same type of weapon was used for both murders and they were buried within five feet of one another is telling. We should know more once my hatchet expert gets here. He won't be able to pinpoint a specific weapon, but he should be able to tell if the same one was used for both murders."

Instead of being impressed by this show of information, Sylvia stiffened.

"What makes you think *I* can't tell you whether or not the same weapon was used for both cases?"

"Um…" Tess swallowed heavily. To point out the obvious—that Sylvia Nerudo was a small-time coroner in a rural county where most people died of the slow and painfully ordinary passage of time—would only result in her daughter losing her job shadowing position.

The scowl starting to darken Gertrude's brow confirmed it. The girl didn't have to open her mouth for Tess to know what was going through her brain right now.

Stop showing off for once in your life.

If you mess this up for me, I'll never forgive you.

Why can't you be more like normal moms?

Tess put on her blandest, most cocktail-party smile. "Are you able to tell? I had no idea."

"I can't *not* tell." Sylvia scowled and crossed her

arms. For such a small person, her aura of intimidation was strong. "Why? Who's your expert?"

"Oh, just a writer friend of mine. I told him there was no need to come all this way, but as soon as he heard about the case, I couldn't keep him away. He should be here tomorrow."

"Mom!"

"What? You like Peter. And he knows all kinds of things about dead bodies. You can ask him your goriest, most gruesome questions."

To Gertrude, the prospect of holding one of her personal heroes hostage so she could pepper him with questions about bodily fluids was one that strongly appealed. The sudden glimmer of excitement in her eyes was unmistakable. To Tess's surprise, a similar flash filled Sylvia's.

"Wait—you don't mean Peter Oblonsky, do you?"

"You know him?"

The answer to that appeared to be a resounding yes. "Are you kidding? Dr. Oblonsky is coming here? To Winthrop? To consult on my case?"

Tess had forgotten that Peter had a doctorate among his many other accolades, but it was clear this woman had his full résumé memorized. "Well, I don't know if he's coming in an *official* capacity, but yes. We try to meet up every few years to chat about the publishing industry. He's been in the business a lot longer than I have. It should be fun."

"Fun? *Fun?*"

"I'll see if he has any free time to stop by. Considering how quickly he booked a flight, I'm guessing he's between deadlines right now. I doubt he'll mind."

The squeak that escaped Sylvia's mouth was Tess's cue to leave. One of the first things being an author had taught her was that it was always good to leave your audience hanging. It was the only way to ensure they'd come back for more.

Grabbing her daughter's backpack and slinging all twenty pounds of it over her shoulder, Tess waved a cheerful—and satisfied—goodbye.

Chapter Six

THE BEST PART ABOUT BEING FRIENDS WITH A sort-of librarian was the all-access pass to the micro-fiche reader after the library closed for the day.

"I could get fired for this, you know." Nicki turned on the ancient, whirring machine and handed Tess the film from 1988. The internet had been rather helpful on the subject of Lucretia Gregory, but information on Annabelle Charles was much more difficult to come by.

It was sad, really. Without modern technology to prop her up, a young woman with her whole life ahead of her had basically vanished. Annabelle's memory was restricted to a few milk cartons and handmade signs buried under decades of missing dogs, babysitting offers, and low-rent band gigs. Tess had to resort to microfiche if she wanted to get any *real* information.

"No one is going to fire you for letting a writer research after hours," Tess said as she pulled out her notebook and pen. "In fact, if I end up solving this murder, you'll probably get a medal of honor. Or a parade. People in this town seem to love parades."

Nicki snorted. "You think you're going to solve a thirty-four-year-old case by reading a few newspaper articles about it?"

"Stranger things have happened. Maybe all it needs is a fresh pair of eyes."

"You're just hoping to find something juicy so you can steal it for your book." Nicki shook her head. Since she was leaning over Tess's shoulder, the long beads of her tassel earrings tickled Tess's cheek. "Admit it. You're hoping she belonged to a cult or dabbled in witchcraft during her cigarette breaks."

"I *have* been thinking about writing a cult book," Tess mused, refusing to be insulted. "But if Annabelle was anything like Lucretia, I won't find anything. Any skeletons Lucretia kept in her closet were as well-hidden as she was."

As cruel as it sounded to sum up a woman—a dead one, no less—so callously, it was nothing but the truth.

By all appearances, Lucretia had been unmarried and childless, her professional appearances restricted to the law firm where she worked as a legal assistant. She'd had a large number of acquaintances on Facebook—along with the requisite outpouring of support after she went missing—but that was about it. No one had offered a reward for her return, and the news outlets had given up on her story as soon as the next big political scandal hit.

Sheriff Boyd had been in office during the investigation, which was where Tess planned to strike next. And by *strike*, she meant strategically lowering his defenses so he didn't take her questions as a personal affront. An open case lingering on his desk for that long—and without any leads to speak of—had to be killing him.

Metaphorically speaking.

Nicki scooted up a chair and settled in with a printed-out spreadsheet while Tess began the monotonous task of skimming the headlines for anything worth note. The company was nice but unexpected.

"Whatcha working on?" Tess asked, her mind only half on the screen.

"Oh, you know." Nicki made a flourishing check mark next to one of the columns. "Just analyzing every single financial transaction Mason Peabody has ever made under the five different shell companies we've been able to link back to him."

Tess pulled a face. "Good God. Don't you have people to do that for you?"

"I *am* the people." Nicki made another mark. Considering the size of the stack of paper in her lap, the task would keep her busy for the next two months. "The good news is I'm saving the Bureau a fortune by printing all this stuff out at the library. If I do end up getting a parade, it'll be for reducing overhead. The Okanogan County Library system, however…"

Tess chuckled and returned her attention to the screen, feeling a little better about the task now that she knew she had a friend to help while away the hours. Getting divorced after fifteen years of not-so-happy marriage had been freeing, but she still sometimes missed having someone share her space.

"So," Tess said after several more minutes of fruitless searching. As usual, cow-tipping episodes and property disputes took up most of the head-lines. "That Jared Wilson is something else, huh?"

Nicki glanced up from her paper and pointed her highlighter at Tess. "Don't."

That glare might be enough to stop criminals dead in their tracks, but it had no power over Tess. "He seems to like you an awful lot," Tess said. "You should see the way he looks at you."

"He looks at everyone that way. He can't help it. He's like an oversized, overeager puppy."

"Aw. You like him."

Nicki rapped the highlighter against Tess's fore-head. "Don't be ridiculous. A puppy might be fun to have around for a few days, but he's going to prove more of a hindrance than a help with this case. Take my word for it. Big, brooding eyes and a bona fide pedigree can only carry a man so far. After that, *I'll* be the one schlepping *him* around."

Tess wasn't one to let a subject drop without a fight, but one of the headlines caught her eye.

"What?" Nicki wasn't slow to pick up on the shift. "Did you find something about her disappearance?"

"Not her disappearance, no." Tess peered close at the screen. She probably needed reading glasses for this type of work, but she wasn't ready to admit it yet. If she squinted hard enough, she could make out most of the fine print. "But it looks like our little Annabelle was a shoplifter. Look—she was arrested in Twisp for taking over three hundred bucks' worth of stuff from an electronics store."

"Stealing a bunch of Beastie Boys cassettes is hardly motive for murder."

"It's no cult, but I can only work with what I'm given." Tess scanned the lines in full before starting over again at the top. "And in this case, I've been given a gift. Check it out—that wasn't her first arrest. What do you think the chances are this girl has an official record?"

"Nuh uh." Nicki put her hands up. "I'm not checking anything for you. You're going to have to bat your eyes at Sheriff Boyd instead."

"I don't bat my eyes at him!"

Nicki blithely ignored her. "Jared isn't the only one who knows how to use his big, brooding eyes to get his way. Throw a little cleavage into the bargain, and I'll bet the sheriff will make you an honorary deputy."

This was so far removed from the truth—Victor Boyd was impervious to eyes and cleavage alike—that Tess could only harrumph. "I don't need my feminine wiles. I'll get him on my side the same way I always do."

"Oh, yeah?" Nicki smirked. "And how's that?"

"With cold, hard logic," Tess said firmly. "And maybe a little bribery on the side."

Chapter Seven

"I'M HERE WITH A PEACE OFFERING, SO DON'T turn me away until you hear me out."

Tess breezed into the sheriff's office bearing a plate of fresh-baked molasses cookies. Instead of pouncing on the opportunity to enjoy a feast at her expense, Sheriff Boyd kept typing at his computer. As he used the good, old-fashioned hunt-and-peck style, even the shortest emails had a way of taking up all his concentration.

"Hello? Did you hear me? I brought your favorite cookies."

"No you didn't. You brought me *Detective Gonzales*'s favorite cookies." He sighed and glanced up. "Someday, you're going to realize that I'm not a fictional character you can push around at will."

"Oh, I've realized it." She fell into the nearest chair. Since she knew that molasses cookies were, in fact, his favorite kind—and that it'd take a pair of pliers and hours of untold torture before he could be prevailed upon to admit it—she put the plate on his desk. "And I'd like to know when I ever pushed you into doing anything. You're the one who always picks up when I call."

He switched his computer off and scrubbed a weary hand along his jaw. Considering the level of scruff that had developed there since the bodies had been discovered, she was guessing he wasn't as close to a solution as he wanted to be. "Funny. I don't remember you calling to make an appointment."

"Because I wanted to make sure you got the cookies while they were still warm," she said. And, because offense was the best defense where this man was concerned, she didn't wait to be invited to continue. "I'm wondering if you can get me the arrest records for Annabelle Charles."

"No." He spoke without hesitation—or surprise.

"But you do have them."

"Of course I have them."

"And the original missing persons file on Lucretia? That you yourself filed?"

When he sighed this time, it was with the long suffering of a man being pressed to death under a pile of rocks. "Must we have this conversation every single time I'm investigating a murder? You aren't entitled to information just because the body was found on your property. In fact, that's a glaring reason *not* to share anything revealing."

She knew it was. She also knew that the more

exhausted the sheriff was, the more likely he was to cave. That was a trick Gertrude used all the time. Requests for increases to her allowance always occurred with greater frequency whenever Tess was approaching a deadline.

She said, "The fact that the police gave up on Annabelle's case makes sense—her disappearance was over thirty years ago, and she seems like a bit of a delinquent—but I can't figure Lucretia's out. Why did you stop looking for her? And why didn't any newspapers call you out for it?"

Instead of answering, the sheriff reached for one of the cookies and took a bite. He chewed slowly and with purpose, his eyes unblinking.

"The only reason I can come up with is because you found evidence that she wasn't actually gone. An abandoned car at the border, maybe, or her credit cards being used a few counties over. Enough to assume that she skipped town on purpose."

He stuffed the rest of the cookie in his mouth. For a man who didn't consider these his favorite, he was eating them awfully fast.

"That's it, isn't it? Chew once for yes and twice for no."

He stopped chewing altogether, which was good enough for her.

"Interesting. If her disappearance was made to look intentional, but it turns out she actually *is* dead, then we're looking at premeditated murder. Or whatever it is when someone goes to elaborate lengths to cover up a death after it happens."

"Accessory after the fact?" the sheriff suggested dryly.

"Yeah. That one." She snapped her fingers. "Which makes it a lot less likely that my grandfather was involved, don't you think? You know how he felt about credit cards. He always paid for everything in cash. He didn't want the IRS keeping tabs on him. And he was hardly in a fit state to start driving cars all over the forest and abandoning them there. That'd be like sending Herb out to conceal evidence. Can you imagine?"

He didn't have to imagine it. Neither did Tess. No sooner had the words escaped her lips than the man in question—Herb, not her grandfather—entered the room.

"If this is about that dead hiker lady, don't look at me," he said in a voice loud enough to be heard by the entire station. Ivy hurried a few steps behind him, obviously trying to get him to save any confessions for the interrogation room, but Herb didn't care for formalities any more than Tess did.

Bless the man.

"It's like I told you at the time. I bought that car from her fair and square. Overpaid for it, too, seeing as how it didn't last longer than two weeks. Duct tape holding every last one of those hoses together."

"Ha!" Tess exclaimed. "I knew it."

Even if she had wanted to keep her triumph to herself, this would have been a hard one to subdue. An abandoned car, just like she'd said. Only instead of leaving it at the border, this one had remained right here in town.

The sheriff cleared his throat. "I don't suppose you've found the receipt for that purchase yet."

"Weren't no receipt. No title, either. A handshake and cash was good enough for my father, which makes it good enough for me." Herb stopped a few feet short of the desk and nodded at Tess. "Good enough for old Melvin, too. You tell him, Tess. He'd have bought the car if I hadn't. He always did like a bargain."

"Don't lump my grandfather in on this," she protested. "He didn't have anything to do with that poor woman's death."

She didn't need to look at the sheriff's face to realize that Herb's presence here didn't bode well for her family's good name. If Herb was being called in to account for Lucretia's car, that meant he was a suspect in her death. Considering his close friendship with her grandfather—and the fact that the body had been found underneath the hardware store floorboards—things were looking none too good for dear old Grandpa.

"She sold the car to you in person?" Tess asked

before either Ivy or Sheriff Boyd took it into their heads to usher her out of there. "You saw her? You talked to her?"

"Course I did. Drove her to the bus station afterward, too, just like she asked." He pointed at Sheriff Boyd. "You remember how it was."

"I remember how you *told* me it was, yes," the sheriff said.

"Did you know the other girl, too?" Tess asked. "The young one who disappeared back in 1988?"

"Tess, now's not the time—"

She held up a hand. "Let him answer if he wants to. You'd have been a young man then, wouldn't you?" Considering how old Herb was now, *young* was pushing it, but Tess wasn't about to quibble over details. Regardless of his physical ability to murder a woman just five short years ago, he'd have been more than capable back in the eighties.

"Who? Annabelle?" Herb blinked. "O' course I knew her. The whole town knew about that nasty piece of—"

"Herb, that's enough." The sheriff spoke with a ferocity unusual in so dry a man.

"Yes, but—"

"Unless you have an attorney present, I think you should keep your thoughts to yourself."

Now it was Tess's turn to protest. "Yes, but—"

"But nothing." The sheriff's ferocity didn't

abate any. "I asked Herb here as a formality, that's all, to follow up on my original investigation. I'd appreciate it if you didn't start accusing him of murder on my behalf."

It spoke well of the sheriff's ethics that he'd advise a potential suspect of his rights before he was required to, but Tess wished—not for the first time—that he wasn't quite so stringent a moralist. He and Detective Gonzales might share a love of cookies, but they took two very different approaches to solving crime. At this point, anything Herb had to say would be of real value.

"Please escort Ms. Harrow out," the sheriff said to Ivy. The fact that he'd reverted to formality wasn't lost on Tess. Neither was the fact that he didn't ask Herb to leave along with her.

"And for the record, I'm keeping these cookies," he said. "Make sure you tell Gertie they're delicious."

———

Instead of taking the thwarted interrogation at the sheriff's office as a sign to back off, Tess used the extra time to make the promised trip up to Peabody Timber.

As soon as Tess stepped into the familiar office to lay the groundwork for Nicki's trap, Mason Peabody leaped up from his desk. *Office* was a generous term for the tin can that sat in the middle of Mason's logging operation in forests of the Okanogan, but it served as his base of operations, so the title fit.

The first time she'd ever visited, she'd been shocked at how out-of-date and understated the building was, a throwback to the seventies that didn't match Mason's overblown personality and expensively cut suits. Now that she knew he was hiding illegal logging practices and channeling dirty money over the Canadian border, it made sense. The less flashy he appeared on the outside, the less likely he was to draw unwelcome questions on the state of his finances.

Then again, the fact that he was quietly and consistently buying up all the real estate in the town of Winthrop wasn't exactly discreet. The area *was* an up-and-coming tourist destination, but there was a limit to how many luxury condos a one-street town needed. By Tess's estimation, that limit was about one.

"You've reconsidered my offer, haven't you?" Mason gave Tess a robust handshake before pulling a chair out for her. Despite his nefarious ways and his desire to take over the sheriff's office so he could cover up as many crimes as he committed, Tess kind of liked the guy. He didn't try to hide the fact that he was as smarmy as they came. She could respect that kind of honesty. "Now that the taint of murder hangs overhead, you've realized what a waste it is to hold on to that property."

Tess wasn't ready to pinpoint Mason as the murderer of those poor women just yet, but she took careful note of this words. It wasn't out of the realm of possibility for him to have planted the bodies there in hopes of driving down her price and convincing her to sell. She'd have to double check with the sheriff to see if the bodies had been moved or removed at any point in their history of interment.

"It's devastating, isn't it?" Tess said. "To think that two actual human beings lost their lives?"

Her not-so-subtle reminder of what they were dealing with caused Mason to grow red around the ears. "Yes. Yes, of course. Terribly sad." He waited all of two seconds before speaking again. "But I'm not wrong, am I? You want to talk options. You're looking for a quick win."

Since she'd promised Nicki she'd get Mason and Jared in the same room together, she heaved a sigh of long suffering and feigned the anxiety of a woman about to experience a major financial downfall.

If Mason had known anything about publishing—particularly publishing at one of the biggest houses in the United States with all the attached foreign sales, translation rights, TV options, and, though she still didn't understand how it worked, gaming rights—he'd have realized that he was talking to a woman who could buy and sell ten of her grandfather's buildings, should she take it in her mind to do so.

But he didn't, and in this case, what he didn't know was definitely going to hurt him.

"I'm not ready to sell, if that's what you're asking," she said as she toyed with a fountain pen on his desk. She lifted her gaze before coyly dropping it again. "But I wouldn't mind if you came out to the store and had a look around. I'm hoping you could give me some advice."

As she expected, Mason took to this request for help like, well, a man being asked for help. Tess might be a professional writer, but sometimes no simile was necessary.

"Well, now. I'd be honored, Ms. Harrow."

"It's just that you probably know a lot more about building than I do, especially when it comes to getting permits and things. Sheriff Boyd is doing his best to turn my poor store into a crime scene. I can't even remove a board these days without his permission."

Nothing more was needed to set events into motion. Mason lived for any opportunity to thwart his nemesis. The speed with which he pulled out his appointment book was almost comical.

"How's tomorrow afternoon?" he asked.

A little sooner than she was expecting, but that, too, was worth note. If *she*'d been the one to plant

dead bodies on someone else's property as a nego-
tiating tactic, she'd want to snoop around the aftermath as soon as possible.

"It's perfect," she said and stood to leave. A pair
of muddied hiking boots stood next to the office
door. Considering how much of Mason's work
took place in the forest, it made sense that he'd
have the footwear necessary to survey his logging
operation, but something about that particular
pair caught her attention.

Tess was something of an expert in men's footwear.
Size, shape, tread… You could solve a lot of crimes if
you knew how a man got from one place to another.
Mason Peabody, currently sporting tight-fitting
oxfords, typically got around in as few steps as possible.

But those boots were well-used. Someone had
taken them deep in the forest and put them through
their paces—something they didn't have much of.
If the frayed laces and scuffed faux leather were any
indication, they weren't an expensive pair.

They were disposable. Easy to throw in a river.
Easier still to burn.

"I didn't know you were into hiking," she said
with a nod down at the shoes. "I've been trying to
get out more—explore the local trails, get to know
the woods. Where do you recommend?"

Mason was sharp enough to smell a trap but not
sharp enough to tell where it was coming from. "I

don't get out as much as I used to. Not for recreational purposes, anyway."

"But you did when you were younger, right? Like… as a teenager?" She was quick to add an excuse for this line of questioning. "Now that Gertie and I are putting down roots, I'm realizing how little there is for kids to do around here. From all I can gather, they spend their weekends tramping around the trails and drinking the forties they swiped from the corner store."

"She seems like she has a good head on her shoulders," Mason said, but with a grin that made Tess think she hit the mark. "But, yeah. I stole my fair share of malt liquor back in the nineties. It's a rite of passage around here."

Since she put Mason's age at around the sheriff's, Tess had no problems with this timeline. If the older bones belonged to a woman who'd gone missing in 1988, Mason could have been involved. He'd have been younger than Gertrude, but that might explain the inexpert butchering.

Every psychopath had to start somewhere.

"That particular rite of passage is what I'm afraid of," Tess said, not altogether lying. True, Gertrude showed more interest in death than she did in underage drinking, but that was simply because she rejected anything ordinary as a matter of course.

"She'll be fine. She's working at the morgue now, right?"

Tess nodded, unsure how to take this. Although it was true that news traveled fast in a town as small as theirs, Mason was hardly the type to keep tabs on a teenager's exploratory career options.

"Well, there you go," Mason said with a laugh intended to solve everything. "You'll never have to wonder where she is late at night."

"She doesn't work the graveyard shift," Tess said, startled. "It's just a few hours after school."

"Really?" Mason shrugged and returned his attention to his desk. "I heard she was getting a lot more involved than that. I guess my sources were incorrect."

Chapter Eight

TESS WAS DEEP IN PLOT OF *FURY UNDER THE Floorboards* when she heard the car pull up. She'd reached a particularly intriguing part of her novel—Detective Gonzales was about to help put his undercover FBI contact in touch with the white-collar criminal he was trying to track—but she was always happy to be interrupted.

"Peter's here!" She slammed her laptop shut and ran to the cabin door, feeling more buoyant than she had in months. Back in Seattle, it had been fairly easy to meet with other writers—and even, on occasion, her editor—but few people visited her out in the middle of nowhere. "Quick, Gertie. Start mixing those cocktails. Peter likes his martinis dry."

"Mom, it's barely two in the afternoon."

"He's a horror writer, honey. Next to romance authors, no one drinks as much as they do."

Gertrude's reply to this was lost under the sound of Tess's squeal at the sight of her old friend. Peter was, in fact, *old* in every sense of the word. He'd long since seen the fresh side of his seventies, and a lifetime spent stooped over his desk and/or a microscope had taken its toll on his posture. He exclusively wore jackets with patches on the elbows and walked with the aid of an elegant silver-tipped cane that matched the rims on his owlish glasses. He'd been the very first writer friend Tess had ever made, and she adored him.

"You told me it was rustic, but I thought that meant one outdoor fountain instead of two." As Peter opened his arms to embrace Tess, the scent of patchouli and old tobacco rose up around her like a second hug. "Love, this is downright medieval."

"Isn't it amazing?" Tess inhaled deeply, allowing herself to bask in his familiar scent before ushering him inside. A single plaid suitcase was all he had with him. "If it gets to be too much, we can always move you to the hotel in town. It's no Ritz, but they have some nice suites. Well, *one* nice suite."

"Don't be daft." In addition to the all the elegant details that denoted Peter as a man of refined habits, he retained a hint of the British accent from his youth. "This place is perfectly Gothic. I might set my next book here."

"Don't you dare. I have dibs on any and all story lines arising from bodies found in the area. So far, this town is proving itself a fount of inspiration."

"So I've gathered." Peter's eyes grew wide behind their spectacles as Gertrude came out bearing a tray with two martini glasses filled to the brim. "Good

God! Don't tell me this is my little baby Gertie. You're practically an adult now."

"Mr. Oboe-ski!" Gertie cried, reverting to the name she'd used back when more than two consonants in a row proved too much for her youthful tongue. In her enthusiasm to greet the newcomer, she almost spilled the drinks, but no one seemed to care.

"So you *do* remember me," he said and accepted one of the glasses. He took a long sip and heaved a satisfied sigh. "And how I like my martinis. You're a blessed angel, my child, and a sight for sore eyes."

"I'm working at a morgue now," Gertrude announced. She handed Tess the tray with the remaining drink and led Peter to the quilt-covered couch at the far end of the room, her tongue running a mile a minute. "Did Mom tell you? They let me scrub in on the autopsies and everything. Well, I have to stand at the back and watch, but I'm still in the room. That's something, isn't it?"

"Indeed. Have they showed you the bone saw yet?"

"Oh, boy. Did they ever. Ms. Sylvie pulled one out for—"

"Wait a minute." Tess stopped in the act of bringing her martini glass to her lips. "*Bone saw?*"

Gertrude waved an impatient hand at her. "Don't be squeamish, Mom. How else are you supposed to get through the osteoid matrix?"

Peter nodded gravely, though Tess could detect

the hint of a smile playing about his lips. "Very durable," he murmured. "One of the strongest organic materials on earth."

Gertrude settled in for a long chat about the different saws used to cut through various parts of the human body—a store of knowledge that Tess had no doubt would come back to haunt her. Peter obliged Gertrude in this, and in all of the subjects that kept them chatting for the next two hours.

As in, a *literal* two hours. Tess counted them, each minute that ticked by making her more impatient to have her friend to herself. Peter was universally beloved wherever he went, yes, but he was supposed to be here to help her solve a murder, not put her daughter on the path to committing them.

She was so desperate that she was about to pull out the typewriter and start working again when Gertrude stood up, stretched, and announced that she had to get started on dinner since it wasn't going to cook itself.

"Don't look at me like that," Tess said when Gertrude followed this up with a pointed glance at her. "I'd be happy with peanut butter and jelly sandwiches. I'll go whip them up right now."

"For the love of my digestion, child, please don't let your mother anywhere near the kitchen. She can plot a crime with the best of them, but get her anywhere near a butcher block..."

Gertrude giggled. "You don't have to tell me. I

once spent a weekend with my friends in town and came back to find that she'd eaten nothing but tuna. And I mean *nothing*. All I found in the kitchen was one fork and like, twelve empty cans."

"Tuna is excellent for heart health, thank you very much," Tess protested, but not without a flicker of shame. She'd eaten that diet on purpose to see if Detective Gonzales could survive for a week on nothing else when he was trapped in the cargo hold of a transport ship. The short answer was that he *could*, but no one with a decent sense of smell was likely to come near him for weeks afterward.

As soon as Gertrude took herself off to whip them up a culinary masterpiece, Tess descended upon her old friend. She felt a little guilty at subjecting him to another two-hour barrage of questions, but he was nothing if not a good sport.

"So. You're going to take a look at those bones for me, aren't you?" she asked, not bothering with a more convenient conversational segue. "You might have to sign some autographs to sweeten up the coroner, but I'm sure she'll let you examine the hatchet marks. When I told her you were coming, she almost died of joy on the spot. I'm mostly interested in whether or not the same weapon was used for both murders. They're almost thirty years apart, but—"

"Wait." Peter put up a hand before Tess could finish her sentence. "You weren't kidding about that?"

Tess sat back, blinking. "What do you mean? Kidding about what?"

"The case. Are you telling me you *really* found two bodies in your grandfather's store? That was the God's honest truth?"

"I gave you all the details in my email." Too many details, if the length of the thing had been any indication. She couldn't help it; words always seemed to flow when they weren't the ones she was *supposed* to be writing. "Both of the bodies belonged to women who went missing in these woods, but with so much time between the cases that no one ever thought to put them together...until they both showed up underneath my floor. No one has told me yet whether the hatchet marks were made pre- or postmortem, but—"

"Pre."

Tess blinked again, this time so forcefully that her contact lens almost popped out of her eye. "How do you know that? I can't get an answer about *anything* out of Sheriff Boyd, and even Gertie doesn't know anything more than the number of marks." She knit her brow. "Unless Sylvia sent you pictures of the bones ahead of time? No, I never gave her your contact info, so I don't see how that's possible."

"Tess, you know the answer to this already. To the whole case."

"I do?"

Peter nodded at her with kind patience. "Two women murdered with multiple axe wounds thirty years apart? Buried under the floorboards of an old, rundown shop in a small town in Washington? The coroner will claim the evidence is inconclusive. The sheriff will find no leads. The district attorney will drop all interest in the case. Until, of course, they realize there's a third missing person they've over-looked, and they can no longer let sleeping dogs lie."

"What are you talking about?"

"I take it they haven't found the third missing person yet."

"Peter, are you a clairvoyant now?" Tess demanded. "Did you sell your soul to the devil like that guy in your last book? The ability to see every-thing…but at the price of being unable to do any-thing about it?"

Peter sounded his rich chuckle—the one that had earned him the nickname Grandfather of the Macabre. "I'm not the one who wrote this book already. Simone Peaky is."

The name nagged at something deep in Tess's memory, but she couldn't quite place it. Peter sat watching her, full of amused patience.

"Simone Peaky?" he urged. "*Let Sleeping Dogs Lie*? Tess, you can't have forgotten. You literally blurbed the book. You called it 'A fast-paced, reckless tale that grabs you by the throat and doesn't let go.'"

"I did?" Tess's eyes widened as that nagging feeling clicked into place. "Oh, shoot! I did say that, didn't I? I remember now. It was a few years ago. The publisher was all over me to give them a soundbite. They wouldn't let my poor agent rest until I gave in."

"So you do recall the book?"

"Well, no." Tess shifted uncomfortably. "I didn't actually *read* it. Honestly, Peter. Who has the time?"

"Tess! I picked it up based solely on your recommendation."

Tess slapped a hand over her mouth to try and hold her laugh back, but she was too late. "Oh, no. Did you? Was it any good?"

"Its quality isn't the point here. The contents are what you need to be concerned with."

Tess groaned inwardly. "You might as well tell me. What is it? Plagiarism? Racist undertones? I'm going to kill my agent for this."

Peter stared at her through narrowed eyes. "I think perhaps you should check and see if you have a copy lying around."

Since the one thing Tess never got around to throwing away was books, there was a good chance the free copy they sent her after publication was lying around here someplace. "Hey, Gertie?" she called, since that was the fastest way to find anything. "Do you recall seeing a book called *Let Sleeping Dogs Lie* on the shelves anywhere?"

Gertrude popped her head through the window separating the small, functional kitchen from the rest of the house, carrying with her the scent of freshly blended basil.

"Yeah, it's on the one above your bed. Anything titled *J* through *O* is up there."

Tess loped off to grab the book in question. The dark cover depicting the back of a girl in a long dress running through the woods had been all the rage for a few years, and this was no exception.

"Okay," Tess said as she returned to her seat. "What page should I turn to?"

"All of them," Peter said. During her absence, Gertrude appeared to have topped up his glass. He was settled in his seat, his cane over his knee and a look of pure enjoyment on his face. "Start at the beginning and don't stop until you reach the two skeletons buried under the floorboards in the quaint little town of Heythrop."

"Heythrop?" Tess echoed. As far as she knew, that wasn't a real place...but the name was close enough to Winthrop to cause goosebumps to break out over her skin.

"Let me know when you get there. I think you'll find the plot *very* interesting."

Chapter Nine

"IT'S WITCHCRAFT, THAT'S WHAT IT IS. THERE'S no other possible explanation."

Tess flipped through the pages of *Let Sleeping Dogs Lie* for the umpteenth time, her fingers cracked and bleeding from the number of paper cuts she'd acquired in the past twelve hours.

"It's uncanny. It's unnatural." She stabbed a bloodied finger at one of the pages. "Just look."

Jared *did* look, but mostly because Tess was waving the book so close under his nose that he didn't have any other choice.

"Her car sat in the field like a dead, bloated whale at sea, festering under the noonday sun as birds of prey circled around, cawing for their dinner." Jared wrinkled his nose. "I don't see what's so bad about that. It's poetic."

"No, not that part." Tess ran her finger down the lines, not bothering to point out that there was nothing poetic about overblown writing. She could hardly believe her name was on the cover of this thing, promising twisty delights. Unless the twist was that birds, whales, and cars in one sentence would eventually make sense, readers were bound for disappointment. "Right here. 'The girl's shiny hoard glittered where it lay. Thirty-seven stolen earrings, one for every hack of the axe against her young, nubile body.'"

Tess threw the book across the room. It hit a pile of precariously stacked two-by-fours near the door and sent them toppling.

"Hey!" Jared protested, but Tess wasn't about to pick up that book again. Unless Simone Peaky had been present at Annabelle's murder, there was no way she could know about the thirty-seven hatchet marks. And since the author *also* mentioned that Lucretia had been killed the same way, Tess was pretty sure the case had just solved itself.

But why that particular book had been sent to Tess to blurb, and why she was reading it only now that she lived in the same Wild West–themed town, albeit with a slightly altered name, was freaking her out a little bit.

Or, you know, a lot.

"I never thought magic was real, but now I have to rethink everything," Tess said. "What else have I been overlooking all these years? Vampires? Crop circles? A perfect system of government?"

"Crop circles *are* real."

Tess turned to stare at Jared, certain he must be baiting her. "Excuse me?"

He grinned at her, his dimples flashing. "They're real. So are aliens. I watched this cool documentary once on how ancient civilizations used to travel back and forth between planets. I could show you, if you want."

Not for the first time, Tess found herself sympathizing with Nicki. An FBI agent who believed in aliens was cute on television, but this man was no Fox Mulder. She tilted her head, eyes narrowed as she mentally corrected herself. In this light, and with that eager expression, he *did* look kind of like a young David Duchovny.

"I'm still looking for a rental, so my hotel room isn't much, but we could order in and—"

A voice interrupted before Jared could finish his sentence, which was probably for the best. Unless Tess was very much mistaken, he'd been about to ask her on a date...to watch an alien documentary.

The dating world was tough on fortysomething divorcées who lived three hours from the nearest Sephora, but it wasn't *that* tough.

"Knock knock!" Mason stepped past the plywood boarding up the front door, looking overdressed for his expedition into town and no less impressive because of it.

Then again, that might have been Tess's relief talking.

"Mason!" Tess rushed forward and offered him

her cheek. He kissed it lightly, "Right on time, as usual. I love a man who's punctual."

"You do?" Jared asked at the same time Mason grunted with self-importance.

"I'm sorry everything is such a mess." Tess led the way into the store, careful to avoid stepping on the boxes of nails that lay scattered haphazardly about. "My new contractor has proven to be worth his weight in gold, but there's an awful lot of work for just one man."

Mason nodded as he took in the exposed nails and fallen stack of lumber. "It's a big job, and one I don't envy you. This is no quick cleanup." He beamed at Jared with the wide, condescending smile that had almost won him a position as county sheriff. "I could probably spare one of my guys for a few days if you need a hand with the framing."

"Really?" Jared asked eagerly.

"Really?" Tess asked suspiciously.

"My brother Adam is good at this sort of thing. I'll see if he has a free day sometime next week."

If Tess was suspicious before, she was downright dubious now. Of all the Peabody triplets, Adam— surly, belligerent, and problematically addicted to alcohol—was the worst. If Mason wanted him inside this building with power tools at his disposal, then it was for no good reason.

"That'd be great, thanks," Jared said. He wiped

his hand on his pants and held it out. "I'm Jared Wil—Wright. Jared Wright. That's it."

Mason eyed him askance. "Don't you know your own name?"

"Of course I do." Jared's cheeks turned pink with embarrassment. "I just told you."

"If you're going to use a false name, boy, I suggest you practice it in the mirror a few times first." Instead of following up on this line of questioning, Mason turned an appraising eye around the shop. "So this is it, huh? I presume the bodies were found somewhere near those floor patches?"

Tess nodded. "Once the new flooring is in, you won't be able to tell where they were, but I'm wondering if I should put down a marker or something."

"A marker?"

"Yeah. A plaque or a red X on the floor or something. People are sure to be curious, and maybe it'll help drive traffic. I'm hoping to get a few visitors who are on murder vacations."

"Uh…" Jared cleared his throat. He was still flushed from his earlier error, the tips of his ears flaming. "People don't go on murder vacations, Tess. I mean, Ms. Harrow."

That slip didn't go unnoticed by Mason, either, though he didn't bother commenting on it this time.

"Sure they do," Tess protested, largely to help Jared save face. She'd never met a worse liar in her life; if he didn't get down on his knees and confess everything by the time this meeting was over, it would be a miracle. "It's called dark tourism. It's when you go to all the super depressing parts of the world to soak in other people's pain. Thousands of people used to visit the Manson Ranch before it became overgrown with weeds."

"Ms. Harrow here is our resident murder expert," Mason explained. He gave a low chuckle. "So you'd better watch out. Try to cheat her out of a few hours' work, and you might end up missing like all the rest. Well, either that or killed off in one of her books. At the end of the day, I don't know which is worse."

Tess glanced sharply at Mason, surprised that he was astute enough to recognize how much of real life—and real people—were in her novels. If he'd read the latest one and seen anything of himself in Randall Bennington, pompous millionaire mining magnate, she needed to be more careful about what she revealed.

"Mason, I'd never kill off someone I consider a friend," she said. "You must know that by now."

"I shouldn't take comfort in that, but I do." He gave her arm a friendly pat. "Now. What's the trouble with this place, and how can we whittle it down to a win-win?"

It had been Tess's intention to pepper Mason with all kinds of questions about building permits and lead piping, to play to his strengths as a man who prided himself on knowing everything about nothing, but she'd been so preoccupied with that devil of a novel that she'd forgotten to prep ahead of time.

This was all Peter's fault. Peter and this Simone Peaky woman. And probably Sheriff Boyd, too, though she hadn't yet figured out how to heap this on his head.

"To be honest, I don't care much about buildings right now," Tess confessed. Technically, she'd already played her part in putting Mason and Jared in the same room together. It was up to Jared to take things from here. "I've had a bit of a shock."

"A shock?" Mason echoed. "Do you need to sit down?"

"No, but I do need some advice." She grabbed the book where it had fallen open—to page 13, naturally—and held it out. "Have you ever read this?"

Mason rubbed a hand along his jaw. "Well, now. I hate to admit it to a writer like you, but I'm not much of a reader."

Big surprise there. She doubted he'd recognize a good sentence if it bit him on the tongue. No one who peppered his speech with as many nonsensical corporate buzzwords as he did could understand linguistic nuance.

"Well, I read it last night."

"The *whole* book?" Jared asked. Mason nodded

in a way signaling that he, too, considered this a feat of undeniable proportions.

"Yes, the whole book," Tess said irritably. Honestly, it was no wonder people thought publishing was a dying industry. Hadn't these men ever fallen under the spell of a well-crafted plotline? "It's the story of Winthrop. Not the people or the buildings or anything, but the murders. *Both* of them. In alarming detail."

To his credit, Mason appeared genuinely shocked. "You mean, someone killed those poor women and then wrote a book about it?"

"Yes? No? Either way, something's not right." She shook her head, conveniently glossing over the fact that she, too, had lifted several salient plot points from the events unfolding around her. She was going to have to go back and change half the plot of *Fury under the Floorboards*; she could hardly plagiarize true events that had already been plagiarized once. Tess continued, "The facts have obviously been changed, but a lot of them are accurate enough to put up a red flag—small details about the women's lives, the way they were killed, the places they were hidden—but it gets worse."

"I don't see how."

Even though Nicki had already assured her that no listening devices had been planted inside this building, Tess dropped her voice to a low hush.

"There's a third dead body in the book. One we're missing. One we've overlooked."

That was the thing Peter had pointed out to her last night, the one discrepancy that bothered him. It bothered her, too, but not for the reasons anyone else thought.

"I don't see why you're bringing this to me," Mason said. He took the book and rifled through the pages, though he didn't linger long enough to read any of them. "It sounds like this Simone Peaky woman is the one you want. Shouldn't you take this to Sheriff Boyd?"

Yes, she should, and she planned to as soon as she got up the nerve.

"Mason, you've lived here your whole life, right? You know all the local history?"

He eyed her askance. "Why do I get the feeling you don't want to talk to me about building permits?"

"Because I need you to tell me everything you know about Sheriff Boyd's sister." She drew a deep breath and looked Mason straight in the eye. He wasn't her ideal source of information, but by his own admission, he'd grown up here. He knew the sights, the sounds, *and* the people.

The people most of all.

"His sister?" Mason echoed.

Tess nodded. "The one who went missing back in 1992. The one who was never found."

The one she was almost certain would end up being body number three.

———

Holding an important conversation to the cacophony of a hammer, a ratcheting screwdriver, and something that sounded like a pigeon dying wasn't the way Tess would have chosen to go about things, but her options were limited.

"At least this way, we won't be overheard," Tess said. Yelled, really—her finger plugging one ear as she and Mason seated themselves on the rickety fire escape that laddered the alleyway. "Jared's not the sharpest crayon in the box, but he knows how to work with his hands."

Mason smirked. "I'll bet he does. Don't worry—your secret's safe with me. I've had many a secretary in my day who worked just as hard off duty as they did on."

"Oh, no. It's not like that. He's—"

"A young, good-looking stranger who just happened to roll into town and start working at your store?" His smirk deepened. "Why do you have him here under a false identity?"

Tess gulped, her mind working fast to come up with a likely excuse, but there was no need.

"You know what? I don't want to know. What

you do with your private life is no business of mine."
Mason shook his head. "But between you and me,
the optics aren't great."

Every part of Tess's being longed to correct this
man—it wasn't okay to sleep with a subordinate,
Jared was practically young enough to be her son,
Nicki would kill her—but she held her tongue. If
Mason wanted to believe that Jared was a plaything
that Tess kept around to while away her lonely
hours, then she wasn't going to stop him.

It was better than the alternative—that he was
a federal agent sent for the sole purpose of working his way into Mason's good graces. Nicki really
would kill her for that one.

"Forget Jared for the moment," she said. Since
the loud pounding abated as she spoke, this was
easy enough to do. After casting a quick, furtive
look around, she lowered her voice and added, "I
already know a little bit about Sheriff Boyd's sister,
but I'm hoping you can fill in the gaps."

Mason shook his head. "Victor and I weren't
close. We attended the same school, but he was
a few years ahead of me. And, I need hardly add,
didn't move in the same circles."

She didn't need him to elaborate. Mason
Peabody was Winthrop royalty—or as close as you
could get to it in a place where every other person
lived in a house made of logs. Born into a wealthy

family, catered to everywhere he turned, and as corrupt as the day was long, he considered himself king of all he could see.

Victor Boyd, on the other hand, was what the world liked to call a self-made man. He'd left home at age sixteen, not long after his sister Kendra had gone missing. He'd thrown himself into law enforcement as a way to compensate for her loss and only moved back to town once he was established in his career.

"Even if you didn't know her personally, you had to have heard the stories," Tess said. "She was written off as a runaway, right? They found a bus ticket and assumed she'd split town, so that was the end of the investigation."

Mason's expression took on a look of interest. "You know about that?"

"I know a lot more than you think—about everyone." It wasn't a threat, but it wasn't not one, either. Tess's observation skills might make her a nuisance, but they also made her the writer she was today. "I also know that Kendra's boyfriend at the time thought Victor was responsible for her disappearance and shot him, but he was never formally charged."

Mason released a low whistle. "Is that what happened? We all knew there'd been an accident, but not the details. No wonder Victor tucked tail and ran."

Like the secretary comments, Tess let that pass,

but it was a struggle. When she wrote about fictional crime, Detective Gonzales intimidated his interrogation victims into revealing the truth. Real life required a lot more tact. And long, deep breaths.

"In the book, the third victim was discovered separately from the other two, buried at the edge of the cemetery in an unmarked grave." Chronologically speaking, she wasn't the third victim but the second one, but Tess let that part pass. "With similar wounds to the other two. All three victims were women, all three were reported missing, and all three were found years later."

"I don't see what this has to do with me."

Tess shook her head, frustrated at her inability to pull her thoughts into a cohesive whole. Too many of the real facts and the fictional plot points overlapped; she was having a difficult time making sense of them. Her primary worry right now had to do with what she'd heard at the sheriff's office about Lucretia selling her car to Herb before being dropped off at the bus station. That tale was too similar to the story of Victor's sister for Tess's peace of mind. She hadn't yet talked to anyone about Annabelle's disappearance, but she was guessing she'd find more of the same.

A girl believed to be on the run. Someone no one bothered to look for.

If what she suspected was true—that there was

a third body in the form of Sheriff Boyd's long-lost sister buried near the cemetery—it was going to break him. And she was going to have to be the one doing the breaking.

"I just need to know what you heard at the time," Tess said. "The story about Kendra running away—did it make sense? Was she that kind of person?"

"Sure. Why not?" Mason splayed his hands. "Like I said, I hardly knew the girl, but people run away from here all the time. Not everyone is cut out for life in a small town."

"Was Annabelle?"

Mason's arms jerked as if pulled by the strings of a puppeteer. He swiveled his head to stare at her, his eyes suddenly so dark that Tess felt as if she was being swallowed whole. "What did you just say?"

"Annabelle Charles. The first victim." Too late, Tess realized that she was a privileged person with privileged access to information—and that the names of the victims hadn't yet been released. Instead of being alarmed, however, she leaned close. "You knew her, didn't you?"

"Of course I knew her." Mason got to his feet, his height suddenly towering and his shoulders broader than Tess remembered them being before. She was more grateful than she could say to have Jared only a few shouts away, his hammer at the ready. "Everyone in town did."

Tess could barely believe her luck. She held her breath, hoping he'd say more.

He did.

"She's the woman who broke up my parents' marriage. She's the reason my father was almost ruined." Mason's lips curled in a grimace. "If she's one of the dead bodies found in your grandfather's store, then all I can say is good riddance."

Chapter Ten

Tess had never seen Sheriff Boyd worked up to such a state before.

She stood back, content to watch from a distance as he hemmed and hawed and stammered. And, of all improbable things, *blushed*.

"Mr. Oblonsky, can I just say what an honor this is?" said the sheriff. Tess could have sworn his hand was trembling as he held it out to the older man. "I've been an admirer of your work for more years than I care to say."

Since Tess had prepped Peter ahead of time, he took this fawning veneration in good humor. He accepted the sheriff's hand and shook warmly, his cane hooked over his forearm. "Of my forensic studies or my fiction?"

"Both," the sheriff said quickly, as if such a thing could have been in question. "I like a good horror story as much as the next guy, but your head wound and blood-spatter reports were a huge part of my early studies."

"Mine, too," Tess admitted, pushing herself off the

wall to join the fan club. She nodded at the sheriff. "That must be why you're willing to admit I get that part of my books right. We both learned from the best."

"You did that research for *Night Nurse*, right?" Sheriff Boyd asked, refusing the bait. As if it would have killed him to compliment her in front of a fellow author. "That book scared the crap out of me when I was a kid. I refused to go the hospital for years after that."

Peter chuckled. "You and about fifty thousand other readers. You should have seen some of the hate mail I got from medical professionals after that book came out. Everyone went to the doctor expecting to come home with only half their internal organs."

"I'd love to know more about where the two overlap—your fiction and your research, I mean. Are you like Tess? Do you dive into forensics as a way to avoid having to work on your books?"

"That's not what I do!" Tess protested, but it was no use. Between Peter Oblonsky and Sheriff Victor Boyd, she had few secrets left.

"You just made the sheriff's whole day." Ivy crept up behind her, a laugh in her voice. "His whole week, actually. I'm sorry to say it, but you've been replaced. Your fame will hold no power over him after this."

Since Tess hadn't been aware that her fame had done her any favors with the sheriff to date, this didn't cut as deep as Ivy intended. "What else can we do to put him in a good mood?" she asked instead. "I'd offer cookies, but we saw how well those went over last time."

"Why does he need to be in a good mood in the first place? You aren't going to try and ask him to deputize you again, are you? I can tell you right now that's never happening. There's literally nothing you could do and nothing you can say to change his mind."

It was on the tip of Tess's tongue to retort that if she *really* wanted a deputy's badge, she'd have one by the year's end, but that wasn't the battle she came here to fight. Taking Ivy by the arm, she led her toward the back of the office, where an ancient fax machine stood next to a copier that had seen its heyday long before Tess had.

"Ivy, we have a problem."

Instead of being alarmed, Ivy heaved a sigh. "Why do I get the feeling that what you're really saying is *I* have a problem?"

"Trust me—this is one that's going to cause us both to suffer." Tess paused and glanced around the busy office, but no one was paying attention to them. "There's a third body."

Ivy covered her eyes with her hand and groaned. "Oh, jeez. The sheriff is going to have a conniption. And I was so sure we covered the entire hardware store. Where was this one? Shoved inside a water heater? Buried in the alley out back? We'd better get Sylvia, stat."

Tess waved a hand at Ivy, signaling for her to keep her voice down. "I don't mean I've literally seen it. I just know there is one."

Ivy peered at her with one eye closed. "Because you found a note left by your deceased grandfather?"

"No, but—"

"Because you can smell the bones with your acute senses?"

"Ivy, this is no time to—"

"Because you're a mystic who's been having visions from beyond the grave?"

Tess had never been so near to stamping her foot in her life. "Will you stop being dramatic and listen?" She reached into her purse and extracted her now-weathered copy of *Let Sleeping Dogs Lie*. "This book overlaps with the murders in a way that has to be more than coincidence. According to this, we're missing one more person."

Ivy didn't take the book from her. "Tess, you do know that novels aren't real, right? I know you've had trouble writing from anything except firsthand experience lately, but the rest of us just make it up as we go."

Tess ignored this slight on her storytelling abilities and tossed the book at Ivy. Ivy, trained to react, caught it.

"Read it, and then you can mock me all you want."

Ivy glanced at the cover before lifting a brow. "'A fast-paced, reckless tale that grabs you by the throat and doesn't let go'? Really? I hope you can do better than this when my book comes out."

Tess groaned. "If that's you asking me for a quote in order to get you to read the book, then yes. Fine. I'll say whatever you want. Just take this seriously." She pointed at the paperback. "That author seems to know an awful lot about the missing women. As in, a *compromising* lot."

"You're saying this Simone Peaky is our murderer? And she confessed in a novel that you helped promote?"

"I'm saying something strange is going on, and I'm afraid Sheriff Boyd isn't going to take it well. One of the victims in the book... Ivy, the clues all line up, and I don't like the way they're shaping up. I think the sheriff's sister is the body we haven't found yet. According to this, we'll find her buried somewhere on the edges of the cemetery."

That got Ivy's attention. Pursing her lips in a soundless whistle, she flipped casually through the pages. "You want to be careful throwing stuff like that around. If the sheriff were to get wind of this..."

"I *know*," Tess said, feeling desperate. "That's why I'm bringing it to you first. Read it and tell me what you think. If I sound like a hysterical scaremonger, then all you have to do is say so, and I'll never bring it up again."

"You're a hysterical scaremonger," Ivy promptly said.

"Ivy!"

A wry grin touched Ivy's lips. "Sorry. I couldn't resist." She glanced at the quote again. "Wait. If you love this book so much, why didn't you bring it in right away? It's been over a week since we found those bodies."

Tess didn't have the patience—or the nerve—to explain to Ivy exactly how the publishing world worked, especially when it came to the favors traded between authors, their agents, and the powerhouses that fueled the industry. She'd find out for herself soon enough. "I forgot about it until Peter reminded me. He's the one who pointed out the similarities and suggested the third victim."

"So…who did it?" Ivy flipped to the back of the book and started scanning the lines. "The murders, I mean? If this book is so insightful, we might as well get some use out of it and solve this dratted thing. Was it dear old Grandpa, after all?"

Tess hesitated. "Yes and no."

"Ha! I knew it. Sheriff Boyd owes me ten bucks."

"Ivy, you don't actually think my grandfather had anything to do with all this, do you?"

The deputy rolled an indifferent shoulder. "The

bodies were under his floor, Tess. I'm a strong believer in Occam's razor. If it looks like a cow pie and it smells like a cow pie, there's no need to taste it and find out for sure."

"That's...not Occam's razor."

"It's close enough to count." Ivy gave up on the pages. "So what's his motive? Love affair gone wrong? Money? Or does he just like the way it feels to kill?"

Tess closed her eyes and counted to ten inside her head. She was starting to get seriously tired of everyone assuming her grandfather had something to do with all this. Whatever happened to innocent until proven guilty? "*If* he did it—and it's a very strong *if*—then it's probably for the same reason everyone else in town did."

"What are you talking about?"

"That's how the book ends. It turns out that both women—I mean, all *three* women—were killed by the whole town in on it together. That's how they died. They were tied up, drugged, and then everyone took turns with a hatchet."

"Um, Tess? You know that's the plot to *Murder on the Orient Express*, right?"

"Of course I know that!"

"Is that why you called the tale 'reckless'?"

Tess counted to ten out loud this time. "There are a few differences, obviously, but yes. I'll admit there are strong Agatha Christie undertones."

"Undertones?"

"Overtones. Directly lifted passages. Who cares?" Tess noticed that Peter and Sheriff Boyd had finished talking and hissed for Ivy to put the book away. If she knew Ivy—and she did—the other woman wouldn't go to bed tonight until she'd read the thing straight through.

Which, good. Tess needed a sounding board for her thoughts, a way to work out the details that were starting to make her feel uneasy about this whole thing. According to Simone Peaky—and, okay, Agatha Christie—the victims had been such unpleasant people that an entire town banded together to do away with them. That was why the number of marks on the bone varied so much. Some of the townspeople had better aim than others.

It would have been an easy enough ending to laugh at—stuff like that didn't happen in real life, regardless of how many writers decided to rehash the same plot—except for the tale that Mason had told her back at the hardware store.

According to him, Annabelle Charles had been a delinquent of the highest degree. Petty theft, armed robbery, extortion schemes in which she slept with married men and then demanded payment to stay quiet about it—there had been no limit to the trouble she'd managed to cause around these parts. Apparently, Mason's dad wasn't the only one to have fallen for Annabelle's charms; he was just the wealthiest.

Twenty thousand dollars had been her price, and it had been paid in full. That hadn't been a lot of money to the Peabodys, but anyone else slapped with that demand would have been hard-pressed to meet it.

Tess had never felt the urge to do away with anyone herself, but she could see how an entire town might feel the compulsion. Especially this town. People who lived this isolated from the rest of the world started to get pretty strange notions after a while.

"Just keep an open mind, okay? That's all I ask." Tess glanced nervously at Peter and the sheriff. They were starting to make their way over, so she had to speak quickly. "And don't say anything to Sheriff Boyd without me. I want to—"

"We're heading over to talk to the coroner," the sheriff said, cutting her short. Since Sheriff Boyd's smile was as wide as Gertrude's had been when she'd first announced her job shadow position, Tess had no fears that they'd been overheard. The people in her life and their obsession with the morgue were starting to become seriously alarming. "Sylvia made me promise to bring Mr. Oblonsky."

"And Mr. Oblonsky is eager to get his hands on

those bones," Peter added, grinning. He rubbed his papery hands together. "I especially want to see how they overlap—"

"With one another," Tess interrupted, her voice firm. She'd warned Peter ahead of time to keep the *Let Sleeping Dogs Lie* tie-ins quiet until she could figure out what to do with the information. "If anyone will be able to tell if the marks are from the same weapon, it's you."

"We'll all go together," Ivy announced. She'd managed to hide the book somewhere while the rest of them were talking, so Tess didn't put up a fight. "By the time we're done with those bones, this murder case won't know what hit it."

Chapter Eleven

"THE BONES ARE GONE."

Gertrude ran out of the morgue to greet them, green scrubs covering her jeans and a look of wicked excitement on her face. Tess started to lick her thumb to wipe away a smear of something wet on her daughter's cheek, but she stopped herself as soon as she recalled where they were. If there was any chance that what touched Gertrude's skin was human in origin, she wanted nothing to do with it.

"What do you mean, the bones are gone?" Ivy asked. "Did Sylvia send them off to get tested? That was a dumb move. She must have known Mr. Oblonsky was coming."

"She *did* know it." Gertrude's eyes shone. "And so did the murderer, because he took them sometime last night. They've been stolen."

Sheriff Boyd was the first to react to this piece of news. Without waiting to hear more, he brushed past the group and swung open the glass doors. Ivy was quick to follow. Tess would have joined in, but manners forced her to wait for Peter, who wasn't as mobile as he used to be. Propping open the door, she lifted her brows as he and Gertrude made their way inside.

"That didn't happen in the book," she said.

Peter chuckled. "No. It seems our murderer has a few surprises left in him. Either that, or your Ms. Sylvie is more careless than she'd like us to believe."

"She isn't," Gertrude insisted. She dashed at the spot on her cheek with the back of her hand, which only caused it to smear. The slight tinge of red made Tess feel nauseated. That was definitely human in origin. "Everything is under tight lock and key—and there's a night guard who keeps watch at this desk all the time. *With* cameras."

That piqued Tess's interest in more ways than one. "You mean there's footage of the theft? Of the murderer?"

"No—that's the thing. All the records have been wiped clean. Ms. Sylvie was about to call the sheriff when you guys came bursting in."

Tess didn't know if they'd been bursting before, but they certainly did now. Even though walking into the morgue like this was probably contaminating a crime scene, Tess refused to be the only person left behind.

Missing bones. Two dead bodies vanished into thin air. The only remaining evidence of murder wiped away.

This was fantastic news. Maybe she wouldn't have to plagiarize Simone Peaky to get a good book out of this, after all.

Gertrude led them expertly through the hallways toward a small, discreet office with Sylvia Nerudo's nameplate on the door. It was already crammed full of people, so the three of them stood awkwardly in the hallway to listen.

"Why didn't you call me the second you noticed the bones were missing?" the sheriff was in the middle of saying. Ivy already had her notebook open and was scrawling notes in her largely illegible handwriting.

It spoke well of the relationship between Sylvia and Sheriff Boyd—and of Sylvia's ability to stand on her own two feet—that the tiny woman didn't back down. "Because missing isn't necessarily the same thing as stolen, and you know it. For all I knew, one of the cleaning staff came through and tossed them in the garbage. I wanted to make sure they weren't misplaced before I called in the whole cavalry."

Considering how many of them were crowded around her, *cavalry* was the right word.

"But you're sure now?" asked the sheriff.

"As sure as I can be," said Sylvia. "There's no evidence of a break-in, but every single one of our cameras malfunctioned at the same time last night. There's no way that's a coincidence."

Peter gently cleared his throat. "And what about the security guard Gertie mentioned?"

Sylvia glanced over at the older man, a quelling lift to her brow. Tess had the delight of seeing the other brow come up to meet it before Sylvia released a sound that could only be described as a squeak.

"Peter Oblonsky. It's actually you."

Peter smiled. "In the flesh...which is more than I can say for these bones I've come to see."

Sylvia's face fell to a comical degree. "Oh, dear. You came all this way. Bought your own ticket. Visited *my* morgue. And—"

Peter smiled with the calm friendliness that set everyone at ease—and that made it so ironic that he wrote and studied such macabre subjects. "Not to worry. Pictures will do just as well at present. I'm sure our good sheriff here will locate the bones in no time."

A flush of pink touched Sylvia's cheeks, but Gertrude was the one who spoke up.

"They're gone, too. No prints, no copies, no files on the computer. It's *awesome*."

Peter blinked, clearly taken aback by this newest turn of events. "But surely your personal notes, your findings..."

"Oh, I can tell you what I found right enough." Sylvia shook her head. "The number of hatchet marks, the angle and placement of the strikes, how the first body contained mostly defensive wounds on the forearms and hands… But without evidence to back it up, I have no way of proving any of it. No court of law would accept my testimony as the sole evidence—and I still haven't been able to pinpoint an exact cause of death."

From the expression on Sheriff Boyd's face, Tess understood Sylvia to be telling the truth. Making sure something could be successfully prosecuted was as by the book as Sheriff Boyd could get. He wasn't likely to proceed without it.

"One would presume the, er, hatchet did the job," Peter said.

Sylvia shook her head. "Not conclusively. Were the women drugged ahead of time? Was there any blunt-force trauma? I'd only just begun my real report. There were so many unanswered questions left."

"Cool. You didn't tell me they might have been drugged," Gertrude said, entirely missing the point.

Tess took that as her cue to grab her daughter by the arm and hightail it out of there. Well, that and the fact that the sheriff was starting to look seriously alarmed. That level of infiltration—of the careful, methodical removal of evidence—suggested a criminal of exceptional skill.

And a criminal who was currently alive to carry it out. If this news didn't clear dear old Grandpa's name, Tess didn't know what would.

"Why don't I take Gertrude and Peter home for

now?" she suggested. "I'm sure you have a lot to do without us getting in your way."

"Mom!" Gertrude protested as she tried—and failed—to yank her arm out of Tess's grasp. "I'm *working*. This is all part of being in the morgue."

Peter's low chuckle did more to pull Gertrude out of that hallway than any amount of tugging Tess might do. "Sorry, Gertie, but I've been in and out of morgues since the seventies. This the first time there's ever been a robbery in one."

"Really?" Gertrude wrinkled her nose. "If *I* were a murderer, I'd steal any of my bodies that got found right away so I could rebury them. If at first you don't succeed, try, try again."

Tess choked.

"An interesting approach, but hardly useful in this instance," Sheriff Boyd said dryly. Without losing a beat, he grabbed the radio clipped to his belt and started barking orders to lock down the morgue. He wasn't even halfway through when he turned and glared at Tess.

Tess strengthened her grip on Gertrude's arm and continued dragging the reluctant teenager away from the scene of the crime.

She might not have all the answers when it came to solving murders, but she did know how to take a hint when it was being leveled warningly at her head.

"Mom, I know I said I wanted to help Sheriff Boyd find the missing bones, but this isn't what I meant."

Gertrude stood at the entrance to the small, quaint cemetery with a frown on her face and that smudge of contamination still on her cheek. Throwing caution to the wind, Tess dug around in her purse until she found a wadded-up tissue. She licked it, dabbed at the teen's face, and was rewarded for her loving care with a screech.

"There were bodily fluids on your face," Tess explained as she dangled the used tissue from finger and thumb. "It was starting to drive me up a wall."

To her surprise—and disgust—Peter poked his forefinger at the tissue and brought it to his lips. Tess barely had time to stifle a gag before he flicked his tongue over the dab of residue left behind.

"Jelly doughnut. Raspberry. Just as I suspected."

Gertrude grinned her appreciation at this show of knowledge, but Tess wasn't so easily won over.

"Peter! What if you were wrong? You might have accidentally eaten a *person*."

"They don't let me get close to anything cool," Gertrude reminded her at the same time Peter chuckled and said, "We passed by a box of doughnuts sitting in the break room."

"I didn't notice that," Tess said, feeling defensive. This was the kind of thing she usually liked to pick up on—a contextual clue that set the scene and answered questions before they were asked—but she'd been distracted by all the murder and theft taking place around them. "And even if I had, there's no way I'd eat anything off that child's face. Kids are disgusting, Peter."

"So are cemeteries, yet here we are."

All three of them returned their attention to the Winthrop Historic Cemetery. It was a place Tess had long planned to visit, a small patch of land set a few miles outside the town proper. Cemeteries were one of the best places to go for character name inspiration, and one that had been standing as long as this one had the additional benefit of being beautiful. For more than a hundred years, residents of Methow Valley had been laid to rest within this two-acre meadow. Wildflowers sprang up around gravestones crumbled with age; more durable plastic blooms nodded brightly above headstones of modern construction.

"I don't get it," Gertrude said, dismissing it all with a blink. "Do you think someone stole the bones and buried them here? Like…out of respect?"

Tess shook her head and handed her daughter a shovel. "Don't be silly. Someone stole those bones because they're the only piece of evidence that exists in this case. Without them, it's virtually impossible to solve, and whoever broke into the morgue knows it."

A visitor to the cemetery, a sixtysomething

man walking a sprightly terrier, took one look at Gertrude's dark hair, dark nails, and shovel and gave them a wide berth.

"Then what are we doing here?" Gertrude demanded. "And why are you going to make me dig?"

Peter answered for Tess. "Because somewhere on the perimeter of this cemetery, we're going to find a third body."

═══════

They didn't find a third body.

To be more accurate, they *did* find one. And then another. And then another. In fact, by the time Tess and Gertrude were covered in sweat and dust that ran in streaked rivulets down their faces, their hands blistered and their moods considerably worn down, they'd found a total of eight.

"I don't know what the rules governing animal desecration in the United States are, but I believe this constitutes a moral crime in the UK," Peter said from the relative comfort of a cemetery bench that doubled as an advertisement for personal injury legal aid. "Five dogs, two cats, and…a hamster? Is that what we've decided to call it?"

"I'm pretty sure it's a guinea pig." Tess ran the back of her hand across her forehead, but all it did was turn the amalgamation of dust and sweat into mud.

"Gertie had one when she was six years old. It was the sweetest little thing. He used to gobble up all the kitchen scraps. Strawberry tops were his favorite."

Gertrude plopped down to the ground, her shovel falling heavily next to her. "This is ridiculous. Mom, we can't keep digging up people's pets. It's weird. And gross."

"You're the one with an interest in anatomy. Why don't you take that guinea pig home and see if you can put his little skeleton back together again?"

"Mom!"

"It was just a suggestion." Tess sighed and fell to the ground next to her daughter. "But don't get too comfortable where you are. We've got to fill in all these graves before we go. I had no idea people used this area as a place to put their pets to rest. I'm just glad Sheriff Boyd wasn't here to witness this."

"Too late," a low, drawling voice said. "He already is."

"Victor!" Tess shot to her feet like a bullet. Her already heated skin flushed uncomfortably, and she was hyperaware of the fact that she was dressed for grave robbing, her hair in a tangled ponytail at the base of her head. "What are you doing here?"

"Gee, Tess. I don't know. Maybe it was the three calls I got informing me that there was a madwoman and her daughter pillaging the local cemetery while an older gentleman egged them on from afar?"

"Oh. Right. Small town." Tess wiped her hands

on the seat of her jeans. "I know how this must look, but you have to understand—"

"Don't."

Tess winced at the note in the sheriff's voice. "We didn't dig up any *people*, I swear. And we never set foot in the actual cemetery. We were just doing a...perimeter check."

"A perimeter check," he echoed flatly. It matched the tight compress of his lips.

"Yep. It occurred to me, as we were driving by, that it'd be a great spot to hide missing bones. You know—in a graveyard? The most obvious place that no one would think to look? I'm thinking about putting it in my book. Can you imagine if Detective Gonzales had to exhume an entire cemetery?"

It said a lot about their history together that nothing about this seemed to surprise the sheriff. In fact, he took a deep breath and completely bypassed her. "The madwoman with a shovel makes sense, but Gertie? Peter? How could you two support her in this?"

Gertrude flushed as guiltily as Tess had. "It's not my fault. I'm a minor. I have to do what my mom says."

By this time, Peter had also risen to his feet and ambled over to join them. He had nothing but complete control over himself, his lips faintly smiling. "To be perfectly honest, *I'm* the one who's responsible. I noticed that some of the soil surrounding the site looked as if had been recently disturbed. The thought occurred to me—ever so slightly, you understand—that anyone disposing of forensic evidence in a hurry might try to use the graveyard as a cover. I'd also suggest you check out any local crematoria, particularly large animal farms in the immediate area."

As if by magic, the grim line of the sheriff's mouth lifted. "Yeah. I thought of that, too. We've also got a watch out on all veterinary clinics, but it's a long shot. Chances are the perp will either sink them in a lake somewhere or bury them in a place we'll never think to look. I doubt we'll see those bodies again."

Tess watched this interaction with mixed feelings. On one hand, she was delighted to be spared Sheriff Boyd's quiet, quelling wrath. On the other, she found it highly insulting that Peter was going to be forgiven for doing *exactly* what she had.

"Don't forget meat grinders," Tess said. "Or wood chippers. If we're making a list, I've got plenty of ideas about how to get rid of a dead body."

Sheriff Boyd raised a brow. "Is that a threat?"

She muffled a laugh. "Only if you plan to arrest me for this slight lapse of judgment." She cast a look over their muddled attempts at finding the third body and found that the rest of her laughter muffled itself. Belatedly, it occurred to her that should it become necessary to tell the sheriff about *Let Sleeping Dogs Lie* and his sister's potential ties to it, he'd realize what they'd been really searching for out here.

If he was annoyed at them *now*, she could only imagine what his feelings would be at that not-so-distant date.

Gertrude heaved herself up from the ground and began shoveling dirt back into their pock-marked holes. Every muscle in Tess's body balked at the sight of so much activity, so she decided to walk the sheriff back to his car instead.

"I can't believe someone broke into the morgue and stole evidence," she said, even though she found that particular twist very easy to believe. The sheriff's steps dawdled next to her, so she assumed this topic of conversation was an acceptable one. "What happens now?"

"As of this precise moment, I'm mostly trying to keep the FBI from getting involved."

"The FBI?" Tess echoed. "Don't we have enough of that around here already?"

He cast her a sideways glance, his expression difficult to read. "My thoughts exactly. But with two bodies, we're looking at a potential serial killer, which is a thing they can't resist." He paused, his steps slowing even further. They were far enough away from Gertrude and Peter that neither one of them bothered to lower their voices. "I just had a long meeting with Nicki. She all but begged me to do what I can to keep the feds out."

"Is that your way of telling me you think she's

the killer? Because I'm pretty sure she was a baby in 1988."

He sighed. "Any official federal presence is likely to spook Mason so far off the grid that her investigation will be set back months, if not years."

"Oh." Tess hadn't thought of that. Although the idea of Nicki putting down more permanent roots in Winthrop was one she strongly supported, she wasn't sure she could put up with Jared for that long. He'd sent her a text that morning of an ancient alien statue that had been unearthed in some cavern or other in Indonesia. As the statue was also alarmingly phallic in size and shape, Tess wasn't sure how she was supposed to take it. "I can see how that might upset her plans. Did she tell you that I managed an introduction between Jared and Mason?"

"She did," he said, and in such a neutral tone that Tess suspected a trap. These suspicions were borne out when he added, "She was also careful to update me about the cover story you fed Mason. Really, Tess? A torrid love affair? That kid is young enough to be your—"

Tess flung up a hand. "I know. It wasn't any of my doing, I swear. Jared forgot his own name, and once Mason picked up on that, it was all downhill from there."

The sheriff snorted in derision. "He forgot his name?"

"Well, his cover name, at any rate. Honestly, I feel sorry for him. I don't think he's going to shape up to be much of an undercover agent." She grinned, unable to help herself. "But he's one heck of a handyman, so at least he has something to fall back on. As soon as he finishes the bookstore, I'm thinking about hiring him to renovate the entire cabin. Gertie wants her own wing."

Instead of sharing her amusement, a shadow descended on the sheriff's face. "I don't know if it's a good idea for you to get too involved in whatever rig he and Nicki are running."

She blinked at how serious he sounded—how stern. "I'd hardly call an undercover federal operation a *rig*."

"I mean it. It's bad enough when you're poking around in *my* cases, but—" He shook himself off, but the shadow remained. "Never mind. Forget I said anything."

"Wait. Victor, *wait*." She put an arm out to stop him, but he'd started moving toward his car again—and this time, there was nothing dawdling about his pace. "What's really going on? What are you afraid of?"

"You mean, other than a double homicide with no leads, little evidence, and two missing bodies?" He shook his head. "Nothing, Tess. Not one tiny thing."

Chapter Twelve

"WHAT DO YOU MEAN, SIMONE PEAKY ISN'T A real person?"

Tess sat at her dining room table with her cell phone in one hand and a finger plugging her free ear. The cabin, normally a quiet retreat, had turned into a noisy game of Yahtzee between Gertrude, Peter, and Nicki—all of whom were laughing uproariously and making it impossible for Tess to hear her agent on the other end of the line.

"It's a pen name, Tess," said Nancy. "A nom de plume. You know how these things work."

It was true. She did. Most of the authors Tess was friends with hid their true personas behind a secure layer of fake names and Schedule Cs. Not only was having a separate business identity better for tax purposes, but there was a much less likely chance that a deranged woman in rural Washington would call you up and demand to speak to you about your murder book *at once*.

"Can't you ring up her agent and ask her to call me? It's urgent."

"If it's urgent, you can email Ms. Peaky on her contact page."

Tess let out a grunt of irritation. "I did that already. Twice. She won't answer me."

"Maybe she's busy. Maybe she's *writing*. You remember, right? That thing authors do when they have a contract? When their hardworking agent has pulled together the deal of a century, and everything hangs on its completion?"

"Hint taken but not accepted," Tess said. "I'm serious, Nancy. I blurbed this woman's book, for crying out loud. Surely you can pull a few strings and hunt her down."

A long pause and an even longer sigh sounded through the phone. "Fine. I'll see what I can do, but I'm not making any promises. This is a tough business, even with a blurb from a bestseller to give you a boost. For all we know, she gave up on being an author years ago and is living her best life in Costa Rica."

"You just said she's probably writing," Tess muttered, but she doubted Nancy heard her. She also doubted Nancy would get any further in the Simone Peaky search than she had herself. Her Google-fu skills were no small matter. If days of searching the web had pulled up no sequels, no future books, and no author appearances, then there was a good chance that Costa Rica story held weight.

Or that Simone doesn't want us to discover who she really is. For all Tess knew, she was actually a serial killer. A criminal on the run.

A resident of this town.

"Stop trying to solve a murder and come play with us," Nicki said. "I think Peter is playing with loaded dice. All he ever seems to roll is sixes. It's starting to freak me out."

"Did you get anywhere on your Simone search?" he asked as he rattled the dice in their cup and tossed them. Contrary to Nicki's warning, it was a succession of ones and twos that would do him little good in securing his upper bonus.

"No." Tess slumped to a chair. "Whoever she is, she's done a good job of hiding her real identity. If I knew a hacker, I might be able to get into the publisher's records or see who her domain is registered to, but..."

Nicki didn't miss her meaning. She threw up her hands in a gesture of surrender. "Don't look at me. I'm not touching this—I'm here strictly as a curious bystander. That book aligning with the murders is just a coincidence. You're always saying how common coincidences are in real life."

It was true. She *did* always say that, especially in any interview she gave. Readers needed to know that a coincidence wasn't a literary shortcut or an author being lazy with the plot. It was a reflection of reality. Just consider how Peter was the *one* person

Tess knew who'd actually read that Simone Peaky book. He was also a forensics expert who dropped everything to come help her in her investigation. That was an aligning of the stars that the *New York Times Book Review* would never let her get away with. She'd have been eviscerated before they got to the second paragraph.

Tess turned next to Gertrude, appraising her daughter as if seeing her for the first time. "You're young. You're edgy. Don't you have an internet friend somewhere who can send me a link to the dark web?"

"Ohmigod, Mom. That's not how it works. It's not a tab you keep open for emergencies."

"Why not? How else are you supposed to get it?"

Peter picked up the dice and rolled again. "I might know of someone who can help you out," he said.

"Wait. What?" Tess swiveled to stare at him. There were those coincidences putting themselves to work again. "You do?"

"Sure. I needed to do some fact checking back when I was working on *Track of Time.* I wanted to make sure the family that got sucked into the computer took an authentic journey. My accountant put me in touch with him. Great kid. MIT grad, used to work for Amazon—if anyone can discover Simone's true identity, it's him."

Considering that Tess had been too scared to

use her laptop for *weeks* after she'd read that book, she believed it. Every static shock she'd suffered had almost sent her into an apoplexy.

"That would be amazing," Tess said. "I've always wanted to have a secret hacker source."

"His rates start at two thousand bucks an hour," Peter said as he passed the dice off to his right. "So make sure you know what to ask for before you call."

Next to her, Nicki snorted. "With a price tag like that, he'd better be able to hack the FBI."

"With a price tag like that," Peter countered, "he can."

Chapter Thirteen

When Tess walked into the bookstore the following day, she encountered a sight that caused fear to shoot all the way down her spine before crawling back up again.

"Adam?" She stopped on the threshold, her hand clutching the frame as Mason's brother finished swiping a metal trowel over her newly erected drywall. "What are you doing here?"

Jared popped his head into the room. He also had a trowel in hand, a swipe of spackle in the shape of a comma beneath his eye. "Mason kept his promise. Adam has been here since eight o'clock helping me get these walls up. Isn't that nice?"

Nice was one word for it, yes. Other options included intrusive, suspicious, and downright dodgy. Mason had lost no time in planting his brother here to keep an eye on things.

"This is awfully generous of you," she said, offering her hand. She wasn't sure whether to be relieved or insulted when Adam just stared at it. Although he and his brothers were identical—their hair the same glinting auburn, their eyes like hard, indifferent stone—no one would ever mistake him for Mason. Whereas Mason was a consummate businessman, polished and pompous down to his Oxfords, she'd never seen Adam in anything but flannel. In fact, he was every inch the handyman Jared was trying to emulate, only the calluses on *his* hands had been earned the hard way.

"I'm not here for you," Adam said and spat on the ground.

This show of hostility did much to assuage Tess's fears. She didn't *love* having her shoes spattered by phlegmy spittle, obviously, but at least it was within the realm of what she expected of this man. Had he welcomed her with open arms, begged her forgiveness and offered to take her to tea, she'd have immediately invested in a handgun. Spit was something she could work with.

"My brother told me to help, so I'm helping," he added, still hostile but no longer projecting bodily fluids. "Don't think this makes us friends."

"Noted. I'm also more than willing to pay you a fair wage, if—"

Adam's lips pursed ominously, so she put her hands up and took a step back.

"If you want," she said quickly. "No pressure. I don't want to take advantage of your time, that's all."

He softened slightly, by which Tess registered an

infinitesimal relaxing of his shoulders. "Just don't ask me to cut down any trees for you, and we'll be good," he said.

Considering that Adam owned one-third of his family's corrupt logging enterprise, Tess was startled into a laugh. "Was that a…logging joke?" she asked.

"It wasn't *not* one" was all the response she got.

Watching this exchange, which was starting to border on friendliness, Jared grinned. He did it so good-naturedly, and with such deep dimples, that Tess found herself returning it.

She realized her mistake almost at once.

"I'm about due for a lunch break if you want to grab a bite," he said, running a hand through his hair. It fell in an almost perfect swoop across his forehead. "I've heard the deli on the corner makes a mean Cubano."

"Oh. Um. Well."

"You don't have to if you don't want to," Jared was quick to add. The flush that touched his cheeks confirmed that what he had in mind was no platonic meal. "I just figured since you came all this way…"

Tess, a master of words and fictional scenarios, struggled to come up with an excuse—a thing that wasn't helped when her stomach gave an ominous rumble. The Cubano at the deli *was* delicious.

"I'm not sure I have time today, but—" She glanced over to find Adam watching them closer than unfriendly interest dictated. With an inward sigh, she realized how little choice she had in the matter. If Mason had mentioned anything about Jared's cover story to his brother, then it behooved her to keep up appearances.

She was a cougar, Jared was her sugar baby, and that was all there was to it.

"Yeah, actually. Lunch sounds great."

"Really? You'll come?" The expression on Jared's face was so pleased—so *eager*—that Tess hastily extended the invitation.

"Why don't you come with us, Adam?" she asked. The radiance on Jared's face dimmed so much that Tess felt like she'd just kicked a puppy. A puppy who obviously didn't know what was good for it, but still. She stared hard at him and added, "That way all *three* of us can get better acquainted. My treat."

Jared might not have been the sharpest tool in the FBI's shed, but he wasn't slow to pick up on her meaning. Any opportunity to further his acquaintance with the Peabody brothers was worth its weight in Cubanos.

And if it just so happened to make her seem less like a creepy old lady who preyed on young, attractive, single men? Even better. Tess had always been a proponent of killing as many birds at a time as possible.

"Okay," Jared said, his sunny mood returned once more. "We've worked hard enough for one morning."

To Tess's surprise, Adam didn't have to be persuaded. With a careless shrug, he said, "I could eat. But I'm warning you ahead of time—I'm not a cheap date."

Apparently, the deli on the corner had a secret menu.

Apparently, the deli on the corner had a secret menu that contained lobster rolls.

Apparently, the deli on the corner had a secret menu that contained lobster rolls selling for thirty bucks a pop.

Tess regretted nothing.

"I can't believe I didn't know about these." Tess slid down in the vinyl booth, her stomach so full of rich, buttery crustacean that someone was going to have to drag her out. "What other secrets does this town contain?"

Across the table, Adam grinned—as in, actually *grinned*, his teeth flashing and an almost cheerful expression in his eyes. "I could tell you, but then I'd have to kill you."

"Don't you think it's a little too soon to be making those kinds of jokes?" Jared asked. He had eaten three lobster rolls of his own, so he was slumped almost as heavily in his seat as Tess.

Only Adam, whose appetite apparently rivaled that of a horse, wasn't slipping into a food coma. "Those women have been dead for years," he said. "I don't see what difference it makes to them now."

"They may have been dead for years, but their bodies were taken from the morgue not more than two days ago," Tess said somewhat tartly. "That's enough of a difference for me."

Before Adam could reply, her napkin slid from her lap and down to the floor. Jared made an effort to grab it, but since that necessitated proximity to a pair of legs that hadn't seen the sharp side of a razor in weeks, she ducked under the table and grabbed it for herself.

And then she promptly sat up so fast that she smacked her head on the underside of the table.

"Ow, ow, ow."

"What happened?" Jared's face ducked down toward hers. "Are you okay?"

Physically, she was fine. Her ears were ringing, and she had some serious qualms about the last time anyone had run a gum-scraper over the bottom of the table, but she'd survive. What wasn't so easy to get over, however, was the sight of Adam's feet sitting shoulder-width apart on the greasy linoleum floor.

She'd been so distracted when she first got to the bookstore that she'd failed to take note of his shoes. No—not shoes. *Boots.* More precisely, a pair of well-worn hiking boots with frayed laces and scuffed faux leather. Unless she was very much mistaken, they were even dirtier than the last time she'd seen them…standing at attention next to the door of Mason's office.

It was almost as if the man wearing them had been tramping through the deepest, darkest parts of the forest. As if he'd gone somewhere to hide evidence he wanted no one to find.

"Tess, what's wrong? You've been down here an awfully long time."

Tess ignored this and popped her head back up where it belonged. The head injury and food coma made good excuses for her sudden discomfiture, so she played them both up as much as possible.

"I'm going to be useless for the rest of the day," she said, smiling in what she hoped was a natural manner. "What with the blunt-force trauma and all this lobster sitting in my gut, what I need is a good, long nap. Or…a hike, maybe?"

Jared blinked at her. "You want to go hiking?"

Tess waved him off, her attention focused on the other side of the table. If Adam was put off by her sudden interest in the great outdoors, he didn't let it show. He was too busy using the prongs of his fork to pick at his teeth.

"You probably know this forest better than anyone." Tess propped her head on her hand and did her best not to gag when Adam fished out a large, fleshy pink lump, examined it, and popped it right back in his mouth. "I've been looking to get into a new hobby. I'd love to know where the best hiking spots are."

"Buy a map," Adam suggested.

"I could ask around, find a few routes," Jared offered. "It might be fun. We could take a picnic."

"Oh, yeah. Good idea."

"How romantic," Adam drawled, his eyes moving back and forth between the two of them. "A quiet, private walk for two. You'd like that."

Tess bit back a sigh. Jared's cover story was being tested again—she was sure of it. Neither Adam nor Mason Peabody was going to relent until she paraded Jared through the town on a leash.

"I *would* like that, actually," Tess said, louder than she intended. And, because she was starting to grow seriously irritated with all the lies and secrets around here, she added, "Although I probably need something easier than your usual route. Your boots look as though you wore them through a swamp."

Adam glanced down at his feet and back up again, his face flushed an embarrassed shade of red. "What's it to you?"

"Oh, nothing. I'd just give a lot to know where you've been going in your spare time. You and Mason both. Doesn't he have boots just like those?"

The red flush on Adam's face transformed from embarrassed to angry. It was on the tip of Tess's tongue to apologize and backtrack—the last thing she needed was an irate Peabody following her home late at night—but support came from an unexpected source.

"It's my fault," Jared said with the air of one making a dramatic confession. He rubbed the side of his nose with a rueful grin. "I left the tap running in the back sink, and it spilled over into the alleyway. It's a mud pit back there. I was going to tell you, but—"

Adam latched onto this with such speed that Tess recognized it for a lie. "You might need to get a few fans back there to dry it up. You'll get rats if you aren't careful."

"Rats?"

"Big, nasty ones." Adam grinned and pushed back from the table. He glanced over the wreckage of their meal. "You're still footing the bill for this, right?"

At that point, Tess would have gladly covered the bill three times over. She was never one to count the cost when something as valuable as information was on the line. And now she knew: Adam Peabody was hiding something in the forest. She didn't know yet what Mason had to do with it, or how she was supposed to find out what his activities entailed— short of skulking in the dark and following Adam wherever he went—but that was okay.

This was what she called progress.

And the best meal she'd eaten in a long time.

———————

"Don't worry. I won't hold you to our picnic." Jared scuffed his toe against the sidewalk outside the diner. "I didn't realize the hiking thing was just a way to get information out of Adam."

A sudden flush of guilt—and something warmer—flooded through her. Jared had helped her out of a tight spot back there at the diner, and for no reason she could discern except that she'd needed it. The least she could do was eat sandwiches and kill mosquitoes with him.

"No. I want to. That would be nice."

He peeked down at her, his dimples starting to peep through. "Really? Like…as a job? To follow Adam?"

"I mean, I wouldn't say no to tailing him through the forest one of these days, but that's not what I meant." She put a hand on his arm and pressed it. The ripple of his muscles under her palm made a few more of those warm feelings rear their scraggly heads. "Thanks for covering for me back there. That was quick thinking."

Jared blushed so hard that Tess couldn't help feeling a little sorry for him. This clearly wasn't a man who was complimented on his brain power very often.

"Thanks," he said, ducking to avoid her gaze. "That means a lot coming from you."

Tess wasn't a woman who was easily flustered by men of any age or physical makeup. She'd spent far too many years at the top of a male-dominated genre to put much stock in anything they said. Some buttered her up. Others belittled her. Most of them bored her. Jared Wilson, however, made her feel a little fluttery.

Maybe it was because he was the opposite of the other men in this town, who'd rather gnaw off their own arms than admit to something as simple as attraction. It might have also been because he was a twentysomething FBI agent with the build of a Greek god.

"I mean it, Jared. I know Nicki isn't the easiest person to work with, but you've been a real help around here—in more ways than one."

"I'm not the one with killer MMA moves and seven best-selling novels," he protested.

"No, but I still like having you around."

His cup, as it were, runneth over. "What is it we suspect Adam of hiding?" he asked, his chest suddenly swelled to two times its normal size. He tilted his head in the direction Adam had gone. "Why were you so freaked out by his boots?"

"Because I saw them the other day in Mason Peabody's office."

"Maybe they bought the same pair? Buy one, get one free?"

Tess shook her head in an attempt to work her thoughts loose. "No. They're not expensive boots. Adam *might* wear them, but Mason wouldn't go anywhere near synthetic leather. When I first saw them, I thought they might be disposable—the kind of boots you wear when you don't want your steps to be traced back to you. But why is Adam wearing them to a construction site? And where are the two of them going that's so muddy?"

Jared cast a look at the forest surrounding the town. This late in the spring, the snowpack had long since melted, but there was no denying that the moisture lingered. It would be easy to go on a short walk and find yourself in a quagmire of difficulties.

"I know what you're thinking, but that isn't it. You saw how he got when I asked about his activities. He was caught red-handed, and he knew it."

"Do you want me to see what I can get out of him?" Jared offered. "Information-wise, I mean? Since we're spending all that time together in the bookstore anyway…"

"No." The word shot out of her like a bullet. Jared had already proven himself the least subtle undercover agent of all time; the last thing she needed was him bumbling around the forest on her behalf.

Aware that she was once again making herself

out to be a jerk of the highest degree, Tess coughed and tried again.

"You have more than enough to do trying to get in good with Mason. Please don't overextend yourself on my behalf."

He took this rebuff in good humor. With a shrug, he shoved his hands deep in his pockets and began making his way back to the bookstore. "Thanks again for lunch, Tess. And when you're ready for that hike…"

She waved him off with a lighter heart than she might have had a few hours ago. "You'll be the first to know, I promise."

Chapter Fourteen

A FEW HOURS AND WAY TOO MUCH LOBSTER-related heartburn later, Tess was attacked on her way to the pharmacy.

One of the nice things about living in a small town was that you didn't have to do things like lock your car or be afraid of people jumping out of the bushes at you on a public street in the full light of day.

Yet that was exactly what Ivy did.

"Gah!" Tess fell back across the pavement, her hand pressed to her chest as she willed her heart rate to slow. The last time she'd seen her doctor, he'd warned her that if she didn't get her blood pressure in control, she'd need to be put on medication. At this moment, with her pulse pounding and her head starting to whirl, she believed it. "Ivy, what on earth is the matter with you? You almost gave me a heart attack."

"Stop making a scene, will you?" She grabbed Tess by the coat sleeve and tugged. "Come on. People are staring."

With the exception of the mail carrier across the street, who gave them both a friendly wave, no one was paying them the least heed, but Tess followed anyway. For one, she really liked this linen jacket, and she didn't want it to wrinkle. For another, she was pretty sure she'd caught a glimpse of *Let Sleeping Dogs Lie* in the back pocket of Ivy's standard olive-green uniform.

They pushed through a thick hedge to a clearing that Tess had never seen before. It was located a few feet from the road, but the shrubs made it appear isolated and—given the season—a little bleak. Scraggly branches reached out like fingers, the ground mushy and damp. A weathered bench offered a place to sit, but there was no way Tess was getting anywhere near it. She liked this skirt, too.

"You have some serious explaining to do," Ivy said. She pulled out the book and slapped it against Tess's chest. The paperback was even more beaten up than it had been two days ago: several of the pages were marked with sticky notes and there were highlighted passages everywhere. "Who is Simone Peaky, and why does she know so much about this case?"

Tess was so relieved to hear that Ivy's interpretation of the book coincided with her own—and that she was prepared to take those interpretations seriously—that she felt tears well up in her eyes. "Oh, thank goodness."

"I tried looking this woman up," Ivy said. "She doesn't exist—did you know that? Nothing but a facade. Every single picture of her on the internet is a goat."

Tess released a shaky laugh and sank to the bench, sacrificing her skirt to the greater good. "I *do* know that, and I'm working on discovering her real identity. I just need a little more time."

Ivy sank onto the bench next to her. It creaked and groaned but held their collective weight.

"Tess, the sheriff needs to see this."

"Agreed."

"I mean it. This woman knows more than she's letting on in these pages. Even if she *is* innocent of the murders, which I have a hard time believing, she could have valuable insight about what happened to Annabelle and Lucretia. And that bit about the third body..."

Tess sighed and dropped her head in her hands.

"I think you should be the one to tell him."

Tess groaned. "Wouldn't you rather tell him yourself and take all the credit? I wouldn't mind. Maybe you'll get a promotion. Maybe you'll be carried through the town on a litter."

Her entreaties didn't work.

"It has to come from you, Tess, or no one. You know that as well as I do."

It was true. She *did* know it. Not because she'd

once blurbed the book and not because she may or may not have emailed Peter's hacker friend in hopes of identifying the real Simone Peaky, but because Sheriff Victor Boyd was her friend.

Theirs might be a new friendship, still wobbling on uncertain legs, but Tess trusted that man with her life. More than her life, if she was being honest. She'd been through a lot this past year, she and Gertrude both, but the one constant had been Victor's gruff, calm acceptance of everything she threw at him. Dead bodies under her floorboards, a murderous Bigfoot rampaging the woods, one of the messiest and most public divorces this town had ever seen…

She drew a deep breath. Telling the sheriff about his sister's possible ties to this case wasn't going to be pretty, but she owed him that much. He might hate her, and he might throw her out of his office for good, but it had to happen.

And it had to happen today.

———

"Ms. Harrow. Just the woman I was hoping to see."

Tess walked through the door to the sheriff's office with a wary step and an even warier expression. If she hadn't already been feeling queasy at the prospect of reopening Victor's sister's missing person case, then that cold, distant *Ms. Harrow* would have done the trick.

"Why?" she demanded, halting on the threshold. "What's happened now?"

She got her answer a few seconds later. The reception area of the sheriff's office wasn't large, but there was enough room for a few chairs and a planter holding a half-dead ficus. Seated underneath the sad, yellowing leaves was a bespectacled old woman who struck fear into nine-tenths of the population around here.

"It's about time you showed up to work." Edna St. Clair was on her feet in seconds. She might be twice Tess's age and barely larger than a child, but Edna wasn't a woman to underestimate. "When I was your age, punching in after working hours would get you fired. *And* blackballed from future employment."

"That's not a bad idea," the sheriff mused, rubbing a hand along his jaw. Despite that *Ms. Harrow* from before, a twinkle lurked in his eye. "In fact, I heartily approve. Consider this your notice, Tess. You're no longer employed by this—or any—government office under my jurisdiction."

"Don't be ridiculous. She's the best deputy you have." Edna coughed and added in a low voice, "Not that there's much competition."

For the first time since she'd encountered Ivy

in the shrubbery, Tess didn't feel like crying. "You hear that, Sheriff? I'm the best deputy you have."

"And the *only* one I'll talk to, so you might as well keep her around for a few more hours." Edna pulled herself up to her almost five-foot height and drew a deep breath. "I have information on the murders."

Tess glanced quickly over at the sheriff, but his expression was still more amused than anything else. That Edna St. Clair supposed Tess to be a member of the police force was her own fault; she *may* have slightly fudged the facts when first meeting this woman last year. She'd tried correcting the older woman on several occasions, but Edna had soundly rejected each attempt.

"What kind of information?" Tess asked, not displeased with this turn of events. Edna was one of the many townspeople who could claim to have been living here for all the disappearances and murders, which made her an ideal source of information.

She was also the most likely to take a gleeful whack at a woman the whole town wanted to get rid of, but that part went without saying. If this story was going to take a *Murder on the Orient Express* turn, Edna would likely turn out to be the ringleader.

"I don't mind if Tess—er, Deputy Harrow— takes your statement, but let's do it in the back." The sheriff pushed open the door behind him and

held it. "I'd like to make this as official as possible…
given the circumstances."

Tess stood politely back and waited for Edna
to precede her through the door. As she stepped
past the sheriff, he stilled her with a light hand on
her shoulder.

"Thank you, Tess," he said, his voice rumbling low
near her ear. "I appreciate you going along with this."

Gratitude was a rare thing to get from a man like
Victor Boyd—especially *unbidden* gratitude—so it
was understandable that Tess was taken slightly aback.

"I owe you one," he added.

Nothing could have been more calculated
to perk her up—or to tighten her stomach in a
knot of anxiety. It didn't loosen even when Edna
informed them both that in *her* day, key witnesses
were offered more than stale coffee and powdered
creamer, and would they please get her a room with
a window so she didn't have to smell the stink of
decades of criminals?

The sheriff indulged Edna with a good humor
that was starting to make Tess nervous. As far as
she knew, there were still two dead bodies recently
stolen from the morgue whose murders he needed
to solve—and without much in the way of a clue to
go on. Had he uncovered something she hadn't? Was
he about to lock up Edna and throw away the key?

"Okay, Edna. Let's hear it." The sheriff made a

big show of pressing the play button on his recording device and moving it to the center of the table. "What do you know about the Harrow homicides?"

"Wait—what?" Tess swiveled her head to stare at the sheriff. "You can't call them the Harrow homicides."

"Sure I can. The bodies were found by Tess Harrow in the middle of Harrow Hardware. What else should I call them?"

She could think of several good names, up to and including the Orient Express murders, the Peaky felonies, or even case number 3197, but she knew a lost cause when it was smirking at her from across the table.

Edna cracked out a sharp laugh. "Harrow homicides is right. I know for a fact that Melvin Harrow was the one who put those bodies under the floorboards."

"You know no such thing," Tess said hotly. "My grandfather didn't have anything to do with it. Tell her, Sheriff Boyd."

"To be fair, we haven't exactly determined that yet. They were found concealed on *his* property, and in a way that suggests he was a participant in the act. You'd notice a giant hole in your floorboards if you showed up one morning, wouldn't you? Or a fresh patch of linoleum that wasn't there before?"

"Maybe," Tess conceded, "but my grandfather hardly pulled himself up out of his grave to bypass morgue security and steal the bodies to save himself from being brought up on charges. He was a tough old man, but he wasn't *that* tough."

Edna's sharp voice pulled Tess back before she could continue the argument. "No, but his granddaughter sure seems like the type, don't you think?"

From the other side of the table, the sheriff choked on something that might have been surprise but was more likely a laugh. Tess would have taken offense, but it was a good point. A granddaughter who committed crimes to save the family name would make an excellent addition to her own book.

"This is all very helpful, Edna, but do you have any proof?" Sheriff Boyd asked. "Until you give us more than a rumor or a feeling, there's not much I can do with this information."

"You're not letting me tell my story," Edna said irritably. She narrowed her eyes at Tess. "Why aren't you writing this down? Isn't that your job?"

Since Tess was eager to get to Edna's theoretical proof, she took the pad of paper the sheriff held out to her and started scrawling notes. *Peaky felonies*, she wrote in heavily underlined pen. *Possible ties to Melvin Harrow?*

This seemed to satisfy Edna, so she kept going.

"I would've turned around home to grab a video camera but it all happened too fast," Edna said, and with an absence of drama that made both the sheriff and Tess sit up straighter. "The first time, anyway."

"The first time?" Tess echoed.

"It was right after that first girl went missing— the Charles girl. Herb Granger and Melvin started banging around the hardware store late one night. I thought they were drunk, as usual, but when I peered closer, it looked like they were doing renovations."

"Renovations?" the sheriff asked, just as Tess said, "Herb?"

"I went to the store the next day, but I couldn't see anything out of the ordinary. It was the same disgusting heap it had always been. *You* remember, Victor. Shelves full of garbage, price stickers placed at random." Edna shrugged. "I figured it was the drink, after all. But the *next* time…"

"In 2018?" Tess asked eagerly. "When Lucretia went missing?"

Edna gave a small start of surprise. "No. Long before that. A few years after Annabelle."

Tess's heart gave an erratic thump. "In 1992?"

"Thereabouts. I don't remember exactly." Edna shrugged as though she hadn't just made Tess's blood turn to ice. "Anyway, it happened again. I *did* grab a camcorder that time, but Herb saw me standing outside and accused me of being a busy-body. *Me.* Can you believe it?"

Since both Tess and the sheriff could believe it, they didn't answer.

Edna released a short huff. "Anyhow, he broke it. The camcorder, I mean. I was mad as fire about it, even if he did replace it as soon as he'd sobered up." She finished her story and sat back, her hands clasped over her stomach. "You see why I'm telling you all this. They were in on it together, your grandfather and Herb. Burying dead people. Drinking to excess. Smashing perfectly good camcorders."

She stated this last one as though it were the most offensive of the lot. Tess would have gladly walked Edna to the door right then and there, but the sheriff wasn't done with her.

"Do you still have that camcorder?" he asked.

"The one Herb bought me? No. I lost that old thing years ago." A slow, creeping smile crossed her wizened face. It took all of Tess's resolution—and then some—not to stand up and run from the room. She trusted that smile as much as she trusted Mason Peabody, Adam Peabody, and a snake. In that order.

"I brought the broken one with me." Edna patted her handbag knowingly. "I thought you might want to see it."

"What are the Peaky felonies?"

Sheriff Boyd lost no time in bagging and tagging the broken camcorder, sweeping it into evidence before Tess could ask to take a look. Not that she imagined there was anything to be gained by it—a broken camcorder that had been sitting under an old woman's bed for thirty years was hardly the clincher in a case like this—but she wouldn't have minded poking around a little.

"Peaky felonies?" she echoed. Too late, she remembered the notes she'd taken during Edna's interview. There, written in her own hand, was the word that tied everything together: *Peaky.*

Mystery author, murderer incarnate, and Kendra Boyd's death knell.

"You underlined it three times." Sheriff Boyd took the notes from her and tossed them on top of the camcorder in the evidence collection box. "Is there something I should know about your grandfather? Something that happened in 1992?"

Tess drew a deep breath. This wasn't how she'd wanted this conversation to go, but few things in life went according to plan. Few things in *her* life, anyway.

"No. Yes. Maybe." She hesitated. "I think you should sit back down, Victor. I've discovered something, and you're not going to like it."

He didn't sit. "Unless it's another set of bones we missed the first time we went through your grandfather's store, I think I can handle it."

Tess bit back a grimace. "Don't be too sure." She pulled the book out of her purse and pushed it across the table, her finger tapping on the author's name. "Simone Peaky. That's where I got the name."

"*Let Sleeping Dogs Lie*?" He picked up the book and glanced at the cover. As soon as he saw the quote, he lifted a brow. "'A fast-paced, reckless—'"

"Don't." Tess held up a hand before he could go any further. She was starting to seriously regret the day she'd typed out those words. "Let's just say I gave them the quote without actually reading the book and leave it at that."

"That doesn't seem very honorable. You lied? To thousands of readers?"

She let that pass. "What you need to pay attention to is the date that book was published."

He flipped to the title page and shrugged. "April 2019. So?"

"That's about a year and a half after Lucretia went missing and was killed, right?"

"Give or take a few weeks, sure." His eyes narrowed, his gaze suddenly more scrutinizing than Tess cared for. She'd never been great at hiding her emotions, and considering the way they were all rushing to the surface of her skin, she wasn't likely to start anytime soon. "Are you saying this is related to her disappearance?"

"I'm saying that the book's plot shares several salient points with our current murder investigation, up to and including a similar-sounding town, two bodies buried under the floorboards of a local shop about thirty years apart, and multiple hatchet wounds on the remains. I'll let you read it for yourself—or ask Ivy—to get the specifics down."

The sheriff seemed inclined to be amused. "Tess, a few coincidences—"

"It's not a coincidence. Not with this level of detail." She forced her heart down out of her throat and back in her chest where it belonged. It was now or never. "And there's more. In the book, there's a third murder victim whose remains we haven't found yet."

The sheriff wasn't slow to pick up on her meaning. "One who died in 1992?"

"Bingo." She grimaced. "A young woman who went missing from her home late one night. She had an overprotective boyfriend, a rackety old truck that was never found…and a younger brother who was the only person who continued searching for her after the police wrote her off as a runaway. In the book, her remains were buried outside the cemetery, which, um, *might* have been what Gertie and I were really looking for that day you caught us digging."

Tess held her breath, waiting for the sheriff's

reaction. Most of the time, she could hazard a fairly good guess as to how he'd receive case updates from her. With incredulity, usually. Amusement, often. And, even though he hated to admit it, gradual and eventual acceptance.

In this instance, he dropped the book like it had bitten him.

"No." He took a step back, his whole body stiff with tension. "I don't believe you."

She reached for his hand, surprised to find that it was ice cold, and tugged. "Sit down, Victor."

"You're always reading into things—making cases overly complicated with your crackpot theories and outlandish claims."

Since her last crackpot theory had turned out to solve an entire murder, she didn't take offense at this. Sometimes, the *least* likely solution was the one you had to watch out for.

"It makes sense," she said quietly. She didn't let go of his hand even though it sat like a cold, dead weight in hers. "You know it does. Two women went missing from this area, their cars and belongings made to look like they were deliberately abandoned. Their bodies were found years later with similar markings on the bones. Your sister's case matches every aspect of it—and now we have Edna claiming she saw something suspicious at my grandfather's hardware store around the time of her disappearance."

She sat and let the words sink in, wishing there was more she could do than clutch at his hand like she was holding a carp.

"Who is Simone Peaky?" he demanded, his eyes hard. Tess was a little frightened at how dark they looked—how glittering—but she forced herself to answer calmly.

"I don't know. Not yet. It's a pen name, but she hasn't written or done anything since this book came out. My agent was the one who took the request for that book blurb, so I have her doing a little research for me. And, ah, I might have another lead on someone who can track her electronic trail. It's not strictly legal, but..."

She allowed the words to sit between them, waiting for him to shut her down. A man as dedicated to rules and authority as this one wasn't likely to take her suggestion of a rogue hacker well.

"Okay. Good. Keep me updated on what you find."

"Wait. What?" Tess bolted to her feet. "Victor—*what*?"

He couldn't quite meet her eyes. "I'll need to keep this book, if you don't mind."

"Consider it yours."

"Who else have you told about it?"

"Pretty much everyone I've met?" She winced. "I'm sorry, but I was trying to make sense of it all, so the truth just kind of popped out. Peter Oblonsky was the one who first brought the book to my attention. Gertrude and Nicki know, obviously. And Ivy. And, um, maybe Mason Peabody?"

The sheriff sighed. It wasn't a surprised sigh so much as a resigned one. He knew her too well to assume that she'd been capable of keeping any of this to herself. Since she wasn't ready to leave him on his own just yet—and because she wasn't brave enough to start asking probing questions about his sister—she changed tack.

"What's the word on the missing bodies, by the way? Do you have any leads on who might have broken in to take them?"

This time, he *did* look at her, but not with anything approaching warmth. As she'd feared, introducing his sister into the conversation—and into this case— had forced him to retreat even further behind his veil of inscrutability. At this point, she wasn't sure she'd ever be able to coax him out of it again.

"Yes," he said and tossed the book unceremoniously onto his growing evidence pile. "I think you might want to talk to your daughter about that."

Chapter Fifteen

"MOM, I SWEAR IT WASN'T ME."

Gertrude clasped her hands in front of her, tears springing to her eyes and a look of stark entreaty on her face.

"I've been *so* careful not to do anything wrong while I was at work. I never touched the bodies or the tools. I didn't push any buttons, even if they are big and red and begging to be pushed. And I definitely didn't have anything to do with the computers or locks. Why would I? I'm just a kid."

Tess knew that taking a teenager's word on faith was something few parents would sign off on, but she nodded and pulled the girl into her arms. Gertrude's streaks of running mascara were sure to rub off on her blouse, but Tess didn't mind. Just about every surface in their house had some kind of makeup residue on it.

"It's okay, honey. I believe you."

"Yeah, but Ms. Sylvie doesn't." The teen's body shook. "I got fired today. She said I can't come back while the investigation is pending. Because I can't be *trusted*."

"She actually said that?"

"Well, no." Gertrude sniffed long and loud. Dashing at her nose with the sleeve of her hoodie, she added, "But it's what she meant. I know it was. She said it was for my safety, and that until they knew how the murderer got in, she couldn't allow me back. Like I care about *that*."

Tess didn't mention that she was in full support of this plan or that Sylvia Nerudo had acted with common sense in implementing it, but that didn't make either of those less true. "I'm sure they'll let you back as soon as the thief is caught. It's probably just a liability issue."

"The other techs were looking at me and whispering all day. They said—" A loud sniffle cut her statement short.

Tess rubbed a hand over her daughter's head. "It doesn't matter what they said. As long as Sylvia doesn't think you did anything wrong, that's all that matters."

"Ugh. Mom, you're not *listening*." Gertrude jerked herself out of her mother's embrace. "It's not me they were talking about. It's you."

"What? How is this my fault?"

"Isn't it obvious?" Gertrude shook her head, her sadness giving way to her more customary irritation. "The bones were found on Great-Grandpa's property. He owned like twelve hatchets and also sold them at the store. He was weird and lonely, and everyone says he hated women."

"That's not fair. He hated everyone equally."

"You're missing the point. *You're* best friends with the sheriff, and *I* was working at the morgue. And then we were caught digging up a cemetery that same day."

Oh, dear. Tess could tell where this was headed.

"They think…" Gertrude sobbed. "They think…"

Tess finished the sentence before her daughter lost it altogether. "They think we broke in and stole the bones to save my grandfather's reputation. They think our whole family is deranged."

If she was being perfectly honest, she didn't blame them. Considering Edna's testimony about the video camera and her grandfather's strange behavior around the time Kendra had gone missing, things were looking none too good. If she were writing this book, Grandpa—and by extension, her—would be suspect number one.

Drawing a deep breath, she fell to the couch in their living room, her bones suddenly feeling as decrepit as the ones that had been stolen.

To her surprise, Gertrude sat next to her.

"What was he like, Great-Grandpa?" she asked. "I mean…he lived all alone in this weird old cabin. You said you only visited him that one time when you were a kid, and he never talked to you. Just sort of let you wander around in the woods. That's what crazed serial killers do, isn't it?"

"Contrary to popular belief, I don't know a lot about the behaviors and activities of crazed serial killers. I've never written about one of those before." Unlike a certain someone no one seemed to know. "But if you'd have asked me a few years ago if he was capable of such a thing... I dunno, Gertie. Loneliness does strange things to people. So does greed."

Gertrude's hand slipped into hers. "But it wasn't him, right? We know that for sure."

"Do we?"

"Obviously. *I* didn't take those bones, and *you* didn't take those bones, so why would anyone else bother? If Great-Grandpa really was the one running around the forest and hacking people to bits, why would anyone else take them?"

Tess sat up so suddenly that her head whirled. "Gertrude Alex Harrow, you beautiful little genius."

"What'd I say?"

Tess shook her head. Until she knew for sure who—or what—she was up against, there were some things a teenager was best left out of. "I'm not sure yet. But there's only one person I can think of who might be as involved in this as Grandpa."

The man who'd helped bury the bodies.

Herb Granger.

If anything had been needed to convince Tess that Gertrude was telling the truth about the rumors surrounding the disappearing bones, her reception in town that afternoon would have done it. There was no telling how or why rumors spread so quickly in a place like this, where social media existed mostly in the form of the church calling tree and chance encounters at the grocery story, but there was no denying that they did. No one went so far as to throw stones at her or start waving pitchforks in her face, but the hostility was palpable.

"I never did trust that old Melvin Harrow," one woman muttered as Tess walked briskly by. "He once told me my Muffin was more like a rat than a dog."

"Some people are addicted to drama, and that's all I have to say on the subject," said another woman—one who Tess *knew* only lived for her next installment of *General Hospital*. "Next thing you know, she'll pretend to 'find' the bones some-place only she knows about."

"What do you think she *did* with them?" another man asked. "Bury them back under the floorboards?"

Needless to say, she wasn't in the greatest of moods by the time she walked up Herb's drive. He lived in a small A-frame house on the north side of the river, a wooded retreat with easy access to the rest of town. The house was old, but Herb's status as a handyman advertised itself in the neatly patched exterior boards and the soaring garage that was easily two times the square footage of the home.

She didn't fail to note that the garage must have been full to capacity, because several cars were parked next to it—one of which she assumed had once belonged to Lucretia Gregory.

"Herb, you have some serious explaining to do." She pounded her fist on the door, the thick wood rattling in its frame. "I know you're in there, so you might as well come out."

No one answered her summons, so she knocked harder. "I mean it. I can see the curtains twitching. You might as well let me in, because I'm not going away until you do."

The curtains swished again, harder this time, but heavy footsteps and the creak of the door indicated that Tess had won. This round, at least.

The old man's grizzled head poked through a narrow opening, the chain on the door and no sign of welcome on his face. "What do you want?"

Tess shoved her foot in the door's opening. "I want you to tell me which car was Lucretia's."

Herb attempted to slam the door, but Tess had been fortunate enough to wear her hiking boots today. Her sense of fashion might be waning the longer she lived out here in the middle of nowhere, but The North Face knew what it was doing when it came to withstanding the elements—and belligerent old men who were almost *definitely* hiding something.

"Nice try, but you aren't getting rid of me that easily. Was it the Outback? I feel like a woman who came all this way to re-create *Wild* would drive the Outback."

Herb's scowl confirmed her theory.

"I'm surprised Sheriff Boyd hasn't impounded it as evidence yet," she said, refusing to be moved by that scowl. "Has he been here to talk to you?"

"No. Why would he? I didn't have nothing to do with those dead girls."

"Are you sure about that? There are witnesses who saw you and Grandpa in the hardware store, Herb. Ones who knew you were up to something late at night."

If Tess hadn't been watching closely, she might have missed the flash of guilt that touched those surly lips. But she *was* watching, and she *didn't* miss it. "I think you and I need to have a talk. And until you come out here and do it, I'm going to go see what that Subaru has to offer."

She slid her foot out of the door and turned away, sauntering toward the garage as though she didn't have a care in the world. In the back of her mind, she knew that baiting a man who may or may not have helped her grandfather murder three innocent women wasn't the smartest way to go about solving a crime, but she had to do *something*. The whole town thought she was a villain. *Sheriff Boyd* thought she was a villain. And if she didn't do something to clear Gertrude's name and get the teen reinstalled at the morgue, her daughter was likely to start viewing her as an evil witch imprisoning her inside a gingerbread house.

She wasn't going to say which one of those bothered her the most, but her throat felt thick every time she thought about that cold look in the sheriff's eyes.

As she approached the Outback, she found that the vehicle hadn't been moved in quite some time. Not only was there a thin layer of dirt and pollen over the top, but tall grass and knobby weeds had sprung up looking like nests around the tires.

It was a nice car—or rather, it *had* been nice back when it was new. It was the forest green color so favored when the car first gained popularity, a rustic hue that matched the woods surrounding it. Bumper stickers proclaiming *Bigfoot Is Real* and *The Mountains Are Calling and I Must Go* suggested that Lucretia's desire to retreat into the woods had been an authentic, if predictable, one.

Tess tried the handle to find that the car was open—an unlooked-for piece of luck that she planned to exploit to the fullest. It smelled musty from underuse, with a slight scent of old man and what she suspected were animal droppings of some kind. Fearful that Herb might be out any minute with a gun—or a hatchet—to stop her, she tugged open the glove box and swept the contents into her hand.

To her disappointment, there was nothing inside but a car cleaning guide and a map that bore a recent publication date. Any signs that Lucretia had disposed of this car in a hurry—or not at all—weren't kept here.

"You won't find nothing," Herb confirmed, his voice ominously close to her neck.

Tess gasped and whirled, but there was nothing threatening in the old man's stance. If anything, he looked amused to find her snooping around. The feeling was reinforced when Tess tucked the map into her pocket only to have Herb laugh out loud. "The sheriff went over this car with a fine-tooth comb back when that lady first went missing. If he didn't find nothing after taking off every blasted panel and screw, what makes you think you can do better?"

To be honest, she *didn't* think she could do better, but that didn't mean she wasn't going to try. "I'm surprised he didn't impound it as evidence," she said.

"He did." Herb tilted his head up at a faded sign hanging on the side of his garage. In faint, almost imperceptible letters, she could just make out K-ep O-t and Po-ice Im-ou-d. Tess blinked up at the sign, all those rusted cars now making sense.

"You mean to tell me that *you* run the local impound?"

He puffed up with something like pride. "Impound lot, long-term storage, towing, junking. You got it, I want it."

"But you're the one it was impounded from," Tess insisted. Surely, that had to be some kind of mistake. Either that, or a legal loophole for committing the perfect crime. Detective Gonzales was going to have to look into it.

"That ol' car's been setting there for years." Herb rolled an indifferent shoulder. "No one cares whether it goes or stays. The radiator's busted, so it ain't going nowhere."

"Then shouldn't you put up a fence or at least lock the car doors? You're practically begging for people to snoop around."

"If you lock the doors," Herb explained, "then they jest break 'em to get in. Easier this way."

Tess found it difficult to argue with this logic—if logic it could be called. She also found it difficult to put up a hue and cry over a car that had obviously been dismissed as evidence. If the sheriff had investigated it when Lucretia first went missing—and if it had been rifled through by every passing criminal who wanted a peek—then it wouldn't be of much use now.

"Well?" Herb demanded, his arms crossing over his chest. He was wiry but strong, his body forged of a lifetime of manual labor. "What do you want? You didn't come all this way to steal car parts."

Tess saw no reason to beat around the bush. "You were friends with my grandfather, weren't you? *Good* friends?"

"Melvin was the best friend I ever had." Herb's arms came down, his belligerent expression not far behind. "Fact is, he was the *only* friend I ever had. I miss him something terrible."

Even though Tess had come here determined to wrest answers from Herb's caustic, recalcitrant grasp, she softened. There was something so honest about the way he spoke, as if he meant every word.

"I'm sorry I didn't come visit you when I first inherited the cabin," she said. "I was so wrapped up in my own problems that I didn't think about the legacy he might have left behind. I should've offered you a chance to go through his things. To see if there were any mementos of him you wanted to keep."

Herb shook his head and tapped his temple. "Everything I need is right here."

Instead of demanding answers about his inter-actions with Lucretia, the camcorder he smashed, or the disappearance of Kendra Boyd, Tess found that her lower lip was wobbling. "I wish you'd tell me about him."

Herb blinked—slowly at first, and then gaining speed. "About Melvin? What d'you want to know?"

The answer to that question was miles long. The amount of backstory Tess had about the man who'd sired her mother wouldn't have filled a single chapter in one of her books. He and her mother had never gotten along, but considering that Tess's entire adolescence had been one long argument with the woman, that wasn't saying much. Her mother was, in a word, a *handful*.

"I know he worked in insurance before he moved out here, and that he hated every minute of it," Tess said. "I know he lived simply and that the hardware store barely made enough money to cover the bills. He wasn't much of a man for talking, and he *definitely* didn't like kids."

She stopped, unable to think of a single other thing to say. He hadn't been much of a reader, which gave them very little in common, and he hadn't made any sort of push to befriend the townsfolk, which meant they were as opposite as two people could get. But he *had* opened his home to her the summer she'd needed it, and as far as she could remember, she hadn't starved. That had to mean something.

"He could have been anything he set his mind

to," Herb said. "I never knew anyone with more gumption."

"Are you sure we're talking about *my* grandfather?" Tess asked. "The man who retreated to the woods and lived without running water for forty years?"

Herb pointed a warning finger at her. "You retreated to the woods and lived without running water for four months. It ain't that far off."

This was true. Although a few months of rusticity could hardly compare with half a lifetime of it, Tess understood the appeal. Living here had brought her and Gertrude close together in ways that she'd thought only existed on TV. They ate dinner together almost every night. They talked about the day's events, shared their troubles, and had so many inside jokes it was difficult to keep track of them all.

Even more telling was the fact that the amount of time her daughter spent with the door to her room shut got smaller the longer they lived out here. Tess wasn't doing so hot at meeting her deadlines, it was true, but even that could be considered a point in the cabin's favor.

She was doing more. She was seeing more. She was *living* more.

Unlike those poor discarded bones.

"Herb, he didn't kill those women, did he?" she asked, unable to stop the question from coming out like that—raw, simple. A little like Grandpa and a lot like Herb.

"Well, now." Herb scratched his jaw. "I don't rightly know."

"What?" Tess felt the ground start to grow unsteady under her feet. The last thing she expected from a blunt-force question was a blunt-force reply. In her experience, that wasn't how murder investigations worked. "Herb. *What?*"

"He never did like that Annabelle Charles. No one did. A nastier piece of work I never—" He cut himself off with a shake of his head. "He had a dog, your granddad, once upon a time. She ran that sweet little spaniel over with her car, and if it was an accident, I'm the Tooth Fairy."

He opened his mouth to showcase several gaps where his teeth used to be. Tess got the point.

"Oh dear," Tess murmured. "What did she do to you?"

"What's that supposed to mean?"

Tess waved her arm around vaguely. "From everything I can gather, there wasn't a single person in this town who liked her—most of them with good reason. What'd she do to you?"

"She killed my friend's dog. Ain't that enough?"

Maybe not enough to out-and-out murder someone, no. But to take a whack with the hatchet? To help bury her body afterward?

Tess was no stranger to that kind of solidarity. She'd bury a body for Gertrude in a hot second. Ivy and Nicki, too, probably. And if Sheriff Boyd asked her? Well…that depended on who the body belonged to.

"And Lucretia?" Tess persisted. "Did my grand-father have a reason to kill her?"

Herb rolled his shoulder in a shrug. "Ain't my place to say. Far as I know, they never met. Why would they? Townies were never his thing."

"She might have come into the hardware store to pick up a few things before her hike," Tess suggested. "Or she could have accidentally stumbled onto his property and…"

"And then sold me her car, walked back to the cabin, and laid down under his hatchet?" Herb snorted. "Girl, you're a fool."

Tess took some measure of relief from this. Annabelle may have been the town pariah, but Lucretia was a stranger to these parts: a tourist, a wanderer. There was no reason for anyone to have harmed her.

Her relief didn't last long. With a sinking heart, Tess realized this was the moment of truth.

"What about Kendra Boyd?" she asked. For reasons she couldn't quite understand, she dropped her voice to a near-whisper. "Is there any reason my grandfather would have wanted to do away with her?"

Instead of showing surprise, Herb's eyes narrowed to serpentine slits. "What does she have to do with anything?"

"She went missing a few years after Annabelle did," Tess said, opting for the simplest route. "And under alarmingly similar circumstances. Without the bodies, there was no real reason to suspect there was any link between them, but now that Annabelle has turned up, who's to say they weren't killed by the same person?"

Herb scowled. His expression didn't bode well for the story about to unfold—another young woman prone to violence and criminal misdeeds in the full light of day—but when he spoke, it was with the same reverence that he'd spoken of her grandfather.

"Kendra Boyd was the best soul this town has ever seen. No one—and I mean *no one*—would've done to her what they done to Annabelle."

"Are you sure? Because I found—"

"Don't go stirring up trouble you know nothing about." Herb raised one craggy finger and pointed it at her. "You're Melvin's kin, so I'll let this one slide, but if you know what's good for you, you'll let sleeping dogs lie."

Tess was so startled by this—the title of the book spoken aloud, almost like an incantation—that she jumped.

"What did you just say?"

"You heard me," Herb said, turning his back on both Tess and the conversation. "Now go away and bother someone else. I'm too old and too tired to play these games."

Tess watched him go, her feet planted to the hard-packed mud. She wanted to go after him and demand answers, but she wouldn't know where to start. There was so much she wanted to know... and even more that she didn't.

For the first time since they'd uncovered the bones under the floor, she wished they'd left her grandfather's hardware store intact. The deeper she dug into this case, the less sense it made.

And the sadder she got for the fate of Sheriff Boyd's long-lost sister.

Chapter Sixteen

THERE WAS ONLY ONE THING TO DO WHEN FACED with the emotional overload of death, missing bones, a teenager kicked out of the morgue, and the startling realization that one's grandfather might end up being a murderer.

"Peter, I need your hacker friend, and I need him stat. He hasn't answered any of my emails, so I need you to make him."

Peter sat at the dining room table in Tess's cabin reading the local newspaper. At the sound of her demand, he glanced up over the top of his glasses. "I'm not sure you understand how hacker friends work."

"Tell him I'll pay extra. Double, if I have to. This is a matter of life or death."

Her plea failed to move him. "As far as I can tell, no one is in imminent danger. Your killer seems content with burglary and tampering with evidence."

"For now," Tess muttered. "But if he's going around and killing women in this town every couple of years, he's due for another one soon. I'd rather it not be me or Gertie, if I can possibly help it."

The prospect of her own death seemed to get a slight reaction. Peter set the newspaper—and his glasses—down.

Which is when Tess brought out the big guns.

"I can't just sit around doing nothing. If there really is a third body—and if it really is Sheriff Boyd's sister—I need to know."

"Why?" Peter asked, his voice gentle.

"Because he deserves the truth."

"Why?" Gentler this time.

"Because no one should have to go that many years without closure. Because he's my friend. Because the one thing he technically gave me permission to do is to track down the author of that book."

"Why?"

Having successfully raised a toddler once already, Tess should have known better than to fall into this trap. Asking why—in a series of softer and more probing ways—was only likely to end up in a loop of annoyance with no end in sight. But she was here and Peter was asking, so she gave in.

"I'm not sure." She sat down at the table opposite him, her whole body falling with a thump. "On that last one, I mean. It's not like Victor to agree to anything that falls outside the lines of his jurisdiction, especially when we're talking about illegal means. The only other time…"

"Yes?" Peter probed. He moved one of his hands over Tess's and held it there. Although the two of them had always been friends, and Tess, in particular, had leaned heavily on Peter to help her navigate the shoals of new authorship, she'd never realized just how much she relied on him.

"He bent the rules a little bit last year. Not much, but enough to help me out of a tight spot." She lifted her eyes to Peter's, annoyed to find that hers were damp. "I think he's asking me to do the same for him. I owe him that much. I owe him a lot more, actually."

Peter gently withdrew his hands. "Then we'll have to see what we can do, won't we?"

"Really?" Tess would have liked to say that all of her excitement was wrapped up in helping Sheriff Boyd—and in solving the mystery of Simone Peaky—but she was never one to lie to herself. The idea of having a conversation with a real hacker was one she cherished a lot more than any rational woman should. "You'll let him know how important this is?"

Peter chuckled, a soft, low sound that did much to dry the dampness of her eyes. "I already have. I was just afraid that once I gave you these powers, you wouldn't stop until you'd probed into the lives and secrets of every single person you know." He paused. "Present company included."

Tess was too excited to be insulted. "Peter, I'd

never do such a thing to you." A thought occurred to her, and she couldn't resist. "Why? Are there skeletons in your closet worth uncovering?"

"Oh, not just skeletons in the closet, my dear." Peter smiled, but there was something off about it that she couldn't place. "I've got monsters under my bed, devils in the details, and an enemy behind every closed door. Enter at your own risk."

———

"Do you take PayPal?"

From the other end of the phone line, something that sounded like a jackhammer cut through the connection. She took it to mean a vehement no.

"Okay, then… How about Venmo? My daughter is always trying to get me to switch."

The jackhammer ceased only to be replaced by the robotic voice of a synthetic speech device. "Lady, do you really think I take payments through *Venmo*?"

"Well, no," Tess admitted. She might not be wholly up to snuff when it came to web-based intrigue, but she wasn't an idiot. "But I can hardly mail you a check. What other options are there?"

"I've withdrawn the ten thousand dollars from your account. That should cover my initial search."

"What? Wait. *What?*" Tess pulled the phone

down from her ear and scrambled to check her banking app. Sure enough, her savings account was down an even ten thousand dollars from where it had been yesterday.

As she lifted the phone back to her ear, she could hear a chuckle—a *human* one.

"Don't worry," the robotic voice said. "I won't take anything more unless we agree on additional terms."

"How did you do that?"

"I could tell you, but that would be another five thousand."

"Never mind," Tess said quickly. She was curious but not *that* curious. She was also going to have to call the bank and have every single one of her accounts closed. This hacker friend of Peter's was scary. "Just tell me what you found out about Simone Peaky."

"Are you sure you want to know? Once you have this information, there's no going back."

Tess hesitated, casting a quick look around the room. She'd waited for a morning when the cabin was empty to make this phone call, but it didn't hurt to double check for prying eyes—or ears. Even though Peter could probably call up this Wingbat99 and get all the details for the low, bargain price of a million dollars, she wanted to be alone when she heard this. Her agent had come up with nothing helpful except the information that the agency representing Simone had gone out of business a few years ago. Anything Wingbat99 found wasn't likely to be good.

"Yeah. Go ahead. We might as well get this over with."

"Cool." The robot paused. "She doesn't exist."

Tess waited for the rest. Then she waited again. Then she waited some more.

"Hello?" She shook the phone. "Are you still there?"

"Yep. Was there anything else you needed?"

Yeah. She needed her ten thousand dollars back. "You're telling me that you spent five hours digging into this woman's background, and the best you can do is nothing? For that much money, I have to at least show my editor a couple of chapters. I'm in the wrong line of work."

The human chuckle sounded again. To Tess's surprise, the voice that followed was equally alive. "I didn't say I *found* nothing. I said she doesn't exist. Simone Peaky is a cover, a fake identity."

Tess wasn't as pleased by this reversion to Wingbat99's human form as she should have been. Although it was nice to think they were building trust, she was starting to develop a serious case of buyer's remorse. "Yes, I know it's a fake name. Authors have them all the time."

"No. Not a pen name. A complete fake. No birth records, no death records, fake social security number. The only known listed address is somewhere in the middle of the Pacific Ocean, and all payments from her one and only publication were run through an offshore account that hasn't been touched. Your woman has no intention of cashing in—or of being found."

"Oh."

"Exactly." Wingbat99 clucked sympathetically. "I feel a little bad, taking all your money only to throw you at a dead end, but a deal's a deal."

"Wait." Tess wasn't ready to give up just yet. "Can't you like…trace her online activity through a specific router or something? I swear that's something they do in spy movies all the time."

"If your woman was a spy, maybe. But she's off grid. Her agent and publisher have plenty of email communication between each other, but anything they got from her was off the books. Electronically speaking, I mean."

Tess grunted in irritation. "And her agency is no longer operational, so I can hardly roll up there and ask them for details."

"Hey! Look at that. You did some investigation on your own."

"I didn't pay ten thousand dollars for your sarcasm. My fifteen-year-old gives me plenty of that for free." She paused, considering. "So, when you say this Simone person hasn't touched any of her offshore accounts, you mean the money's just sitting there?"

"Yep. She didn't get much of an advance, if that makes a difference."

It didn't. Tess could think of only three reasons why someone would hide money overseas and then leave it there for years at a time. The first: that she was inordinately rich. The second: that she was scared of being traced.

The third: that she was dead.

"It's weird, right?" Aware that she was running up the meter—and that Wingbat99 had every capability of charging her for it—she rushed to finish. "In all your years of peering into people's private lives, have you ever seen anything like this?"

"Someone who goes to extreme lengths to keep themselves hidden? Of course. It happens a lot more than you think. You, of all people, should know how easy it is to hide in plain sight. You and your daughter both."

Tess sighed. As much as she hated to admit it, Wingbat99 was right. No part of her own past was hidden, but that didn't mean she hadn't been burned—and burned hard—by the other people in her life.

She was also starting to feel like Simone was a dead end—and that Peter was right. Wingbat99 wasn't as overpriced as he seemed. It would have taken her weeks, if not longer, to follow up with Simone's agent—and she doubted whether he knew just how shrouded in mystery his client was. In her experience, agents asked few questions as long as the checks kept clearing.

"While we're on the subject of your daughter, I could tell you what Gertrude's been Google searching lately," Wingbat99 said. "For a fee, of course. I've got several parents who have me on retainer to keep an eye on their kids' activities."

Tess refused to fall for it. "Nice try. I'll bet you the entire ten thousand dollars you stole from me that the only things she's searched for are fan fiction of the *Nightwave* graphic novel series, all kinds of gross body decay forensics, and the best places to find missing skeletons in Washington State."

"That's…pretty close, actually."

She knew it was. Her relationship with her daughter might be an odd one, but she liked to think they understood one another. "Where are the best places to find missing skeletons in Washington State, by the way?" she asked. "As one amateur investigator to another?"

"As one amateur investigator to another, I suggest you find a new hobby."

———

Tess wasn't sure if watching two men swing hammers and perform free manual labor counted as a hobby, but it was rapidly becoming one of her favorite things to do.

"Are you sure I can't get either one of you a drink?" she asked as she reached into the cooler she'd brought along with her to the hardware store. It contained, among other things, several sandwiches from the grocery store, lest the two men decided they wanted her to spring for lunch again. She could get way with expensing a meal like that one time, but she shuddered to think of what her accountant would say if she made it a regular occurrence. "I have sweet tea, soda, performance-enhancing water…"

"Do I look like I need performance-enhancing water?" Jared asked as he hoisted a literal sledge-hammer over one shoulder.

Before Tess could figure out how best to reply, Adam snorted and said, "You know those things are a scam designed for Karens like you, right? Most people just pee out all those extra vitamins. There's only so many the body can hold before it goes to waste."

Tess resented the implication that she was a Karen, but she was glad to get Adam talking. Most of the time, the only way he replied to her was with grunts or monosyllables—usually combined into one guttural noise.

"I dunno," she said. "The blue raspberry ones taste pretty good."

He stared at her for a moment before holding

out his hand. "Fine. I'll take one. But blue raspberry isn't a real thing. It's just regular raspberry that they dye blue so it doesn't get confused with all the other red flavors."

Tess lifted herself off the seat and held out the drink in question, but she didn't let go right away. "You seem to know a lot of random, esoteric facts."

"And you seem to use a lot of big, unnecessary words."

Tess found herself flashing him a genuine smile. As much as she hated to admit it, the guy was growing on her. He had zero interest in impressing her—or, she suspected, anyone. There was something to respect in that.

"I could put some vodka in it, if you need a little boost," she offered.

He practically yanked the drink from her. "I'm not *that* much of an alcoholic," he muttered. He directed one of his grunts at Jared. "I'm taking ten. We can test out that plumbing seal when I get back."

Tess paid close attention to his feet as he stomped away, but he wasn't wearing the hiking boots this time. These looked like well-worn construction boots, once a bright tan but now faded to an indeterminate gray.

"I know," Jared said, his gaze following Tess's. "He hasn't worn the muddy boots since you pointed them out. I think he knows something's up."

"Interesting," Tess said.

"And you probably shouldn't mention the vodka stuff too much. I've been keeping pretty close tabs on him, and he spends a lot of time at the bar. Like, *a lot*. I think he might have a real problem."

"Interesting," she said again.

Instead of accepting this at face value, Jared cocked his head at her, an eager, almost childlike expression on his face. "Why is that interesting?"

Tess wasn't exactly sure. So far, nothing about Adam set off any *real* alarm bells—it was more of a gentle tinkling—but she'd learned a long time ago to listen to every sound. "I'm just impressed by how much work you're putting into this whole thing, that's all. At this rate, you'll get hired onto Mason's crew in no time."

Jared flushed with sudden pleasure.

"You should try taking Adam out for lobster rolls again," she added. "He seemed to really like those."

Jared's flush deepened even more, although Tess couldn't imagine what she'd said to evoke it.

Until he spoke.

"I really liked that, too," he said, his eyelashes fluttering. "Having lunch, I mean. With you."

Tess knew it behooved her to shut this conversation down—and to shut it down fast. Long, decadent eyelashes had always been one of her weaknesses. Her own were stubby, short, and impervious to mascara. She patted the cooler to distract herself. "Then you're in luck. I packed enough sandwiches to see you two through to the end of the day. Not lobster, obviously, but there should be a tuna salad in there. The roast beef looks a little questionable, but no one has died from eating at the grocery store deli. Not that I know of, anyway."

"Tess…" Jared began, but Tess was up and on her feet before he could finish whatever it was he planned to say.

"I should probably head home and get to work," she said. It wasn't a complete lie. In addition to falling woefully behind on her deadline, she owed a popular online magazine a thousand words on what it meant to be a single working mother living and toiling in the middle of nowhere. It promised to be a scintillating read. "You'll let me know if you need anything?"

Although Jared looked as though he wanted to argue, he seemed to recognize defeat—and Tess's capacity for avoiding difficult conversations. "Of course," he said. "Thanks again for everything you're doing to help me out. So far, Adam isn't doing much to smooth my path, but that's okay. I'm not a man to give up easily."

Tess suspected that Jared was talking about a lot more than just getting in good with Mason and his logging crew, but she refused to let herself dwell on it. With a bright smile and a promise to replenish the sandwich supplies tomorrow, she made good her escape.

After all, those thousand magazine words weren't going to write themselves. Unless, of course, she could convince Peter or Gertrude to do it for her—or, if desperation took over, the expensive and highly questionable Wingbat99.

Chapter Seventeen

TESS MANAGED TO EKE OUT HER ARTICLE *AND* insert a particularly entertaining hacker twist in her novel before Peter and Gertrude came home from running errands.

"Well?" Peter asked as he moved carefully through the cabin door, his cane hooked over one arm and a bag of groceries clasped in the other. "How'd it go with Wingbat this morning?"

"Would it be weird if I said I really liked him? I think we might become friends."

Peter chuckled. "Don't be fooled. That's social engineering at its best. The charm is part of the package deal."

"Really?" Tess had always assumed that hackers were social misfits, living off Mountain Dew and whole bags of Doritos in the dark. A humorous hacker who could manipulate her like playing a drum opened up a whole new world of possibilities. "Does this mean you've met him?"

Peter seemed offended by this. "Of course not. The last thing I need is a dinner guest who can hack into every single one of my guests' financial accounts before the end of the first course." He paused and handed her the bag of groceries. One look at the truffle butter perched on top, and Tess knew she was done for. "Speaking of, we're having a dinner party tonight."

"Peter, have you lost your mind? We can't have a dinner party in the middle of a murder investigation."

"Certainly, we can. People have to eat, don't they?"

In this, he was seconded by Gertrude, who pranced through the door with several more grocery bags in tow. If that child had accompanied Peter anywhere they sold truffle butter, they were in for quite a night. That was a fifty-mile drive, at the very least.

"Who's coming to this grand dinner of ours?" Tess asked as she peeked inside one of the grocery bags. The sight of several marbled rib eyes had her rethinking her pessimism. She'd eat with the devil himself if it meant a medium-rare steak soaked in truffle butter.

"Nicki, obviously," Gertrude said as she started pulling out an array of root vegetables that Tess would have been hard-pressed to identify. "And you and me and Peter."

"Oh. Is that all? That should be fun."

Peter coughed gently. "Your coroner friend is also coming."

"Sylvia Nerudo?" Tess said. "Really? I'm surprised

she'd be willing to eat with us, considering the current theory about my role in the bones' disappearance."

One look at the warning shake of Peter's head, and Tess wished the words unsaid.

"Don't mess this up for me, Mom," Gertrude said, her voice and lower lip wobbling in tandem. "The only way we could get her to come at all was by promising that Peter would sign her old copies of *Forensic Magazine*. And even then, it wasn't easy."

All at once, Tess realized that this dinner party had nothing to do with her, and everything to do with getting her daughter back in Sylvia's good graces. Instead of being upset, Tess had to suppress every urge she had to throw herself in Peter's arms. This was his doing, she knew—a way to smooth the waters, to try and repair the damages wrought by the theft of those bodies.

"I'll be on my best behavior," Tess promised. "I mean it, Gertie. I won't even mention the murders unless someone else brings them up first."

Gertrude's look of doubt didn't do much to make Tess feel better, but at least the teen continued unloading groceries with something approaching enthusiasm. In a lower aside to Peter, Tess said, "Thank you for this, Peter. If anything can get that woman back on our side, it's shop talk with an expert like yourself."

"You should probably know that I also invited

Sheriff Boyd," Peter said by way of answer. "I'm sorry, Tess, but he wouldn't come. He said he was too busy with the investigation."

She did her best not to take this to heart, but it was difficult. "Did he mention anything about the book?"

She thought, but didn't ask, *or me?*

Peter grimaced. "No, but he said he needed to oversee a search around the cemetery's perimeter. Apparently, he doesn't feel we did a thorough enough job the first time."

———

Tess held true to her promise not to talk about the murders unless someone else mentioned them first. She'd been afraid, when everyone first poured in, marveling over the smell of roasted meat and the transformation of the dining room table with a white tablecloth and a pair of silver candlesticks, that it would be a difficult promise to keep.

It wasn't. Mostly because the murders were literally the only thing anyone could talk about.

"I'm going to have to get my hands on a copy of this book you guys keep talking about," Sylvia said, sitting back in her seat. She had a glass of wine in her hand and a look of mellow enjoyment on her face. At first, she'd been a little stiff, but good food and the relaxed atmosphere had gone a long way in putting her at ease. She even looked different as the evening wore on; the curly hair that had been bound in a bun at her nape now unfolded in salt-and-pepper waves around her shoulders, her shoes off and her feet tucked underneath her. "You wouldn't happen to have any at the library, would you?"

Nicki shook her head. "Not that I've been able to find. We had a copy when it first came out, but it went missing."

"Missing?" Tess echoed, her head swiveling to stare at Nicki. The last time library books had started suddenly disappearing, it had ended up helping them solve a murder. "You mean recently?"

Nicki laughed. She looked as relaxed as Sylvia did, her body encased in a long, colorful sheath dress that only a woman with 20 percent body fat could pull off. "No. I mean it was lost to the system years ago. You wouldn't believe how few of the books we lend out around here get returned. It's better now that the bookmobile makes regular rounds, but our losses account for about half the annual book budget."

"Oh." Tess wasn't sure whether that made the situation better or worse. It would have been nice to solve another murder based on a catalog card, but she needed there to be *some* variation in her Detective Gonzales series. "Can you at least look up who checked it out before it went rogue?"

"I already did." Nicki grinned and pulled a slip of paper out of a pocket that had hitherto gone undetected. "I don't recognize any of the names, but that's no surprise. The book came out before I started working here."

Tess scanned the list eagerly, but nothing jumped out at her. Two women who lived in Omak checked it out before a man in Tonasket failed to return it along with thirteen other books, with titles that ranged from popular thrillers to one questionably titled *Cooking with Roadkill*.

"Ew." Gertrude read over Tess's shoulder. "People don't really cook roadkill, do they?"

"Protein is protein," Sylvia said with a shrug. "I'd rather eat a raccoon off the side of the street than most types of seafood. I've heard raccoon's pretty tough, so you have to be creative how you cook it."

Gertrude perked up to a degree that sent every alarm bell in Tess's body ringing. "Huh. I'll have to look into it. That might be a fun challenge."

It was on the tip of Tess's tongue to forbid any and all culinary efforts related to dead animals scraped off the pavement, but Peter spoke up first.

"You're awfully interested in this criminal investigation for a librarian," he said.

Nicki proved herself every inch the undercover agent that Jared would never be. With a light, trilling laugh, she leaned across the table toward Peter.

"I know, right? Having Tess move here was a dream come true for me. I've always been an armchair detective, even as a kid. I blame Nancy Drew. I used to go through every floor of our apartment building, asking if my neighbors had lost anything they wanted found."

"And did they?" Peter asked, an amused smile playing about his lips.

"Only one. This lady who lived above us asked how good I was at tracking down cheating husbands. I was three days into the investigation before my mom found out and shut it down."

Everyone at the table laughed and relaxed even more, Tess going so far as to unbutton the top of her jeans to avoid losing all circulation to her legs. That truffle butter was no joke.

"Nancy Drew was my gateway drug, too," Sylvia said. She brushed a lock of her hair behind her ear. "Obviously, I didn't go the detective route—or the librarian one—but forensic pathology was a natural progression. Science was always my thing, and I like knowing I'm putting in my piece of the puzzle whenever a body comes through my doors."

This was all Gertrude needed to latch on— and latch hard. "How come you never worked in a bigger city?" she asked, her chin propped on her hand. "I mean, Winthrop is fine and all, but just think of how many more murdered people you'd get somewhere like Seattle or Spokane."

"Or London," Peter put in. "I'd never have been able to complete my research if I didn't have a fully rotating stock of corpses to test my theories."

"You'd be surprised how much excitement crops up in a place like this," Sylvia said. "I was published, once upon a time. It wasn't *Forensic Magazine*, but one of the colleges down South was interested in how our cooler climates worked on organ matter."

Since there was every likelihood Gertrude would continue delving deep into organ matter, corpses, and roadkill cuisine for hours if Tess didn't intervene, she turned the topic to a slightly less gory subject.

"What about other kinds of forensics?" she asked, thinking of the map she'd pulled from Lucretia's glove box. She'd spent a good hour looking it over, but no one had the foresight to mark out body locations with a big red X. There wasn't even a circled pencil mark to help guide her. It had been used—that much she knew from the inexpert way it was refolded—but she had no idea why. These days, almost everything was on Google Maps anyway. "Like the kind where you pull fingerprints out of thin air or on an old treasure map?"

"No amount of research is ever going to get you fingerprints from air," Peter said, amused.

"But the treasure map is entirely possible," Sylvia said, turning toward her. "Getting prints from paper is one of those things that you can do with a home science kit. Why? Do you have one?"

It hadn't been Tess's intention to pull out the map tonight, mostly because no one knew that she'd gone to visit Herb. Tying Herb to the case almost certainly tied her grandfather to it, and she wasn't ready to throw him on the pyre of her suspicions just yet. But she had three highly capable and intelligent experts in all things criminal justice sitting at her table right now. It seemed a shame not to use them.

"Not a treasure map, exactly." She pushed back from the table and unlocked the top drawer of her desk. The *Guide to Okanogan County* sat exactly where she left it. "And I don't know that I need literal prints lifted off. But I'd be interested to know if someone planned a route somewhere along these roadways. Don't people usually trace those things with their fingers? That would leave oils behind, right? So you could tell where they wanted to go?"

From the way Peter and Sylvia broke out into the scientific processes behind sweat, latent residue, and skin cells, Tess guessed that her theory was right. Especially when she saw how hard Nicki was struggling not to join their conversation. Being an FBI agent who was only supposed to know about the Dewey Decimal System had to be a real struggle sometimes.

"This is the best dinner party ever," Gertrude said, listening in rapt wonder as Peter and Sylvia started listing off everything they'd need to get started. "I take it all back, Mom. For once, you didn't ruin anything."

━━━━━━

"We'll need some kind of sealable chamber, obviously," Sylvia said, quickly taking the lead on the proceedings. She turned to Tess with a raised brow. "How's your Tupperware game?"

"Strong," Gertrude answered for her. The teen sprang up from the table and ran to the kitchen without losing a beat. "What are we talking? Quart? Gallon? The huge one that Mom sometimes uses to soak the bunions on her feet?"

"Gertie!"

"The foot one should be fine," Sylvia called back.

"Just make sure you wash it first," Nicki added with a grin. She rolled her eyes toward Tess in sympathetic amity. "It's your own fault, you know. You raised her."

"If I'd have known she'd grow up and spill all my deep, dark secrets, I'd have handed her over to the wolves when I had the chance," Tess muttered, but with a strong feeling of pride. Gertrude was throwing herself heart and soul into this project, her expression lit from within. Despite all the setbacks to her burgeoning forensic career, she refused to be kept down for long.

Tess wasn't the only one to notice.

"I'm sorry I had to ban her from the morgue," Sylvia said as she sidled closer. She kept her voice low. "I love having her around—I really do—but I wouldn't be able to live with myself if anything happened while she's under my watch."

"I take that to mean there are still no leads about who broke in?"

Sylvia shook her head. "None that I've heard of. Just a lot of rumor and conjecture."

Tess didn't pretend to misunderstand her. "Gertie and I didn't have anything to do with it, if that's what you're thinking. I've done a lot of things in the name of research, but breaking and entering isn't one of them."

The silence that greeted this statement did little to make Tess feel better. "What is it?" she asked. "What aren't you telling me?"

Sylvia tilted her head and stepped back toward the opposite end of the living room. Everyone else was busy arguing over Tupperware and ambient heat sources, so they managed to go unnoticed.

"I don't know what you've heard from Sheriff Boyd…" Sylvia paused and waited for Tess to respond, but all she managed was a shake of the head. At this point, the things she'd heard from Sheriff Boyd would hardly fill a teaspoon. "Well, it's looking more and more like a professional job."

"What do you mean, professional?"

"Sophisticated," Sylvia said. When Tess didn't respond right away, she added, lower this time, "Expensive. Someone went to a lot of trouble to make sure they wouldn't get found."

This sounded so much like what Wingbat99 had told her—that Simone Peaky was a woman buried under several layers of protection—that Tess gulped. But Sylvia wasn't done yet.

"Not only were there no prints or signs of a break-in, but the security feed was wiped on every level." Sylvia lowered her voice even more. "We keep an on-site record of the feed, obviously, but it's also set to automatically update to the cloud. Whoever got in there hacked in from the outside."

"Hacked in?" Tess echoed, her gaze shooting quickly to Peter and back to Sylvia again. "Are you serious?"

"I've lived in this county for almost my whole life, and I've never seen anything like it. Most of the crimes we see around here are smash-and-grab type affairs—someone's drunk uncle acting up again or a pair of delinquents holding up the gas station for drug money. Whoever's behind the missing bodies knows what they're doing." Sylvia nodded over at where Gertrude and Peter were testing out the seals of the different Tupperware lids. "I'm only telling you this so you understand what I'm up against. What we all are. I don't want to see an innocent kid getting hurt."

Tess was having a difficult time assimilating all this, and not just because keeping an innocent kid from getting hurt was also high on her priority list. There were only a few people she could think of who might have the means and the contacts to carry out that kind of elaborate scheme.

Mason Peabody was one of them. Peter Oblonsky was another.

Before she could speak, Nicki drew up, her brows raised high and a smile quirking the corner of her lips. "I hate to interrupt what looks like an important conversation, but we're going to need some iodine crystals if we want to pull this thing off."

"I have some at the morgue," Sylvia said doubtfully. "But it's a long drive there and back."

"Don't be absurd." Peter joined them, looking the picture of grandfatherly indulgence. "There's no need to go all that way. I spotted a wilderness survival kit underneath the sink earlier. The water-purification tablets should do the trick."

"I have a wilderness survival kit underneath the sink?" Tess asked. "Why do you know that and I don't?"

"Because I'm a prying old man with nothing but time on my hands," he said silkily. "Didn't you know? No one in the world makes for a more dangerous houseguest. Now let's get this thing started, shall we? I'm dying to know what we'll find on your map."

Chapter Eighteen

"I've decided where we should go on our hike."

Instead of waylaying Jared at the bookstore, Tess skipped the middleman and went straight to his hotel room. Like so many of the other buildings—and people—in this town, the hotel was dressed up in full Western-themed decor. Pictures of horses bucking well-shaped cowboys, more animal horns than were seemly, and golden-hued wood paneling greeted Tess's eye no matter which way she turned.

Jared himself was no exception. Although he was dressed casually in tight-fitting jeans and an even tighter-fitting T-shirt, the shirt boasted that he'd been a finalist in the 2017 Rodeo of Kings. It even had strategic holes and paint spatters that made it seem as though he'd worn it every day since.

Noticing her noticing it, he grinned and tugged ruefully at the sleeve. "It's better if you don't ask."

As if she could help herself *now*. "Because you stole it from a rodeo cowboy who's bent on vengeance, or because you were actually there?"

"A magician never reveals his secrets." He held up his palms for her inspection. "Look. I also finally got some of those calluses you wanted. Real ones and everything."

To be honest, they looked more like deeply painful and possibly infected blisters than anything else, but that wasn't what Tess came here to talk about. She held up the map, now covered in a series of inky, blue blots that showcased every spot where a person had touched it. Since all five of them had handled it last night, there was no shortage of blots.

Even with their cross contamination, however, there was no mistaking where the map had been traced the most. A random spot in the wilderness, remarkable only for how unremarkable it looked, had been the focal point.

The whole process had been fascinating, and Tess was definitely going to have Detective Gonzales whip out a survival kit in the wilderness to make use of her newfound knowledge. She'd expected some kind of chemical extravagance, but all they'd done was pour a few iodine crystals out into the bottom of the Tupperware, unfold the map on top, seal the container tightly, and then apply gentle heat to the bottom. Within seconds, the blue fingerprints started to appear.

Tess would have been hard-pressed to say whether she or Gertrude had been more excited by the findings. Even Sylvia and Nicki had allowed themselves to be beguiled into enthusiasm.

Peter, however, had only looked knowingly on.

"You want to go here?" Jared asked as he took the map from her hands and studied it. He stabbed a finger at the blue smudge. "What is it?"

"I don't know," Tess admitted. Neither had anyone else last night, although conjectures had run wild. Since she'd refused to say where she got the map—or why she cared so much about where it led—those conjectures had run the gamut from murder-related destinations to a wild-goose chase that would only end up with someone being eaten by a bear. "With any luck, it's where we'll find the missing bones. Or the third body."

Jared dropped the map like it was on fire. "Shouldn't you give this to the police?"

Tess had thought about it—she really had. Taking Sheriff Boyd a peace offering in the form of a map belonging to Herb Granger had been her initial plan, but she'd driven past the cemetery on her way to town and reconsidered.

Not content with the perimeter check that Tess and Gertrude had undertaken, the sheriff had widened the cemetery search by a good fifty feet. He'd also enlisted the aid of a ground-penetrating radar. At least, that was what Tess assumed it was. Ivy had been pushing what looked like a lawn mower slowly over the ground while the sheriff sat nearby, staring at a laptop screen. Several deputies standing off to one side and leaning on dirty shovels indicated that they'd already found—and dug up—several sets of bones.

Guinea pigs, probably. And from the grim faces of the entire crew, she was guessing they weren't too happy about it.

Tess scooped the map up and tucked it into her pocket. "I'm mostly kidding about the dead body part," she admitted. "Chances are it'll only take us to a fishing hole or scenic outlook. I just want to check it out and see what's there, and I'd rather not go by myself. Please, Jared? I packed a picnic and everything."

Technically, Gertrude had been the one to pack the picnic, but Tess wasn't kidding about not wanting to go by herself. Gertrude was at school today. Nicki was busy with the bookmobile, and the sheriff and Ivy were out for obvious reasons. As for Peter, well, he was a sweet old man who walked with the aid of a cane. She didn't want to have to carry him down the mountain when they were done.

Jared cast a quick look over his shoulder to the interior of his room. Tess caught a glimpse of the opposite wall. It was hung with photos of the Peabody family, what looked like dozens of printed-out sheets of financial records, and, to both her surprise and delight, actual red yarn strung between them. Somebody was getting serious about his investigation.

"If you're busy, I understand," she said quickly. "I should have called ahead."

"No, it's great. It's perfect. I want to." She noticed a tinge of pink touching his ears when he swallowed and tried again. "What I mean is, I'd be honored to come with you. Even if all we end up finding is a fishing hole."

———

Some men were born to lead. Others were born to follow.

And some men were put on God's green earth for the sole purpose of hiking up mountains like Tarzan taking a Sunday stroll.

"Come on, Tess. You can do it. Just a few more feet."

Tess looked up and gauged the distance between herself and Jared. Even with the sun glaring directly into her eyes, she knew him for a liar. That wasn't a few feet. That was an insurmountable distance.

"You'll have to go on without me," she panted as she sank to her knees. She didn't have far to go. There was such a slope to the ground underneath her that she was practically moving in a vertical direction. "I give up. Tell Gertie I love her and to burn the box underneath my bed without looking inside. There are some things a daughter was never meant to see."

His low chuckle only served to make her more exhausted. Anyone who could hike five miles in an upward direction and laugh about it was obviously not someone she could be friends with, let alone—

"Here. I'll help." He was by her side before she even realized he'd trotted down the mountain. "Put your arms around my neck."

She did as he asked, but only because she had no say in the matter. In a Herculean display of athleticism, he swooped her into his arms. She clung to him like a woman fearful of falling to her death, but there was no need. He leaped up the distance without breaking into a sweat—which was good, because Tess was sweating more than enough for the both of them.

The views from up here were gorgeous, a sweeping vista of trees, the swelling undulations of several nearby mountains, and more trees. Tess felt breathless from the climb and from the fact that Jared hadn't yet put her down.

"Sorry," he said as she wriggled out of his grasp and slid her boots to the solid earth. The man was obviously capable of superhuman feats of endurance, but she found she preferred to stand at a cliff's edge on her own two feet. "I got carried away."

"So did I, apparently. How are we supposed to get back down again?"

He grinned. "Don't worry. I won't abandon you up here. Nicki would never forgive me if I lost her best friend in the wilderness."

The fluttering that had been making its presence known behind Tess's rib cage picked up in earnest. It was one thing to have a strapping young thing carry her around like she weighed no more than a heroine from a Gothic novel; it was quite another to hear that other people considered she and Nicki to be best friends.

"Really? Did she call me that herself, or..." Tess's voice trailed off as she continued taking in the 360-degree views. There were several other mountains in the area that far surpassed this one in terms of height, but this one had the advantage of being the muddiest.

So muddy, in fact, that anyone walking this way would be sure to track large clumps of it back down with them.

"Did you walk that way?" She stabbed a finger in the direction of a winding trail that lay ahead of them. It was a continuation of the path they'd taken up here, faint but distinguishable...and marked by a series of muddied footprints.

Footprints that looked an awful lot like the ones a pair of cheap hiking boots might leave behind.

"No." Jared came up next to her, his gaze following hers. "I didn't want to go too far. I wanted to make sure you were okay."

Another time, this sweet gesture might have had an impact on Tess, but not now. Not when her every warning instinct was sitting up and demanding attention. "I don't suppose you brought that ankle gun with you, did you?" she asked.

"Are you kidding?" Jared cast her a sideways glance. "I never leave home without it."

"I think you'd better pull it out." Tess gulped. "It rained last night, which means these footprints should have been washed away. They're fresh."

She didn't have to ask twice. Without taking his eyes from the trail, Jared reached down and extracted the gun from his ankle holster. The first time Tess had seen it, she'd felt nothing but fear. Her feelings this go around were much warmer. Whatever else might be said about this man, he was capable. And obedient.

"What do you want to do now?" he asked. "Should we check it out, or did you want to head back to town and call it in?"

As handy as it was to have a Sheriff Boyd or a Nicki Nickerson keeping an eye on things, Tess could really get used to having her own personal FBI agent who had no problems letting her call the shots.

"Let's take a look around," she said with a decisive

nod. That gun—and the man holding it—did a lot to bolster her confidence. "We're almost to the spot on the map. We might as well see where it leads."

He nodded and gestured for her to get behind him. She found herself clinging to his belt loops as they moved slowly forward, their steps following that of their mysterious visitor.

Tess wasn't sure which one of them saw him first. Afterward, when she was sprawled on her bottom and covered from head to toe in mud, she thought it might have been her. In the moment, however, with Jared's whole body leaping to action with the same speed he'd shown when he tackled her, she suspected it was him.

"Adam?" Jared called as soon as a familiar auburn head popped into view. The Peabody brother—whichever one it was—turned at the sound of his voice. "Adam, is that you?"

The Peabody took off like a shot. Jared wasn't slow to follow. That was what accounted for Tess's unseemly plunge into the mud. Since she was still holding onto his belt loops, she surged forward with him. Since she wasn't a two-hundred-pound FBI agent at the top of his game, however, she didn't do anything more than surge. As the two men took off into the woods, she flailed, flapped, and ultimately fell.

It wasn't the worst thing in the world, despite

the fact that her jeans were soaked through and a clump of something wet and heavy hung from the back of her head. As the sound of pursuit and breaking branches trailed off into the distance, she noticed that she wasn't alone up here.

A few feet forward, hidden behind a copse of trees and brush, stood a small structure that might once have been a cabin but was now more of a dilapidated shack. She'd seen similar ones in these parts before; most of them were abandoned ranger's stations or public hiking huts that had been put up as a place for people to rest their weary bones. Although Tess's bones were plenty weary, she had no intention of sitting down.

"Hello?" she called as she drew closer, careful to give herself a wide berth in case another Peabody decided to pop out at her. "Is anyone here?"

No one was—or, if they were, they weren't willing to own up to it. Grabbing a stout stick in case someone jumped out at her, Tess tiptoed up to the door, which was a generous term for a piece of oiled canvas that hung in a flap over the open frame. She poked the stick inside and, when nothing jumped out to attack it, followed with her body.

It took her eyes a moment to adjust to the darkness. Any light the windows might have let in were blocked by similar pieces of oilcloth hanging over them from the inside. The result was gloomy, but

Tess had to admit they were effective. The temperature inside wasn't cozy, but it wasn't die-of-exposure-cold, either.

The reason for that became evident when Tess placed a hand near the top of a pot-bellied woodstove in one corner. Heat radiated off the surface—not scalding, but the kind of simmering that comes from a fire allowed to quietly bank itself.

"What the…?" She turned and took in the rest of the cabin at a glance. Signs of habitation were everywhere—in the sleeping bag neatly rolled out on top of a cot in one corner, in the row of freshly cleaned mugs next to a dishwashing bucket, and definitely in the stack of paperback books on top of a wooden crate that had been tipped on its side to be used as a table.

The writer inside Tess couldn't resist. Yes, there was every chance that another Peabody would emerge to murder her where she stood, and she really ought to go out there and make sure Jared was okay, but she always made it a point to snoop on other people's bookshelves.

A few romances from a well-known author, an untouched copy of *War and Peace*, and a Reader's Digest collection of favorites from the fifties didn't hint at much, but the bottom book on the stack caused Tess to drop the entire lot.

She didn't know why she was surprised.

Everything about this case revolved around one author and one book—neither of which she could claim for herself.

It was *Let Sleeping Dogs Lie* by Simone Peaky. And for reasons Tess couldn't even begin to understand, the copy was signed by the author herself.

Chapter Nineteen

Tess wanted to get down the mountain and to safety as soon as possible. Jared wanted to stay at the cabin to see if anyone planned to return for the night.

Adam Peabody smirked and defied either of them to tell him what was wrong about staying in an abandoned shack that few people knew about and even fewer cared to find.

"Feel free to take a look around, if you want," he said, standing with his arms crossed in the entryway to the cabin. He looked about as dirty as Tess felt, thanks to yet another flying tackle from boy wonder over there.

Jared, it was hardly necessary to say, didn't look the least bit winded from his efforts in chasing, taking down, and escorting Adam Peabody back to the cabin. He hadn't fired a shot, either, which Tess felt to be a considerable point in his favor.

"Go ahead. I've got nothing to hide," Adam added with a gesture around the cabin. "All I'm guilty of is sleeping on public land and reading some stupid book that everyone in town is already talking about."

Tess shared a look with Jared. None of what Adam just said was incorrect. As far as she could tell, these cabins operated on a first-come, first-served basis, and he wouldn't be the first man to find solace in these kinds of surroundings. But his sudden flight from the scene spoke volumes about his being found here. And if that was his copy of *War and Peace*—not to mention the Sisters of Sunshine Bay romance series—then she'd eat the oilcloth over the door. Something strange was going on around here.

"This book is signed," she said as Jared took Adam up on the offer to look around the cabin. He moved slowly and methodically, his FBI training taking over in a big way. "Where did you get it?"

"I don't know." Adam shrugged, strangely blasé about the man currently poking through his belongings. "A bookstore. The library. Does it matter?"

Yes, it did matter, especially since this book clearly wasn't one of the rogue copies from Nicki's bookmobile. Tess was about to point that out when Jared cleared his throat.

"There's enough food up here to last several weeks," he said as he lifted the top off a cooler in one corner. The cooler was old and weathered, but the fact that all the perishables were under a tight seal indicated that whoever had been staying here knew a thing or two about the wilderness.

That was how you kept bears from getting in.

Tess knew all about avoiding bears. Of everything she feared in the wilderness, bears topped the list.

She lifted out a container of egg salad, popped the seal, and took a healthy sniff. "And this is brand new. You literally just brought this up here."

"So? I was in town restocking supplies. I had a craving."

Tess glanced down at his mud-caked boots and narrowed her eyes. "Does your brother Mason know you come up here?"

"Mason?" Adam's whole body gave a stiff jerk. "Of course not. He wouldn't come near this place if it was the last shelter on earth. He hates the woods."

"But he runs a logging company," Jared pointed out—rather reasonably, Tess thought.

"Exactly." Adam released a short, barking laugh. "He won't stop until he's ripped out every last tree."

That was when Tess knew Adam for the liar he was. One of the ways Mason managed to move so much money through his company—and with a trail so convoluted that it required two undercover federal agents to track it—was because he participated in sustainable logging. No sooner did they clear out a patch of land than they reseeded it—usually at an exorbitant cost to the company, and often in areas where no actual logging had been done. There were many environmental consulting organizations on his payroll—and, according to Nicki, not all of them were shells. Mason might be a scoundrel and a thief, but he ran a surprisingly eco-friendly operation.

Tess whipped out her phone and started snapping photos of the cabin. She made sure to include the stack of books, the bedding, and the food stores.

The copy of *Let Sleeping Dogs Lie*, however, she tucked into her purse.

"Hey!" Adam protested. "I said you could look around, not take my things."

"I'll buy you a new one," Tess promised.

"But that one is signed by the author."

"I'll track another one down on eBay. You won't know the difference."

"That shows what you know," Adam muttered. "It's the only one in existence."

To Tess, that was as good as a confession—but a confession of *what*, she couldn't say. Like so many other people in and around this town, Adam was more tied up in the murders and the missing bones than he was letting on. Unfortunately, he was too young to be held liable for the first murder, and she could hardly envision him as the criminal mastermind who'd hacked into the computer system at the morgue. He hadn't even been able to properly run away from Jared on a terrain that gave him the full advantage.

"I take this to mean you don't want me at the bookstore anymore," Adam added sullenly.

Tess wasn't so lost to common sense that she

was willing to let things go *that* far. "What? Why? You two have been making such good progress."

"Really?" Jared asked, just as Adam furrowed his brow and said the same thing.

"You don't mind if I keep coming?" Adam asked. "Even though you followed me up here?"

"We didn't—" Jared began, but he heard Tess's warning hiss and stopped himself short. Honestly, it was as though this man had never undertaken espionage and intrigue before.

"*We didn't* mean to scare you, but you were acting so suspiciously that we couldn't help but follow you up here," Tess lied. To admit that they'd only found this place because of a map—a map that she'd found on Herb's property in a car that had once belonged to Lucretia Gregory—would only tip Adam off. "But if all you're doing is camping, I don't see what it has to do with us."

"So you're not going to tell the sheriff about this place?"

"I mean, I might mention it in casual conversation, but—" She took one look at his clouding expression and changed her mind. "No. If you'd rather I didn't, we can keep this between us."

He grunted in what Tess took to understand was gratitude.

"And you're not going to make me move everything out of here?"

"I doubt I have that power," Tess confessed, though Jared and his gun might have helped move things along, should she decide to go that path.

"And you're not going to say I have to stop helping?"

Of all Adam's questions, that one seemed to weigh the heaviest on his mind. A less suspicious woman might take that to mean that he loved bookstores or that he was enjoying his time with Jared, but Tess's suspicions had long since taken over this conversation.

What Adam was scared to lose—what he didn't want to miss—was access to the half-built bookstore. There was something inside those four walls that he wanted.

Considering that the only items of value in there were a few power tools, some vastly overpriced bamboo flooring, and the espresso machine that had been delivered yesterday, she was guessing that the something he wanted was more sinister in its makeup.

Something like a third body.

"It's up to Jared," Tess said, since she didn't want it to look like she was too eager.

She was eager, though. If Adam thought there might be a body somewhere inside there—if he *knew* it—then it was her duty to plant cameras, sit on a stake out, and do whatever else was necessary to make sure she witnessed him finding it.

"Well?" she prodded, trying not to sound as ferocious as she felt. If Jared failed to pick up the hint, if he messed this up for her in any way...

"I don't see why not," Jared said with the boyish grin that made him look so innocent. "I'm used to having Adam around now. I'd feel lonely to go back to working all by myself."

"Then it's settled." Tess clapped her hands before either of them could say anything more. "Starting tomorrow, you'll both work twice as hard and get the bookstore done before the original estimate. It's a deal."

Both men were so outraged at this peremptory command—and at Tess's audacity in issuing it—that no more questions or accusations were raised. They left the cabin as a cheerful trio: one thriller-writer-turned-amateur-investigator, one undercover FBI agent, and a man Tess knew was hiding something.

Now all she had to do was figure out what.

Chapter Twenty

NATURALLY, TESS HAD EVERY INTENTION OF telling Sheriff Boyd about the hike. No sooner had she and Jared parted ways, the still-full picnic in hand, then she made a beeline for the cemetery.

From the look of things, the sheriff's department wasn't having any more luck locating the mystery missing body than Tess and Gertrude had. Even with radars, a full team of young, fit deputies, and the willful determination of a sheriff that few people were willing to cross, you couldn't make bodies materialize out of thin air.

"What happened to you?" Ivy asked by way of greeting. "You look like you fell halfway down a mountain to get here."

Tess glanced down at her muddied disgrace of an outfit and laughed. "That's not far off, actually. You, on the other hand, are remarkably clean for someone digging up half a cemetery."

Ivy didn't answer her laugh with one of her own. "Technically, we're only digging up *around* the cemetery. And in about ten minutes, we won't even be doing that anymore."

Tess's heart sank. It had always been a long shot, but hope had a way of holding out in situations like these. Drat the thing. "You didn't find anything?"

"No, and if you're here to talk to Sheriff Boyd, I wouldn't. He's not happy about wasting all this time on a wild-goose chase."

Of course he wasn't—and of course Tess knew who he'd blame for it. Not Simone Peaky for writing the book, and not Peter for introducing it into the case. Not even Ivy for corroborating her own fears.

Tess was going to take the blame for this one, and there was nothing she could do about it but square her shoulders and face the inevitable.

"Where is he?" she asked, holding her hand up to her eyes as she scanned the cemetery. A tall figure stood near the back, standing under the branches of a barren elm. "Never mind. I think I found him."

"Wait—you're not going to talk to him, are you?" Ivy's eyes grew wide, and she gave a discreet shake of her head. "I wouldn't. Not now. Not if you want to keep your skin intact. He's already made two grown men cry today."

Tess drew a deep breath and steeled her resolve. Making grown men cry was something she did on the regular. Scaring *her* off would take a lot more than that.

"Don't say I didn't warn you," Ivy muttered as Tess picked her way across the cemetery. The team had been careful not to disturb the eternal rest of any of the people who were officially—and legally—interred there, but as Tess walked, she scanned the ground for any signs of a disturbance. There weren't any to speak of, but that didn't mean much. If someone had buried a body here in the nineties, there'd be no way to tell. Not without exhuming every single person in here.

Her steps slowed as she approached the sheriff's form, which seemed gaunt and aloof in this setting. His head cocked at the sound of her footsteps, but he didn't turn to look at her. He was too busy staring down at a single headstone carved with two names, both of which bore the surname of Boyd.

"Your parents?" she asked quietly as she came to a halt a few feet away.

"They died shortly after Kendra disappeared," he said. His voice was even quieter than hers, and she had to lean close to hear it. Victor's familiar scent wrapped an invisible hand around her heart and squeezed. "There's room in this plot for one more. They were always so sure she was gone; they made me promise to put her here if her body was ever recovered."

Tess didn't want to think about what would happen if she already was here—if their killer had a sense of humor so sick and twisted that not even *she* would've dared to put it in a book.

"I'm sorry you went through all that trouble for nothing," Tess said.

Instead of agreeing with her, Sheriff Boyd grunted. He also glanced at her, his expression flat but not hard, resigned but not angry.

More than anything, he looked like he needed a hug.

"At least it gave us something concrete to do. My guys hate not having any leads." He sighed. "But that's the story, isn't it? Word for word."

Tess wasn't sure she followed. "What do you mean?"

"That's what happened in the book, remember? The coroner has inconclusive evidence—which, considering our coroner doesn't have *any* evidence, seems fitting. The sheriff doesn't find anything worth note—a thing I think we can all agree is true, considering how few leads I have to go on. Eventually, the district attorney drops interest, and that's that."

"Until they find the third body," Tess prompted. "Then everything comes together."

The look the sheriff gave her was so bleak, she gave in and wrapped her arms around him. To her surprise, he didn't push her away. He didn't exactly fall into her embrace, but the fact that he let her hold him at all—and in full public view—was telling. Especially since the longer she stood there, her arms refusing to let that powerful chest go, the more he started to relax against her.

"There is no third body, Tess," he said, his voice so low that she felt its vibrations more than she heard the actual words. "You and I both know that. Just like we know those women weren't killed by a mob of townspeople bent on vengeance."

"From the sound of things, Annabelle had enough enemies for it to happen."

"Yes, but Lucretia was a stranger to these parts. She didn't." He paused. "And neither did my sister."

Herb's words from before flashed through Tess's brain, his avowal that Kendra Boyd was a good person—a *great* person—and someone no one would want to harm. "I wish you'd tell me more about her," Tess said. When the sheriff winced and pulled away, she hurried to add, "Not because of the stupid case. I mean, I *do* think she's relevant, and I'm not ready to give up on that *Sleeping Dogs* book just yet, but it seems like you could use someone to talk to."

"To say what?" he asked. "That I loved her? That I miss her? That my life has never been the same since she left?"

"Yes."

The sheriff drew a deep, ragged breath. "I loved her. I miss her. My life has never been the same since she left."

Tess stood and waited, a lump caught in her throat. For the longest moment, she was afraid that was all she was getting—a few terse sentences and the soft breathing of a man who rarely allowed himself a soft *anything*—but he sighed and continued.

"The only reason I put the whole team on the cemetery to look for that missing body is because there's justifiable cause," he said. His eyes met Tess's, but she didn't think he was looking at her. Not really. "I don't believe half the garbage in that book, but the author got one thing right: there's a link between Annabelle Charles, Lucretia Gregory, and Kendra Boyd."

Tess was almost afraid to ask, but she forced herself to do it anyway. "Beyond the obvious?"

He tilted his head in agreement, a lock of his silky hair falling across his forehead. Tess longed to brush it away, but she balled her hand and shoved it behind her back instead. She didn't want to do anything to disrupt the moment. Not when she was getting so *close*.

She might never solve this dratted case, but she might, if she tried hard enough, solve the man.

"No one cared enough to look very hard for any of them," he said. "Myself included. That's the part that bothers me the most. I was just a kid when Annabelle Charles ran her reign of terror around here, but I heard the stories. We all did—me and my sister, everyone

we went to school with. When Annabelle went missing, most of the town sighed in relief and looked the
other way. When Lucretia disappeared, there wasn't
the same kind of hatred to fuel a quick cover-up,
but no one pushed. She'd indicated to several of her
coworkers that she was leaving, determined to find
a way out of a lifestyle and a career she didn't enjoy.
With Herb's testimony that she sold him her car and
the bus depot's confirmation that the ticket had been
used, it made sense. A quick getaway, a fresh start.
Who hasn't dreamed of that?"

Tess found herself nodding along. In many
ways, that was exactly what she'd done when she
and Gertrude had first come to this town. They'd
needed a retreat from the world and all the people
in it. Sometimes, disappearing from life was the
solution you never knew you needed.

He blew out a long breath, sending that lock of
hair fluttering. "And Kendra…well. She was my
favorite person in the whole world, but she wasn't
without her problems."

"She was older than you by several years, wasn't
she?" Tess asked gently.

He glanced over, almost surprised to find her standing there. "Yeah. Four years, actually. As kids, we were
pretty close, but toward the end…" He took pity on
Tess's balled-up hand and brushed the hair away from
his forehead. "I don't know. Something happened

240 TAMARA BERRY

to her, and she changed almost overnight. She fell in with a bad crowd. Her boyfriend—I told you about him—was a good-for-nothing pothead who was one failed class away from never finishing high school. She fought with our parents almost every single day. She constantly threatened to pack everything up and leave, and I think she'd have done it, only…"

"Only she didn't want to leave you behind?" Tess guessed.

Victor released a low curse and kicked at his parents' headstone. "She *promised* she wouldn't go without me. She said she was going to wait. Until I was eighteen and had finished high school. Until we could get an apartment somewhere and make our own way in the world. Together."

Tess stood and quietly digested this story. Victor must have taken her silence as a condemnation of his actions, because he immediately launched into a defensive position.

"It's why I never bought that story about her running off to Seattle. Was it the most obvious answer? Yes. Would she have done it without telling me? No. *No.*" He spoke with so much emotion that it set off something wild inside Tess's rib cage. "And I knew it. I was the only person who knew it. I knew about Kendra and I knew about Lucretia and I knew about Annabelle. Why the *devil* didn't I put it all together before now?"

She had plenty of ways to answer that question. Because he was a human being who made mistakes. Because he was desperate to believe that his sister was still alive, even if it meant ignoring the evidence right in front of him.

Because one man was never meant to bear this kind of burden alone.

Tess didn't say any of this aloud. The last thing Victor Boyd wanted to hear from her was a bunch of balmy platitudes that didn't mean anything. She knew this man well enough to realize that there was only one thing that could help him heal, and that was finding the killer.

Even if they never found Kendra's body, even if she remained a missing person for the rest of their lives, he needed to close two of the three cases if he wanted a chance at happiness. And Tess, who may have only started this investigation to clear her grandfather's name, needed that as much as he did.

Which was why she did the only thing she could think of. Pulling the newest copy of *Let Sleeping Dogs Lie* out of her bag, she handed it to him.

He groaned. "What now?"

"I know it's not what you want to hear, but I found this book on top of a mountain."

"Of course you did. Which mountain?"

She pointed in a vaguely northeastern direction.

"I don't know the names of every hill around here, but I have a map if you want the exact location. There's some kind of old shack there—an abandoned ranger's station or something."

He nodded as though this made perfect sense. "Ramsey Peak. There used to be a fire watchtower up there back in the fifties."

Tess blinked in surprise. "You know it?"

"Of course. Every kid who grew up in this town threw a party there at least once." He relaxed enough to lift his lips in a light smile. "I think nine-tenths of us lost our virginity up there, too."

This new conversational direction was one Tess would have gladly taken, were it not for the fact that they were standing on his parents' grave and discussing the agony of his sister's disappearance. The idea of this man doing something so untoward as losing his innocence in a dilapidated shack was one she'd have to revisit at a future date.

"Including the Peabody boys?" Tess inquired.

"Yes." The sheriff was shrewd enough to sense the shift, both in the subject matter and in Tess's tone. "Why? What did you find?"

"Adam Peabody and enough supplies for him to hide out there for at least two weeks." She pointed at the book. "And some light reading material to keep him occupied while he did it. This copy of the book is *signed*, Victor."

"I think you'd better start this story from the beginning," the sheriff said.

With that, all traces of memory and emotion disappeared. As she launched into her tale of the map, the climb up the mountain, and Adam's determination to return to the bookstore even in light of these new revelations, the investigative spirit took over as if by magic.

Just like Tess knew it would.

———

"I'd like it stated for the record that I in no way, shape, or form condone the use of a teddy bear to catch a murderer," said Sheriff Boyd early the next morning.

Tess paused in the act of ripping the stuffing out of the teddy bear in question. "The record notes your concerns." She pulled out the small mechanical device that was attached to a miniature camera in the bear's right eye. "And to be clear, the bear isn't part of this. I just need his guts."

Sheriff Boyd took the camera from her and examined it. "You really used to spy on Gertie's babysitters with this thing?"

"I never *spied* on them. I was protecting my child. There's no telling what kinds of things people will get up to when they think no one is watching."

He cast a very obvious glance around the

half-finished bookshop, which seemed eerie and skeletal in the dim morning light. Tess had chosen to do this particular activity when the town was as quiet as possible, for the obvious reason of not wanting any of the Peabody brothers to see what she was up to.

"Does that include setting up a surveillance system in hopes of catching a man in the act of…" the sheriff trailed off before picking up the thread again. "What, exactly, do we suspect Adam of wanting with this place? I'm having a hard time keeping track."

"You didn't have to come with me," she pointed out. In fact, she was surprised that he'd agreed to this. And not just because of the questionable legal ramifications. Although there was nothing stopping her from putting cameras in any and all corners of a bookstore she owned, having the sheriff help her find the best hiding spot and set it up so the battery operated on a self-generating loop was a bit out of the ordinary.

Tess shook her head and continued, "If you'd seen how eager Adam was to get back here, how upset he got at the prospect of losing his all-hammer access, you'd have agreed with me. Are you absolutely sure your deputies checked every possible place where another body might be buried in here?"

"Not absolutely sure, no." The sheriff skimmed his flashlight over the floor, which was almost completely intact now. "But your little boyfriend had this place down to the studs. If *he* didn't find anything…"

"Jared Wilson isn't my little boyfriend."

He cleared his throat. "I'm sorry. Your large boyfriend."

"Victor! I'm not dating him. We went on *one* hike together, and it was mostly a cover so I could check out the destination on Herb's map without drawing suspicion."

Instead of taking comfort from this, Sheriff Boyd looked at her through narrowed, darkly appraising eyes. "So what you're saying is, when you invite a man to help you with an investigation, he shouldn't read anything into it?"

Tess felt as though something tight grasped her by the throat and refused to let go. "Victor…"

"I'd suggest you mount this inside one of the knots in that wood paneling near the door," he said conversationally. "Since there's already an electrical panel for the light switches, it should be easy enough to wire it in without anyone noticing. As long as you remember to back up and erase the footage every day, you'll be able to run this thing for years."

"Victor," she said again, more firmly this time. He tilted his head and waited. Since she hadn't thought much beyond getting his attention and forcing him to return to the topic at hand, he had to wait for quite some time.

"Well?" he prodded.

She had no idea what compelled her to act. Maybe it was the fact that he was still looking rough around the edges from that conversation in the cemetery. Perhaps it had more to do with the fact that she'd detected an oh-so-delicious hint of jealousy in the way he talked about Jared. More than likely, it was the inevitable outcome when two people were plunged into danger over and over again.

Whatever the cause, Tess had her arms around his neck and her lips pressed against his before she realized what she was doing.

Not that she regretted the impulse. She'd been close to this man enough times to recognize his latent strength, to know that he was as firm and unyielding in physique as he was in every other aspect of his life.

What she hadn't known—and what she'd never be able to forget—was how soft his mouth felt on top of hers. Instead of being surprised by Tess's sudden catapult into his arms, he caught her. In fact, she couldn't swear that she was the one who instigated the kiss. The moment she crossed the room and over the invisible barrier that had kept them apart for so long, he was as invested in the embrace as she was.

"Do you always have to throw your whole body weight at me?" he grumbled as she nudged him toward the wall. It wasn't her fault—she had to do *something* when he lifted a hand to the back of her head and tangled it in her hair. She'd never been the type to meekly accept overtures like that. When a man held her head so he could deepen the kiss, she had to retaliate by pressing her whole body against his. It was science. Equal and opposite forces and all that.

"If it's too much for you, then why are you trying to cop a feel?"

"I'm not trying to cop a feel," he growled against her mouth. "I'm trying to keep from toppling over."

As he followed this remark up by copping a feel with so much enthusiasm that Tess gasped, she didn't take it to heart. Especially when he stopped there, drawing back with a ragged breath that said all the things that neither of them were willing to put into words. Instead of letting her go right away, he pressed his forehead softly against hers, allowing their breath to mingle as their heart rates slowed.

Tess would have been happy to keep going—happier still to tug this man to the floor and see what two equal and opposite forces could do when they put their backs in it—but there was something so sweetly romantic in that gesture, so un-Victor-like, that it sent a thrill through her.

"For the record, I invited you to help me with this investigation because I respect your opinion," she said as soon as her head cleared enough to form a coherent thought.

"There's no need for flattery. You already got what you want."

She laughed. "Are you always this grumpy after a woman kisses you? If I'd have known that, I'd have kept my thoughts—and my hands—to myself."

"You didn't kiss me," he returned, still sounding adorably grumpy. "*I* kissed you. You just made it easier for me to reach your lips."

"So…what you're saying is, all I have to do is get a little bit close…" She brought her mouth so near to his that she could almost taste the minty sweetness of his breath. "And you'll do the rest?"

He wanted to fight it, Tess could tell. A man as proud as this one had to be led rather than driven, but something about the morning air and the quiet of the bookstore was getting to them both. With a muttered growl of protest, he brought his mouth to hers once again…only to send them both falling to the floor.

"What the—" The second Victor's lips touched hers, the back of Tess's calf hit a cardboard box she couldn't remember putting there. Her weight was so off-balance that she went down with a thud, and, since her arms were still wrapped firmly around Victor's neck, he went with her.

It had been so long since Tess had enjoyed the

weight of a man on top of her that she didn't register the pain right away. She liked the warm bulk of him, the strong, hard lines stretched out on top of her body.

What she didn't like, however, was the round, knobby ridge pressing into her back like a tiny fist.

"Ow, ow, ow," she said as she rolled out from underneath him. The box she'd hit was crushed almost flat, its contents starting to scatter around her. She thought she heard the clacking of something ceramic, but that wasn't right. She remembered now that Nicki had brought a few more boxes of books from the library in an effort to strengthen her cover story for meeting with Jared.

"Don't be so dramatic," Victor said, a laugh curving his lips. "I was careful to catch myself before I—"

His voice cut out in a manner that could only be described as *dramatic*.

"What?" she asked, disliking the look on his face. It was too similar to the one he'd worn back at the cemetery—that bleak, distant self-reproach. "What's wrong?"

"Don't move," he warned and started to slowly pick himself up. "Stay right where you are."

Only through supreme force of will was Tess able to keep her limbs from flailing out. "Oh, God. Is it a spider? So help me, Victor, if it's a spider, I'm going to—"

"No, Tess," he said, his voice so quiet that she had

to strain to hear it. What she didn't have to strain to do, however, was see him reach for the radio at his hip. "It's not a spider. It's another set of bones."

Chapter Twenty-One

"YOU HAVE THE RIGHT TO REMAIN SILENT," Ivy said, a much-too-wide grin on her face as she slipped a pair of handcuffs on Tess. They pinched at her wrists—and not in a fun way. "You have the right to refuse to answer questions. Anything you say may be—"

"You can stop now," Tess said irritably. She rolled her eyes toward the sheriff, almost as annoyed with him as she was with Ivy. "Are you really going to let her haul me away like this? I'm not resisting arrest. We could just as easily walk across the street like decent human beings."

Sheriff Boyd—she refused to call him Victor after this—sighed. "Ivy, is that really necessary?"

"Oh, it's necessary." Ivy clapped a hand on Tess's shoulder. "How many times do you think I'm going to get a chance to drag Tess off to a jail cell? I intend to enjoy myself."

That made exactly one of them. From the moment Tess had found herself lying in yet another a pile of bones, she'd felt a heavy weight in the pit of her stomach. She wasn't such an expert that she could tell the difference between this body and the two missing ones, but her instincts warned her that they'd finally found the mysterious third victim.

Kendra Boyd. In a box. At my bookstore.

"It's a formality," Sheriff Boyd promised, his eyes not quite meeting Tess's. She wanted to point out that there was a smudge of her lipstick at the corner of his mouth, but she didn't dare.

Okay, the optics were bad. That a box of bones was sitting on the floor of her bookstore, when two sets had recently gone missing and she was the primary suspect in their theft, was hardly a point in her favor. But everyone in this room right now—Sheriff Boyd and Ivy Bell and Sylvia Nerudo—knew she wasn't a murderer.

They *knew* it.

"Just let the townspeople see that we've taken Tess in, fill out the paperwork, and then put her in my office until I can get away," the sheriff said.

"Uh…in your office?" Ivy echoed. "Are you sure you want to leave her alone in there?"

"Ivy!" Tess was really starting to get tired of this. "I'm not going to do anything."

"Fine. Put her in lockup. Just…" Sheriff Boyd sighed and pinched the bridge of his nose. Since the moment Sylvia had come rushing in, half-rumpled with sleep and carrying a body bag, he'd been careful not to look at her. Not at Tess and not at the coroner and *definitely* not at a body that could very well turn out to be his sister's. "I'm sorry, Tess. I don't have a choice. You know that as well as I do."

She took pity on him.

"Don't worry about it. I've always thought it would be good research to spend all day in a jail cell. Experience all the discomforts and indignities firsthand, you know?" She held out her handcuffed wrists so Ivy could lead her away. "Let's get my shame parade over with. You'll stop them if they throw rotten produce at me, right?"

Ivy snorted. "Sure thing. All the tomatoes I can eat."

Ivy led her triumphantly away, a spring in her step and a mischievous smile on her lips. Neither one of those things lasted very long. They only made it a few steps outside the door when the sound of voices reached them from inside the bookstore.

"Victor, take a look at this. Unless I'm mistaken, these are hatchet marks."

Just like that, Ivy's smile fell. Tess's mood, which was already dropping faster than the forest temperatures at night, plummeted along with it.

"Ivy," she said, her words barely above a whisper.

"I know," Ivy said, equally hushed. "Just put one foot in front of the other."

The task was easier said than done—not

because the townspeople came out to boo and hiss, which they didn't, and not because Tess's ankle was twisted from where she'd hit the box, which it was, but because the farther she got from that bookstore, the more she felt that something terrible was in the air.

"Who could have done such a thing?" she asked before they'd made it halfway. She didn't know if she was asking about the murder or the fact that the killer had seen fit to put the body somewhere she was sure to find it, but it didn't matter. There was no answer either way.

"Don't try to get inside the head of a murderer," Ivy said by way of reply. "It's not a place anyone should stay for long."

Tess did her best to stay out of the murderer's mind as they walked into the sheriff's office. She remained out of it as she was fingerprinted and booked. She even stayed clear when Ivy pulled open the door to the lockup, which was a fancy name for a small, windowless room near the back.

As soon as she sat down and Ivy offered to grab her a snack from the vending machine, however, she was done for.

"No, I don't want a snack. I want to be back in the bookstore. I want to help."

"I know you do," Ivy said, and with so much sympathy that Tess suspected she'd seen that bit of wayward lipstick. "But the best thing you can do right now is sit here. Quietly."

The emphasis of that last bit wasn't lost on her. "Aren't I at least supposed to get a phone call before you abandon me?"

"Who would you call?"

The thought of calling Gertrude and Peter to explain this newest turn of events wasn't one that appealed, and Tess wasn't sure she was ready to face all the questions Nicki would have about Tess being inside the bookstore early in the morning with Victor Boyd. And Jared was *definitely* out for those same reasons.

"Never mind," she said. "I'll save it for it later."

In the normal course of events, Tess would have been bored out of her mind, stripped as she was of her cell phone and her notepad. But after only half an hour of sitting in that empty room with nothing but her thoughts to keep her company, Ivy poked her head through the door.

"Inmate, you've got a visitor."

"It wasn't funny the first ten times you called me that, and it's not funny now," Tess said, but the prospect of having someone to help her while away the time wasn't unwelcome. "Who is it?"

Edna St. Clair came breezing in before Ivy could announce her—or issue a warning. "Ha! I heard they threw you in the clink. It's about time." The older woman sailed past the rows of desks and planted herself outside Tess's cell. "How's it feel to be on that side of the bars for once?"

Tess sighed. Since she had nothing but time on her hands, it seemed like a good moment to clarify things. "Edna, you know I'm not really a police officer, right?"

Edna blinked at her from behind a pair of owlish glasses. "Yes, you are."

"No, I'm not. I'm an author. I write books."

Edna planted her feet more firmly on the floor, a martial glint of determination in her eyes. "But you're here all the time. And you're always poking around asking questions you shouldn't."

Ivy snorted. "She has you there."

"Is there a reason you've come all this way?" Tess asked, giving up and giving in. Some battles were simply never meant to be won. "I'm not up for bail yet, and unless you had another video camera out last night... Wait. Edna, *please* tell me you had another video camera out last night. And that you captured footage of whoever put those bones inside my bookstore."

Ivy grabbed the back of two chairs and dragged them toward the front of Tess's cell. Planting herself in one, she gestured politely for Edna to take the other.

She didn't, of course.

"If I sit in that chair, I won't be getting up again

until I'm dead," she said, staring at the low seat and cushioned back. "When you get to be as old as me, none of your muscles work the way they're supposed to."

"Edna, I saw you out pulling weeds in your front yard yesterday like a woman half your age," Ivy said.

Edna moaned and put her hand on her back in a show of theatrics. "And I'll be paying for it for weeks." Before she could continue lamenting the loss of her joints and tendons, she turned to Tess with an outstretched finger. "I saw that young man of yours skulking around your bookshop last night. That's what I came here to say."

Ivy and Tess both jumped to their feet at the same time.

"Why didn't you say that earlier?" Ivy demanded, just as Tess groaned and said, "For the last time, he's not my young man. We went on *one* walk together."

"One walk, my sciatica." Edna snorted. "You two have been sauntering around this town, giggling like teenagers, ever since you moved here. We had a name for that kind of thing, back when I was a young lady. You'd have been known as—"

"Thank you, Edna," Ivy interrupted, caught between annoyance and laughter. "I think we've both been called that particular word enough times in our lives."

Tess wasn't so easily amused. "But I don't understand. Are you talking about the *sheriff*? Sheriff Boyd? You saw him at my bookstore last night?"

Edna released a loud snort. "Who else would I be talking about?"

Tess could think of several answers to that question, all of which made more sense than the sheriff. Adam Peabody had a lot to be held accountable for, including that mysterious shack up at the top of the mountain, a signed copy of Simone Peaky's book, and the fact that he was obsessed with her bookstore. Mason Peabody was kind of obsessed with it, too, now that she thought about it. He'd been the one to suggest his brother work there in the first place. Jared Wilson had his own set of keys, and Nicki routinely brought in boxes of books as a way to meet with her undercover partner.

So, yeah. People had been buzzing around the bookstore for weeks—some for good reasons; others for reasons Tess had yet to work out.

Ivy, however, had no such qualms. She reached into her pocket and pulled out her notebook, her fingers rapid as they flipped the pages. "Edna, I need you to start this from the top. At what time did you see the sheriff at the bookstore?"

"Late. It was dark. I was coming home from bingo at the church and decided to walk that way, just to make sure everything was all right." Edna rolled an eye at Tess. "You don't have to thank me. I'm happy to keep watch over things."

Tess was pretty sure that what Edna was happy to do was cram her nose deep into other people's business, but she refrained from saying so. She was too interested in the rest of this tale. There was nothing wrong with Sheriff Boyd patrolling the area, especially given the kind of activity that had been taking place at the bookstore lately, but it was odd that he hadn't mentioned it.

"Did he go inside, or was he just passing by?" Ivy asked.

"Ivy, you don't think—?" Tess began, but Ivy held up a finger to silence her.

"I don't know," Edna said, a furrow in her brow. "His car pulled up and stopped in front of the building, but then it crept around to the back. I thought it was odd because he didn't have his headlights on. He could have hit something out there. He could have hit *me*."

Ivy's gaze flashed over to Tess's before quickly shifting back again. "His car? You mean his truck, or his squad car?"

"Squad car," Edna said, and with a swiftness that gave her words weight. "You can always tell his because it's the one with the hammer marks in the bumper."

This was true. A group of angry bikers had once taken offense at the way the sheriff escorted them out of a bar and wreaked their vengeance on his squad car. Ivy was always on him to get it fixed, but he said he liked the way it looked, like a badge of honor.

"I'm sure he was just doing a perimeter check," Tess said. And, because it seemed important to make the clarification, "It's not what you think, Edna. We're just friends."

Edna snorted in derision. "And I'm the high priestess of Methow Valley."

"No, really. It's not like tha—" Tess closed her mouth before she could finish her sentence. Technically, it *was* like that. Granted, their kiss had been interrupted by the sudden appearance of corpse number three, and there was still a lot that needed to be said between them, but that kiss had been a long time coming.

From the way her stomach grew suddenly tight, that kiss wasn't the only thing Tess and Victor had been working up to. Anxiety and concern mixed with something warmer, something almost uncomfortably hot. It was *killing* her not to be with him right now, to hold his hand or simply stand nearby as he processed the evidence that was likely to lead to confirmation of his sister's death.

When Tess didn't say anything, Ivy jumped in to

fill the conversational gap. "I don't give two shakes of a cat's tail what Tess and the sheriff get up to in their downtime, and neither should you. What happened next?"

"I told you already." Edna set her jaw. "I don't know. One minute, I was watching his car creep around the building like he didn't want anyone to see, and the next..."

Tess and Ivy leaned in close, their breath as close to bated as it could get. As authors, they could both learn something from this woman when it came to drawing out tension. Edna was the type who could milk the drama out of a butchered cow.

"All the streetlights in the middle of the town came on at once. It was the strangest thing. I've never seen them do that before."

Tess was startled by this new piece of information, but Ivy nodded like it made perfect sense. "We got a call around eleven p.m. last night. Apparently, half the bulbs burned out. There was some kind of glitch in the system that made them surge all at once."

"A glitch in the system?" Tess echoed.

Edna harrumphed. "That was no glitch. Whoever turned them on didn't want me to see what was going on inside the bookstore. I was blinded for a full two minutes. By the time I got my vision back, the sheriff was gone and all the doors were locked. I couldn't get in to see what he'd been up to."

"Or he was never there to begin with," Ivy said in a low voice meant only for Tess's ears.

For once, however, Tess didn't agree with the deputy. Edna wasn't always the most trustworthy source of information, and there was a good chance she was exaggerating for effect, but something about this story was setting off alarm bells.

"Who controls the streetlights?" Tess asked.

Ivy shrugged. "They run on an automatic system. It sometimes acts up, but that's true of anything tech-related in this town. A few years ago, the fire alarm at the high school went off every three hours like clockwork. We couldn't figure out what was wrong for days, but it turned out one of the students hacked into the system to get out of a chemistry test and then forgot to change the setting back afterward."

Those were the exact words Tess had hoped not to hear.

"You mean someone might have hacked into the system and flooded the whole street of lights on purpose?" she demanded.

"If they did, I want damages," Edna proclaimed. "There's still a fuzzy spot in my right eye. I'll never be able to drive again."

Ivy snorted. "Nice try, Edna. We confiscated your driver's license last month when you hit that parked bicycle. You're never driving again as it is."

Tess wasn't so easily amused. She didn't believe for one minute that Sheriff Boyd had anything to do with the body inside her bookstore, but that bit about the lights was alarming…and not just because it gave someone the perfect opportunity to slip inside the store and leave her a gift she'd have much rather been without.

There was only one person she could think of who could hack a remote system like that, and only one person who might have a reason for doing so.

His name was Wingbat99.

⸻

"I'm ready for my phone call now," Tess announced as soon as Ivy returned from escorting Edna out the door. The trip to the front of the office and back should have taken all of two minutes, but the clock on the opposite wall indicated that it had taken five times that.

Tess was guessing Ivy had a few more questions for Edna. Questions she didn't want Tess overhearing.

"Why?" Ivy asked suspiciously. "Who are you going to talk to?"

"I can't tell you that," Tess said. And, because she was never any good at keeping secrets, especially when so much was at stake, she added, "A guy named Wingbat99. He's my hacker-for-hire."

Ivy's only sign of surprise was a carefully arched brow. "You have a hacker-for-hire? Do I want to know?"

"I have the sheriff's permission to use him, if that helps." Tess wrinkled her nose before amending her statement. "Well, he doesn't *technically* know about Wingbat, but he said I can use whatever means are necessary to try and find the missing body. I won't tell him if you don't."

"But you already found the missing body," Ivy pointed out.

Yes, Tess had, and that was what worried her. The timing of everything—the way all roads kept leading back to her bookstore—was starting to feel like a lot more than a series of coincidences.

"Please? I can't just sit here waiting for Sheriff Boyd to wrap things up. I have to do *something*, or I'll start climbing the walls." She paused and allowed a slow smile to creep over her face. "Have you ever heard me sing 'The Song That Never Ends'? I'm really good. I only need a few hours before my voice is warmed up enough to actually hit those high notes."

Ivy sighed. "Fine, but only if you let me listen in on the call. I've never met a hacker before."

Tess couldn't think of a good excuse to keep Ivy off the other line, so she agreed. Ivy was so pleased that she even released Tess from the holding room and let her sit at the desk like a normal person while she did it.

"You have to promise not to say a word," Tess said as she lifted the receiver and punched in the number Peter had given her. He'd made her memorize it like a spy recalling the coordinates of nuclear bomb—a thing she'd found ridiculous at the time, but fully appreciated in this moment. "Here goes nothing."

The phone rang exactly three times before the robotic voice picked up. "Wet 'n' Ready Cleaning Service, where the only thing hotter than our mops are our rates," it said. "How may I direct your call?"

"It's Tess Harrow. I need your help."

There was a slight pause and a whirring sound before the robotic voice cut off. When Wingbat99 spoke again, it was with his regular voice. "Sorry, Tess, but I wouldn't even bail my mom out of jail when she got arrested for shoplifting last year. You're on your own for this one."

"How did you know—?" she began, but there was no need to ask.

"And tell whoever is listening in on the other receiver that they won't be able to trace me. If MI6 couldn't track me down when I was literally calling from inside their building, your small-town sheriff station doesn't have a chance."

"It's my friend Ivy, and she's not trying to trace you," Tess said.

"Hey!" Ivy shot her an annoyed glance. "What'd you give me away for?"

"I didn't give you away. He knows already."

"He might have been able to track us to the police station, but he didn't know I was listening in," Ivy grumble. "He was fishing."

Wingbat99 chuckled deeply. "That's true, actually. You'd be surprised what people give up without realizing it."

"See? I told you." Ivy clicked her tongue triumphantly, but she didn't hang up the receiver. "For what it's worth, Tess is telling the truth. We're not trying to trace you. Tess wanted me here for moral support."

What Tess really wanted was to be left alone to make her phone call in peace, but she knew better than to try. "Do you know anything about the streetlights surging in the middle of Winthrop late last night?" Tess asked.

"Well, now. That's an interesting question."

Ivy and Tess shared a quick look.

"Interesting how?" Ivy asked.

"Ivy, this is my two thousand bucks. Let me ask the questions," Tess said.

Ivy's eyes practically started from their sockets. "Two *thousand* dollars? He'd better have the answers to Blackbeard's missing treasure for that much."

"Oh, that was found a few years ago," Wingbat99

said breezily. "A friend of mine tracked it down off the coast of Virginia. He sold it off in pieces to private collectors, so no one knows where he got it."

Tess strongly suspected Wingbat99 of making things up to impress them, but Ivy fell for the trap. "No way," she breathed.

"Ivy, *focus.*" Tess loosened her grip on the phone, which was so tight she was starting to develop a cramp in her fingers. "Wingbat, what do you know about the lights?"

"If you're asking me whether or not I caused that surge, the answer is no. But I looked into that town of yours back when you first contacted me— all part of the package deal, you understand—and there was a bit of an anomaly."

"What kind of anomaly?" Tess demanded.

"The whole thing is wired to a single system. The government computers and infrastructure, I mean. It happens in small towns sometimes, especially ones that update all their tech at once. Here. Watch."

Ivy and Tess sat, slightly bewildered, as every single one of the computers around the room flashed before turning off again.

"Did you do that?" Tess asked, eyes wide.

Ivy's eyes weren't just wide—they were livid. "Are you telling me our entire department is compromised? That anyone can get in and look at our case files?"

"Well, not *anyone*. I'm kind of the best in the business." Wingbat99 paused a moment. "But I could name you five or six who could get in easily enough."

Ivy was too busy grumbling to pay much attention to this, but the implication wasn't lost on Tess. "Wingbat, is the morgue on this system you're talking about?"

"Yeah. Morgue, sheriff's department, schools, all two of the traffic lights you guys have there, the electricity grid. If it's got a government stamp on it, it's mine."

Ivy finally understood. She shot Tess a glance before releasing a low whistle. "The missing files and security footage at the morgue. You think whoever hacked in and erased all their information also flashed those lights last night."

Yes, Tess did. She also thought that Wingbat99 could, if given enough incentive, tell her exactly who that someone was. "If I were to ask you to do some poking around, could you find out who got into the lights last night and the morgue system a few weeks ago? Without anyone knowing about it, I mean?"

"Yeah, but it'll cost you. That kind of information can be dangerous to access."

Tess believed it. Anyone who'd gone to these lengths to steal two bodies—and then deposit a third one in her bookstore under cover of night—was up to no good. Tess had no idea what *kind* of no good, but since she was the one currently being held inside a sheriff's office, she didn't like where things were headed.

Being blamed for the missing bodies and files at the morgue hadn't been pleasant, but since the evidence had been all circumstantial, it didn't mean much. Other than her daughter working there as an intern, there'd been no proof that she—or her grandfather—was involved.

But the body being purposefully placed in her bookstore was something else. Especially when added to the other two bodies under the floorboards and the *Let Sleeping Dogs Lie* book with her blurb on the cover.

Someone wanted Tess to be deeply involved in this case. Someone was going out of their way to make sure she was a part of it.

And considering how long ago that book had been published, they'd been planning this for quite some time.

Chapter Twenty-Two

THE FIRST THING SHERIFF BOYD DID WHEN HE entered the station to find Tess sitting at his desk, her hands free of handcuffs and the door to the jail cell standing wide open, was demand to know where Ivy was.

"She went to check on Edna St. Clair," Tess said without getting up. There was no need. In three powerful strides, he'd managed to cross the whole floor.

"Edna was here? Again?"

"Yes, and Ivy is afraid she might be the next murder victim. She knows too much." A rueful smile touched Tess's lips. "I'd say she's exaggerating, but there's a chance she's right. I'm starting to think none of us should be out wandering alone."

In Victor's eyes, admitting her own fallibility as a human being and a woman was tantamount to confessing to a crime. He dragged the nearest chair across the floor and parked it on the other side of his desk. "What did Edna say? What happened?"

The poor man already had so much on his plate

that Tess hesitated. That, just as much as her heavily slumped shoulders, only caused his alarm to grow.

"You might as well tell me," he said. "I can legally keep you here for twenty-four hours before I have to release you."

The threat had little power over Tess—mostly because being in protective custody was starting to sound quite nice, provided Gertrude could be in here with her.

"What were you doing creeping around the bookstore last night?" she asked by way of answer.

His eyes narrowed but he allowed the conversation to veer off course. "What are you talking about? I wasn't creeping around the bookstore last night."

"You didn't drive your squad car around the side of the building with your lights off?"

"What? No, of course not. I've been meaning to send someone over to warn you about the amount of construction debris you have building up in that alleyway, but…"

Tess wasn't able to laugh at this attempt at a joke, but she did manage a feeble smile.

"What's this about, Tess?" the sheriff asked. "You know I always park it at the station for the night. There aren't enough squad cars for everyone to take one home."

She nodded. She *did* know that, and it confirmed what she'd suspected when Edna had first shared her story. An empty, accessible vehicle that anyone could have stolen from the police station meant that, well, there had been an empty, accessible vehicle that anyone could have stolen from the police station. There was no limit to who could have taken it out for a joyride.

"And you didn't see a bright flash when all the streetlights flooded at once?" she persisted.

"I got the report this morning, but I wasn't here when it happened. I was at home." He leaned earnestly across the desk, his hands hovering above hers. "Tess, what do you know?"

"That's what Edna saw last night. *Your* squad car and *my* bookstore were getting up to no good together."

With a sigh, she set about relaying Edna's tale. It took a few minutes to run through every aspect— including that Ivy had taken detailed notes and could corroborate each part—but it wasn't until she introduced her phone call to Wingbat99 that Victor showed signs of animation.

"And you think this hacker friend of yours is telling the truth?" he asked as soon as she was done. "That someone is remotely accessing our system?"

"It makes sense. If he can do it, then anyone can."

"Someone who wanted to cover up their theft of two bodies from the morgue?"

She tilted her head in assent.

"The same someone who then handed over a third body in the dead of night using an elaborate ruse involving one of my squad vehicles and a hackable lighting system?"

Tess shifted uncomfortably in her seat. This was where things got admittedly murky. "I don't know. Yes? Maybe? I find it hard to believe that Edna made any of that up. Besides—someone broke in and planted that body in a place I'd stumble upon it. Literally. When would they have done it if not last night?"

When the sheriff didn't answer right away, Tess pushed on. This next part was painful, but it needed to be said.

"Was it a woman?" she asked as gently as she could. "The bones in the bookstore?"

Victor's mouth formed a flat line. "It was a woman."

She unclasped her hands and gripped the sheriff's by the wrist before he could make a move to stop her. His hands were cold to the touch. "What else did Sylvia say?"

"Not much." Victor allowed his fingers to become entwined with hers. "She'll know more in a few days, but from what she can tell, the hatchet marks are similar enough to the other two to make a convincing case, even without the original bodies. She's no Peter Oblonsky, but she's respected in the field. Between her testimony and the third body, we might be able to pull something together...provided we find a suspect."

"And, uh, do we have one of those?"

Victor's grim expression confirmed what Tess already knew: fat chance. It was part of what made all this so frustrating. Not only were they missing the actual bodies of the deceased, but there didn't seem to be any evil criminal mastermind looming on the horizon. Or—if Tess wanted to be perfectly frank—a motive.

"I put a team of deputies on rotation guarding the morgue," Victor added as his rubbed his thumb back and forth along the back of Tess's hand. She didn't think he was aware he was doing it, but she liked the soothing pattern the wide pad of his thumb made against her skin. "No one's getting in there this time without my knowing about it."

Tess was about to ask if that was really necessary—to point out that a murderer who placed a body inside her bookstore wasn't likely to come back the next day to spring it out of the morgue—but she didn't have an opportunity. As soon as she opened her mouth, the door to the station swung mercilessly open, the wood slamming against the opposite wall with a crack.

"Jared!" Before Tess even fully registered the presence of the younger man, she yanked her hands out of Victor's and shoved them in her lap. She had no idea *why* she did it, and the flash of swift, sudden pain on Victor's face made her wish it undone, but it was too late. "What are you doing here?"

"You have no legal grounds to keep this woman under observation," he said, stalking into the room in a way that seemed to add six inches onto his already impressive height. He was always attractive, but something about the hard set of his anger seemed to enhance every one of his qualities. His cheekbones grew more chiseled, his powerful thighs swelled, and there was nary a sign of a dimple anywhere. "I demand you release her at once."

"Uh, Jared?" Tess ventured as she got to her feet. "Maybe now's not the best time to—"

"You know as well as I do that she had nothing to do with those murders." He crossed his arms over his chest and glared at Sheriff Boyd. "I'd like to know the charges."

If Tess thought an irate, crusading Jared Wilson was a sight to behold, he was nothing compared to the cold, furious sheriff rising to his full height. He wasn't as tall as Jared by several inches, and his build was much more weather-beaten, but none of that seemed to matter. This man of the law, who ruled his county with a firm yet kind hand, who refused to let the devastation of his personal life creep into his professional one, wasn't one Tess would willingly tackle.

At least, not right now.

"I'm holding her for questioning. That gives me twenty-four hours before I need to charge her for anything. Ninety-six, if I want to start adding the bodies stacking up on her property and take it to the nearest judge. Murder might not be something you take seriously where you come from, but we aren't so willing to look the other way."

"Ninety-six hours?" Tess said, but she might as well have stayed silent for all the attention the two other men paid her.

Jared strode forward and grabbed Tess by the upper arm. Since there was already enough fighting taking place in this room, she stood passively and let him. "Please. I could have you and your job tossed out in half that time. You might not know who I am, but—"

"Oh, I know all about you," the sheriff said at his most drawling. "And I know who your daddy is. Too bad the deputy director of the FBI doesn't make the rules around here. *I* do."

"Wait—the *deputy director*? Of the whole FBI?" Tess whirled to face Jared. "Really?"

A touch of color crept up Jared's cheeks, but he didn't back down. "I think he might have a little pull, even in a place as backward as this. You want me to call him and find out?"

For the longest moment, Tess thought Victor might actually do it—to call this bluff and force

Jared's hand, to see how far he could push the younger man. But it was nonsensical for a lot of reasons, most of which had to do with the fact that she *wasn't* under arrest, and she *didn't* have anything to do with the murders.

"You know what?" Victor threw up his hands. "You can have her. I have better things to do."

This time, Tess really *did* intervene. She rejected the notion that any man—no matter how many badges he carried or what kind of FBI royalty he descended from—could "have" her. "Would the two of you please stop acting like a pair of deer with your antlers locked? We're on the same team, remember? The team that's trying to figure out who's been killing a bunch of women around here?"

Both men had the decency to look ashamed of themselves, but their antlers stayed locked.

"Then do me a favor and get him out of here, would you?" Victor asked. "I don't have the time or the patience for this right now." His gaze landed everywhere but on Tess before finally settling on Jared. "And before you start waving your father at me again, let me remind you that your cover in this town depends on *my* generosity and *my* willingness to look the other way. You and Nicki both. I'm not without some clout of my own around here."

Already, some of Jared's swelling confidence

started to deflate. Tess deemed it best to get him out of there before the sheriff really started to light into him; when in the right mood, the sheriff could reduce even the most hardened of criminals to tears. This untried, desperate-to-impress federal agent didn't stand a chance.

"Come on," she said, laying a gentle hand on Jared's forearm. Almost at once, she could feel the muscles underneath starting to relax. "Your white knight heroics have succeeded...for now. Let's leave before the dragon decides to retaliate."

She tossed a playful look at Victor over her shoulder as she led Jared away, but he didn't appreciate being compared to a dragon. His gaze was hard and his jaw harder, his expression so flat that something inside her cried out. Until the body they'd found was identified for certain, Sheriff Boyd was in for a difficult time. A friend—a *good* one—wouldn't leave him to his own reflections.

It was on the tip of her tongue to send Jared on his way, but Ivy appeared before she could form the words.

"Is he back?" Ivy asked and, without waiting for an answer, pushed through to the offices beyond. "Thank goodness. Sheriff Boyd, you're not going to believe what—"

That decided it for her. As long as the sheriff had work to keep him busy, as long as there were clues and facts and conjectures to bear him company, he didn't need Tess. Not really. Not in any way that mattered.

"Saved by the Ivy Bell," she said under her breath as she dragged Jared the rest of the way out the door.

───────

"You don't know it yet, but you just dodged a serious bullet. What on *earth* were you thinking bursting in on us like that?"

Jared showed an alarming lack of remorse for his actions.

"I've been around law enforcement my whole life, and I've never met a man like that one," he said as Tess led him out of the sheriff's office and down the street. Feeling as though she'd already pushed her luck enough for one day, she went in the opposite direction of the bookstore. "He might be the sheriff, but he had no right to keep you under lock and key."

"I *wasn't* under lock and key," she pointed out. "In case you failed to notice, I was sitting at the desk like a free woman."

He was careful not to meet her gaze. "You know what I mean. He was trying to intimidate you by leveraging his position of authority. He was *using* you."

She didn't bother correcting this assumption.

For one thing, she wasn't about to explain the complicated dynamics of her relationship with Victor Boyd to a man she'd only known a few weeks. For another, she was pretty sure Jared had grossly misunderstood the scene he'd walked into.

"Be that as it may, there was no need for you to burst in like that. I had things handled just fine on my own." Since Jared showed every sign of arguing this point, she turned the conversation. "Jared, are you really the son of the deputy director? Of the *whole* FBI?"

This, at least, had the capability of bringing an abashed look to his face. "It's not what you think. I don't usually go around waving his name every time I want something, but this was an emergency. You needed me."

There was something so sweetly touching about this that Tess found herself softening toward him. She also found herself interested in what a man with his pedigree was doing out in the middle of nowhere, jumping on a half-finished case where he was clearly neither wanted nor needed.

"No wonder Nicki refuses to warm up to you," she said with a rueful shake of her head. "That kind of family connection might be great for your career, but it can't be winning you a whole lot of friends."

His face fell. "You have no idea."

Tess would have said something more along

these lines, but a flash of movement across the street drew her attention.

"Wait—is that Herb?" Tess grabbed Jared by the front of his well-worn flannel and tugged. She laid herself flat against the brick wall outside the bar, surprised when Jared pressed the entire length of his body in a protective curl against hers.

"What? Where?" Jared made a motion toward his ankle holster. It took all of Tess's strength—and then some—to keep him from whipping out his gun.

"If you keep flashing that thing every chance you get, your cover is going to be blown by the end of the month," she said, but she gestured toward the end of the street, where Lucretia's forest green Subaru Outback was creeping toward the edge of town. Sure enough, when she glanced in the driver's-side window, it was to find Herb's familiar wispy white head behind the wheel. "That lying jerk. He told me the car hadn't worked in years."

Jared was interested enough in Herb's movements to follow her gaze, but not so interested he moved his body from where it was pressing her into the wall.

"Herb? You mean the guy with the map?"

"He's not just the guy with the map. He's also one of my grandfather's oldest friends. They spent a lot of time in that hardware store together. *And* he claims he bought that car from Lucretia before she disappeared."

For once in his life, Jared wasn't slow to follow along. "You want me to tail him? See where he goes?"

"*Can* you?" she asked before coughing and quickly amending her statement. "I mean, *would* you? That'd be great."

His brows knit a little at that first outburst, but he didn't allow the expression to linger. "Don't worry," he said. "I might not be much of a hand at lying, but I'm getting pretty good at tailing people. Ever since our lunch with Adam, I've barely let him out of my sight."

"And have you found anything interesting?"

"Other than the fact that he spends most of his time sitting alone in a bar? No." He paused. "But that's what I'm trying to tell you. Following people around is the one thing I'm good at. No one ever seems to realize I'm there until it's too late."

There was such a strange timbre to his voice—in another man, Tess might call it wistful—that she hesitated a second too long.

"I won't let you down, Tess," he said, more resolute this time. "You can count on me."

With that, he took himself off in hot pursuit of their quarry—but not before he swooped close and pressed a hot, hard smack on Tess's lips. The kiss was so unexpected, and so surprisingly determined, that she could only stare up at him in response.

By the time she'd reassembled her wits, he was

already strolling quickly down the street, his hands in his pockets and a whistle on his lips. To look at him, he was just a man heading toward his work truck, but he moved with deceptive speed.

Huh. There was more to Jared Wilson than met the eye.

Which, considering how her lips still tingled and her body felt oddly limp in all the places it had touched his, seemed about right.

———————

The next day, Tess hopped into the bookmobile as soon as the opportunity afforded itself. Waiting only until she verified that the vehicle was empty, she threw herself into the chair next to the librarian. A huge stack of papers sat on Nicki's lap, and she was twirling a highlighter through her fingers as she pored over them, but neither of those stopped Tess from demanding answers.

"Nicki, why didn't you tell me how high-ranking Jared's dad is?"

Nicki glanced up but quickly returned her attention back to her work. "I did tell you, remember? I warned you not to have anything to do with him, but you didn't listen. You never listen."

"You said that he had a powerful father, not *the* most powerful father."

Nicki rolled her shoulder. "Does it matter? I told you I'm stuck with him whether I like it or not. Why? What's he done this time? I swear to God, if he said anything to blow my cover with Mason…"

"No, no," Tess was quick to respond. "Nothing like that. Just a little personal altercation with Victor yesterday."

That caused Nicki to lose her concentration. Her brow arched so high it practically touched her hairline. "How personal?"

More personal than Tess was willing to go into right now, that was for sure. Not that it mattered. As soon as Nicki noticed the flush on Tess's cheeks, her federally sanctioned investigative skills kicked into gear.

"Oh my God, he kissed you, didn't he? I knew he would, the little rat. His kind always does."

Curiosity won out over Tess's sudden—and immediate—desire to flee. "What do you mean, *his kind*? Hot young men who are good with hammers? Federal agents in the prime of their lives? Because those are the only answers I'm willing to accept at this time."

Nicki snorted. "Nice try. You're cute, but you're not that cute. Jared is a walking, talking daddy complex if I ever saw one."

"Nicki, you wretch. His dad has nothing to do with this."

"That must have been one heck of a kiss." Nicki cast her a knowing glance. "Tess, he's a twenty-something himbo who will never live up to his father's expectations. Of course he's going after a rich, successful cougar who can wipe the floor with him emotionally, physically, and intellectually. It'd be weird if he *hadn't* taken one look at you and fallen immediately in love."

Tess wasn't sure which part of this outraged her—or pleased her—the most. "I'm not a cougar! And Jared isn't in love with me. It's more like…"

"A puppy dog following its owner? A trained monkey endlessly crashing his cymbals? A young man who's so desperate for parental approval that he'll latch onto the first authority figure to fall for his dimples?"

"Nicki!" Tess's protest was drowned out by her own laughter. "If you were a real friend, you'd tell me to go for it. How many times in my life am I going to get propositioned by someone who looks like a Greek statue?"

"*Did* he proposition you?" For the first time, Nicki showed signs of approval. "I didn't think he had it in him. Good for you. I mean, I absolutely forbid you to have an affair with that useless lump of a man, but good for you."

Since Jared hadn't propositioned Tess—not really—she was quick to change the subject. She nodded down at the papers in Nicki's lap. "What are we working on, by the way? More financial records? That's not a very fun way to spend your time."

Nicki shook her head and turned the papers so Tess could see them. The name Peter Oblonsky appeared at the top, followed by gruesome photos of dead bodies in various states of decay. "Just a little light reading. Peter was telling me all about his work, so I couldn't resist. There's a whole catalog in our library system dedicated to him. I had no idea you knew such fancy people."

"I *am* fancy people," Tess retorted. She lifted the pages and flipped through them. "This does seem like a lot. Did he write all these?"

"Not all of them, no." Nicki pulled out a few sheets from the bottom. The report she handed Tess was much smaller and less impressive than Peter's body of work, but she recognized Sylvia's name at the top. "Apparently, we have quite the collection of forensic experts in our midst. Who knew?"

Since the research article Nicki handed Tess was on cognitive bias in the field of forensic pathology, she wasn't long in handing it back. As interesting as that kind of work was, it wasn't going to help her figure out who was behind the murders.

"I take it you heard about the latest body in my bookstore," Tess said.

Nicki winced. "They're saying it's a young

woman—and that the age of the bones is similar to what you and that dratted book predicted. Is it the sheriff's sister?"

Tess shook her head, allowing her hair to fall over her face to hide her expression. Nicki teasing her about Jared's crush was fine, but Tess didn't think she could bear it if she applied that same irreverence to Victor. "We haven't heard yet, but Sylvia should know in a few days." A sudden fear clutched at her chest. "Nicki, when I started all this, I never thought—"

Nicki's hand shot out and gripped Tess's. "I know, sweetie. None of us did. It's why I'm poring over all these old forensic reports and why your friend Peter hasn't slept in days. It's why Gertie has been haunting the morgue like a ghost begging to be let in from the cold and why you're breaking just about every law you can to compile evidence."

Tess was more grateful for Nicki's understanding than words—her stock-in-trade—could say.

"Unless I'm very much mistaken, it's also why you have my partner running all over town doing your errands instead of helping me nail Mason Peabody and his greedy enterprise to the ground." Nicki sighed. "Don't worry. I'm not upset. The busier you keep him, the less babysitting I have to do."

"He's not doing my errands," Tess protested, but with a guilty flush. With any luck, he was on

Herb's tail as they spoke, following the older man to uncover whatever he was hiding.

"And I'm not late for a book fair in Riverside," Nicki said as she sat back and started highlighting a few more passages in one of Peter's research papers. She paused long enough to point the highlighter at Tess. "But if anyone asks, I ran out of gas somewhere off US 97. You'll swear that on your life."

Chapter Twenty-Three

WITH THE BOOKSTORE CLOSED OFF DUE TO THE ongoing investigation and Sheriff Boyd refusing to take her calls, Tess had very little to do but wait.

And wait.

And wait some more.

"I can't take this much longer." She jerked herself up from the porch swing overlooking the land out behind her grandfather's cabin. Never had that patch of remote wilderness looked so bleak. Even the weather seemed to feel the oppression of inactivity, the clouds hanging low and depressed in the sky. "There has to be *something* we can do to move this investigation along."

Gertrude glanced up from the book she was reading—a huge, ten-pound textbook revealing the delights of *Criminological and Forensic Pathology*. "I thought you said Jared had a few leads."

Tess tried to glare at her daughter in warning, but Gertrude was impervious to maternal scolds and solicitude alike.

"Wasn't he going to try and get all buddy-buddy

with Adam Peabody to get answers? Or follow Herb to the kill site?" Gertrude's brow wrinkled. "Or both? I'm having a hard time keeping track of what you're making him do."

"I'm not *making* him do anything," Tess said irritably. Honestly, between her daughter and Nicki, they were painting her to be some kind of predator. "Of his own volition, he offered to try a few things, but nothing has panned out. Apparently, Herb was just driving to some junkyard near Mazama, and all Adam does is drink alone at a bar."

"What about Wingbat?" Peter asked, emerging out onto the porch in time to hear this last part. "Has he had anything to say about the light system?"

"No." Tess sighed and turned her back on the forest. Nature was only making her irritable. "And I have to say, I'm not very happy about his lack of communication. What's the point of being a hacker if you can't even send an encrypted email to update me on things every now and then?"

As if on cue, Tess's phone rang. Both she and Gertrude dived for it at the same time, but Gertrude had the textbook in her lap to account for. Tess got there first.

"Hello?" she asked, breathless. "Wingbat, is that you? Were you just listening to us?"

"Of course it's not Wingbat," came the sheriff's irritated voice. "It's me. Sylvia just called. The report is in."

"And?"

The sheriff blew out a long breath that told Tess nothing. And everything. "I think you should head into town. You're going to want to hear this for yourself."

———

"The victim's name is Yasmine Kope," Sylvia said.

Tess sat and stared across the desk at Sylvia Nerudo, her eyeballs dry from the lack of blinking. "I'm sorry. What? That can't possibly be right."

Sylvia turned her case file so Tess could read it. "I know. I was just as surprised as you were." She tapped on what looked to be a yearbook photo from eons past. "She was nineteen at the time of her death. Cause is inconclusive, but the multiple hatchet marks we found on her bones probably had something to do with it."

Tess twisted her head to peer up at Sheriff Boyd, who was standing over her shoulder with a grim set to his mouth. If he was at all pleased to learn that the body they'd discovered wasn't that of his long-lost sister, he was doing a phenomenal job of hiding it.

"I still don't understand," Tess said, unable to tear her gaze from Victor. "Who is Yasmine Kope, and why haven't we heard of her until now?"

That got the sheriff moving. "I knew Yasmine. We all did. She was homecoming royalty, valedictorian, and rodeo queen six years running. She was headed to—what was it, Sylvia—University of Texas? Alabama? Something like that."

"Alabama." Sylvia nodded. "I remember because she was working on perfecting her southern accent before she left. She was the president of the thespian club, too."

None of this was helping clarify things for Tess. That Yasmine Kope was a peer of these two, she understood. That she was a young lady of remarkable talents was also clear. But how or why *her* body should be the one that showed up in the bookstore, she had no clue.

Her brows knit tightly together. "When did she go missing?"

"She didn't. That's the problem." Sheriff Boyd lifted the file from the desk. His appraisal was perfunctory at best, making Tess think he'd long since memorized the words emblazoned on the page. "She went to college. I remember that much for sure. There was a going away party, Sylvia—I was there. *Kendra* was there. We all watched her pile into her car, stuffed to the roof with her belongings, and waved as she headed out."

"Did you hear from her after that?"

"Yes? No? How the devil should I know?" A dark

thundercloud of a scowl settled on the sheriff's face. "Kendra went missing a few days later, and then I was in the hospital for two months recovering from those blasted bullet wounds. Yasmine's rosy future as the belle of the South was the last thing on my mind."

Tess hated to poke an obviously wounded bear, but the question had to be asked. "There's no police report of her disappearance?"

The wounded bear didn't disappoint. "Of course there was no report. That was the first thing I checked. What kind of idiot do you take me for?"

Sylvia winced at the volume—and vehemence—of the sheriff's outburst, but Tess welcomed it like a baptismal cleansing. A Victor Boyd who was capable of yelling at her was a Victor Boyd who wasn't completely beaten down.

"What about her parents? Grandparents? Have you contacted her next of kin to find out what they know?"

He rose up to his full height and crossed his arms. "I didn't call you here to walk me through entry-level investigation steps. She only had one living parent at the time—a drunk waste of space who packed up and left town not long after she did. And before you ask whether or not I looked him up, yes, I did. He died a few years ago. Pancreatic cancer."

Like the rest of his outburst, none of this

bothered Tess. "If you didn't want my input on how to go about solving this, what *am* I doing here? I mean, I appreciate the heads-up, obviously, but I didn't put that woman's body in the bookstore. And none of this is even remotely close to what happened in *Let Sleeping Dogs Lie*."

Mentioning the book was a mistake. Sheriff Boyd opened his mouth and closed it again. "That book has been a pain in my neck since the moment you brought it to this town. It cost me thousands of dollars in overtime to search the cemetery, not to mention the amount of time we've wasted following a bunch of dead-end leads that only exist inside the head of some crackpot writer. How am I supposed to justify that to the financial board? To the taxpayers?"

Tess knew, without asking, that the *crackpot writer* he was talking about wasn't Simone Peaky. It was her. She also knew that his anger—if that was what you could call it—had less to do with his frustration over the case and more to do with the fact that he was left, once again, without any answers about his sister's disappearance.

"Since the body was found in your bookstore, I thought you might want to know that you've been cleared of all charges," he said stiffly. "That's all. I wouldn't want your boyfriend crashing in and accusing me of abuse of power again."

"Victor, you know very well he's not my—" she began, but that was a mistake, too. The use of the sheriff's name—and in that supplicating voice—pushed him the rest of the way over the edge.

"Sylvia, I'm taking these files with me as well as the backups so I can keep them under lock and key. You'll make sure you check in with the deputy posted outside before you head out for the night?"

"Sure thing, Sheriff Boyd," Sylvia said. "We should know a little more in a few days. I'll keep you apprised of what we find." She stood and escorted Victor to the door. Tess made a move to follow her, but a low hiss from the coroner stopped her.

While she waited for Sylvia to return from walking the sheriff out, Tess poked at the knickknacks on the desk. As these amounted to a pair of bookends that appeared to be made out of real human skulls and a photo of a young, smiling Sylvia standing on the edge of a cliff while attached to a hang glider, they didn't keep her occupied for long.

"That was in Hawaii," Sylvia said as she came back into the office. She nodded down at the picture. "Kahului. Some of the best winds you'll find in the world."

"Oh." Tess's knowledge of extreme sports wasn't large, so she nodded politely. "It's beautiful."

"Beautiful but terrifying. Your daughter already said she plans to go as soon as she turns eighteen."

"*What*?" Tess knocked over the picture in her sudden alarm. "To fly around with a kite strapped to her back? Over my dead body."

Even though Tess regretted the tactless words as soon as they left her lips, Sylvia chuckled and put the picture back in its place. "Don't be too surprised. A lot of the people who work in this field seek out high-adrenaline activities. There's something about being surrounded by death all the time that makes you want to feel alive, you know? To put off the inevitable, if only for a few terrifying seconds." She shrugged. "But you're her mother. I'm sure you know best."

Tess *did* know best, and Gertrude was going to get an earful when she got home, but that wasn't the most pressing issue right now.

"What is it?" Tess asked, not mincing matters. "What do you want to tell me that you didn't want the sheriff to overhear?"

Sylvia's look grew sharp. "What makes you think that's why I wanted you to stay back?"

Because Tess understood people. Because Tess understood Sheriff Boyd. Because Tess knew that however little authorities liked her interference on cases like this, her insights almost always ended up being valuable.

She didn't say any of this aloud. Instead, she stood there until Sylvia gave in.

"Fine. Yes. There *is* something I wanted to run by you." Sylvia drummed her fingers in a nervous pattern on top of her desk. "I should be telling Sheriff Boyd, or even Ivy, but I wanted your advice first. There's a chance that what I found is nothing, and I'll regret even mentioning it, but…"

Tess leaned forward and stilled the other woman's nervous movements with her hand. "You can trust me. I want this case solved just as much as you do."

Sylvia's gaze met hers in a flash of understanding. Her nervous drumming stopped. "Sand," she announced.

"Sand?"

She nodded. "Not much, and not enough to be conclusive, but there were sand particles clinging to a few of the bones. I'm not saying they have anything to do with the murder—in fact, I'd be surprised if they did—but they could hint at the location where our bones were buried before they were, uh, relocated to your bookstore."

Tess was able to piece that much together on her own. "So you think they were brought here from a beach? As in…the ocean?"

Sylvia shook her head, her mouth pursed tightly. Faint lines etched her upper lip. "No, not the ocean. These were bigger particles with mica bits in them, debris from the mountain that had been repeatedly worn down. It happens in areas of the Methow

River where heavy flow leads to a quieter pool—a swimming hole, if you will."

Tess nodded. That made scientific sense to her, though she could always check with Peter later. "Are there any of those around here?" she asked.

She knew the answer before Sylvia said it out loud.

"I can think of only one area with the right conditions that's also remote enough not to have been disturbed for the past thirty years."

Tess didn't want to hear it. She wanted to cover her ears, run from the room, and pretend she'd never heard of someone named Yasmine Kope.

Sylvia said it anyway.

"It's on Sheriff Boyd's property—the property both he and Kendra grew up on."

Chapter Twenty-Four

THE OBVIOUS SOLUTION TO TESS'S PROBLEM WAS to drive up to Sheriff Boyd's house, come up with an excuse to patrol his property, and discover for herself if there had been any digging activity on or near the riverbed.

This was untenable for several reasons, most of which had to do with Tess's reluctance to intrude upon a man who wasn't very happy with her right now. Also, the bookmobile was parked right across the street from the morgue. It made the most sense to start there.

"Nicki, do you have a property map for the county somewhere in your system? Something with records of ownership and copies of all the deeds?"

Nicki glanced up from the stack of books she was checking out for the niece of the man who ran the drugstore. There were several other patrons browsing the blue bookmobile, so there wasn't an opportunity for a discussion of any depth, but that was fine. There were only so many fires Tess could put out at once.

In this case, she planned to take an extinguisher to any and all notions that Sheriff Boyd or his sister had done away with a friend of theirs. If there were sand particles on those bones, then there *had* to be some other location around here that fit the bill. She didn't care how many people stole the sheriff's vehicle and creeped around the bookstore at night. Or how many hackers got into the city's system and flashed the streetlights to draw attention to it. Or if Sylvia had found a signed confession pinned to the body instead of a tiny bit of sand.

Sheriff Boyd would no more murder a bunch of innocent women than he would murder *her*—and Tess could say that with absolute certainty. In the short time she'd been living here, she'd given him more than enough provocation to do away with her. Yet here she was. Still breathing. Still standing.

Someone was trying to make it look like Sheriff Boyd was implicated in all this—the same way they'd tried to make *her* look implicated by burying the bones inside her grandfather's store and stealing them out from underneath Gertrude's nose.

Well, too bad. That wasn't happening on Tess's watch. Not while she had breath left in her body. Which, considering how many women seemed to go missing around here, might not be long.

"I can probably rustle some old county maps up for you, but I don't see why." Nicki bade farewell to the young woman with her stack of Nora Roberts novels and groaned as the implication of what Tess was asking sank in. "Oh, jeez. Please tell me we aren't on the hunt for even more bodies. Aren't the three we have enough? You're starting to get downright greedy."

Tess chuckled but shook her head. "It's more of a personal project. Let's just say I'm interested in the geological phenomena around these parts."

"For...a novel?"

"Sure. Let's go with that."

Although Nicki narrowed her eyes, Tess didn't elaborate. Sounds had a way of carrying inside this tin can of a bookmobile, and the last thing she wanted was for that nice family in the back to know she was trying to discover if they owned a piece of land ideal for the long-term storage of human remains.

"I don't know how detailed the records that are open to the public are going to get," Nicki said. "Any questions you have are better directed to Sheriff Boyd."

Tess's visible wince caused Nicki to laugh.

"Otis Lincoln will also do in a pinch. In fact, he's probably your best bet. Both his father and his grandfather were the mayor before he took up the position. No one knows this area like he does."

Tess perked. Otis Lincoln and his wife, Mya,

were good people—and even more to the point, they liked her. It might have been more accurate to say they liked *Gertrude*, especially considering her daughter's friendship with their two sons, Tommy and Timmy, but not everything needed to be spelled out.

"That's a good idea, actually. Thanks."

Nicki sighed. "Don't sound so surprised. Most of my ideas are good ones. It's just that you're usually too busy admiring your own to notice."

"Off the top of my head, there's only one location that fits the bill." Otis sat back in a recliner, his ankle propped on a footrest and a bag of melting ice over the top. He winced as he adjusted his position. "And that's—"

"I know," Tess said before he could form the words. "Sheriff Boyd's property. I heard. I was hoping you might have more personalized suggestions. You're out on those bike trails all the time. Surely there must be somewhere else."

Otis paused to consider. He might be the mayor of this town, but his real love was the rental bike shop he ran with his wife. That love explained why he was currently nursing a sprained ankle as well as why an entire wall of the house was taken up with rusted gears and cycling posters. And why Mya kept topping up Tess's glass of sauvignon blanc. These were people who knew how to relax.

"Not that I can think of, no. Our part of the river isn't much of a place for swimming. The water levels are too low in the summer, and no one in their right mind would try it this time of year. Spring runoff is no joke."

"That's not very helpful." Since Tess was well into her second glass, she wasn't as upset as she might have been otherwise. "And there's no one with, say, a backyard volleyball court or sandpit for their kids?"

She thought but didn't add, *and enough space to bury a body?* The sheriff was friends with Otis. The last thing she wanted was for any of this to get back to him.

None of that seemed to matter. Otis was a good enough mayor to put a few of the pieces together. He shook his head. "If this is about you trying to find where those missing bodies might be buried, I don't think I can help. I also think you're barking up the wrong tree. Our murderer is probably long gone by now."

That was the first time Tess had heard anything to that effect. She immediately perked up and set her wineglass aside. "What do you mean? So far, all the clues lead to someone local. Someone who's operating in our midst at this very moment."

He shook his head, a frown tugging at his beard. Like many men who'd shaved their heads to hide male-pattern baldness, Otis sported a proud and robust face of hair. "A resident *could* be the one behind the disappearing and reappearing bodies, of course, but who's to say anything about the original murders? Do you know how many people pass through town every year? We get a lot of tourists, not to mention visitors just driving through on their way to and from Seattle. Anyone could have killed those women and disappeared from all town records."

"But *you* lived here the whole time, right?" Tess asked.

Instead of taking offense, Otis chuckled warmly. "Yes, which goes to show what a wild-goose chase you're on. We're a small town, but most of us have been here for decades. If you're going to start looking into every single local, you'll be searching for years."

Tess tapped her teeth impatiently. Everything Otis was saying was true, which was what made things so frustrating. She *knew* she didn't have a good suspect. That's why she was trying to find one.

"Well, I know Herb was here, because he was friends with my grandfather. He's also the one who bought Lucretia's car."

"A thing he never once tried to hide," Mya

pointed out gently. She was a soft-spoken woman, small of stature and physically fit thanks to her family's cycling obsession. "He used to drive that rackety old thing all over town. I remember dodging it on several street corners."

"Edna St. Clair was here, too," Tess continued, naming one of the only other residents she knew personally. In a way, she was starting to hope the old woman had done it. It might explain why she kept popping up with clues that only made Tess's job harder.

"True," Otis admitted. "So was her sister, who passed two years ago. And the couple who lives across the street from her. And most of the sheriff's administrative team. And the entire Rotary Club. And—"

"Point taken." Tess held up her hands in surrender. "I'm searching for a needle in a haystack."

Mya cleared her throat as she lifted the bag of ice from her husband's ankle and plopped a fresh one onto it. "What makes you so sure the clues lead to someone local, anyway?" she asked. "The bones being stolen from the morgue looks bad, yes, and I'll admit that it's strange for a third body to just show up in your bookstore. But there have been reports of the murder investigation all over the national news. Maybe the murderer saw them and came dashing to town to cover his tracks. If you ask me, you'd be better off looking for anyone who's staying at the hotel or just visiting for a few days."

Tess jerked so fast that her wine sloshed over the edge of her glass. "What? Why would you say that?"

Mya shrugged as she handed Tess the cold towel that had been sitting between Otis's foot and the ice bag. "I'm not a thriller writer, obviously, but it seems like an easy enough solution to me." She paused, her tone completely free of irony. "Don't you have an older gentleman staying with you right now? For all you know, he's the one behind it all. Maybe he's only paying you a visit to finish what he started."

Tess managed to laugh alongside Otis and Mya, and even to finish her glass of wine, but she didn't linger much after that. It wasn't that she *believed* what Mya was implying, or even that it made any narrative sense. It was just that for some strange reason, she no longer felt like chatting about murder.

That had to be a first for the illustrious Tess Harrow.

Chapter Twenty-Five

"Wingbat, can I call you back? Now's not a good time."

Of every understatement Tess had made in her lifetime, this was the one to cap them all. Not only was it bad time for a chat, but it was a bad *location* for it. She was currently squatting next to the river on the edge of Sheriff Boyd's property, her head low and her voice lower.

"Is that your hacker?" Jared asked eagerly. "What's he saying? Did he figure out who got into the lighting system?"

"Shhh!" Tess waved her hand to try and silence her companion—and to get him to squat down with her. *Her* stature might make it easy to hide in the spiky fronds of a juniper bush, but Jared was practically visible from space. The last thing she needed—or wanted—when trying to clandestinely comb private property in hopes of finding a burial site was a man as loud and obtrusive as Jared Wilson.

Unfortunately, it was equally difficult to leave a loud, obtrusive man standing in the middle of town, which was how she got into this mess in the first place. She'd hoped to creep up here unobserved while the sheriff was busy with a press conference, but Jared had guessed what she was up to and refused to let her go alone.

For your safety, he'd said. *There's no telling what a man like Sheriff Boyd will do if he finds you.*

Yes, there was. He'd yell. He'd fume. He'd order Tess to go home and stop acting like she had anything to do with his case.

But try telling *that* to the Boy Scout over there. Gallantry had demanded he accompany Tess, and as it turned out, gallantry was the one thing Tess was powerless to overcome.

"Does Sheriff Boyd know you're currently standing on the edge of his property?" Wingbat asked by way of answer. "I've never met the guy, obviously, and his social media game is seriously lacking, but all the articles I've read paint him as a bit of a hard-ass."

"Are you tracking my location right now?" Tess demanded.

"Some people pay me good money for that. Do you know how many mobsters' kids I'm currently watching? I'm a kidnapper's worst nightmare."

Tess sighed and did her best to crouch lower. She had no idea how visible this area was from the sheriff's modest ranch-style house, but she wasn't taking any risks. His truck had pulled up not more than five minutes ago.

"Do you want me to talk to him for you?" Jared asked, still in a voice that was about sixty decibels too loud for their setting.

"It's fine. I'm fine. Stop fussing." Since Tess didn't see any way out of this except the most direct route, she sighed and gave in. On the phone, anyway. "Okay, I'll bite. What did you discover, and how quickly can you give me the details?"

Wingbat's low chuckle sounded like a death knell in her ear. "Faster than you think. The hacker who got into your town's system to override the morgue security and streetlights?"

Tess's nerves felt as though they were stretching off into eternity. "Well?"

"Doesn't exist."

"What? Are you kidding?" In her sudden surprise, Tess almost toppled over into the churning waters of the swimming hole. Otis hadn't been kidding about the spring runoff; this was probably a lovely spot in the summer, but it was downright dangerous this time of year.

Fortunately—or unfortunately, depending on how you looked at it—Jared was ready and waiting to catch her. He had his arms around her and was dragging her back from the water's edge before she realized what was happening. By that time, the phone was pulled so far down from her ear that she couldn't make out the words Wingbat was saying.

"Careful," Jared warned as he steadied her. "I can only save you if you stay out of the water. After that, you're on your own. I can't swim."

"What kind of grown man can't swim?" she asked. Without waiting to hear Jared's response, she pulled the phone up to ear and hissed, "What do you mean, there is no hacker? You couldn't find him?"

"There's no one to find," came Wingbat's easy reply. "I got into the system with no problems—as I expected—but there was no sign that anyone had been there before me. Not off-site, anyway."

Jared watched her curiously, his head tilted to try and catch what Wingbat was saying.

"I don't understand," she said. "You mean, the systems weren't accessed at all? Then how did someone erase all the files and flash the lights at just the right moment?"

"Easy. They did it from where you are. There's no need to hack in if you have access to a government computer. Your bad guy is right there in town with you. He's probably been operating under your nose this whole time."

Tess wasn't prepared for how this piece of news, following hard on the heels of Mya's playful accusation, would hit her. Her knees buckled under her, and she was once again falling to the sand below. This time, she flung a hand up to prevent Jared from coming to her rescue.

"Wingbat, what level of expertise would be needed to do that? Are we talking a legitimate hacker? A computer science degree expert? Or just some kid who spends too much time playing Roblox?"

Wingbat laughed. Even though he meant no harm by it, the sound left Tess feeling cold all over. "Somewhere between the second and third. I doubt a full degree would be required, but you'd need a basic working knowledge of how interface accessibility works."

That answer didn't help matters any. "You mean someone who's done his research and excels at new subjects?" she asked. "Like, for example, Peter Oblonsky?"

"Yeah, actually." Wingbat sounded surprised. "Peter could do it without batting an eye. That man picks up information faster than any client I've ever had before. Ah, present company included, of course."

"Very funny," Tess muttered, but her heart wasn't in it.

"If there's nothing else you need from me, I'm taking six grand from your account and calling it a day."

Even that didn't have the power to move her. "Fine. Take it. Whatever."

A curious silence fell over the conversation. "Are you okay? You sound weird—weirder than usual, I mean. Considering the size of the royalty payment that was just deposited into your account, you should be out celebrating."

He was right. A royalty check was normally a cause for celebration—a reason to break out a bottle of pink champagne and give Gertrude carte blanche to whip up whatever culinary masterpiece she had her eye on that month.

This time, however, the celebration would have to wait. Especially since Tess caught a movement out of the corner of her eye just as Jared pounced forward in his full protect and serve mode.

"Don't—" she warned at the exact moment Sheriff Boyd came crashing through the juniper bush, looking exactly as pleased to see her prowling around his property as she'd anticipated. The moment he caught sight of them, he stopped short, his hand at his hip as though he'd like nothing more than to draw his weapon and point it at them.

Jared, too, showed an alarming tendency to reach for his gun, but Tess stopped them both by sighing and heaving herself to her feet.

"Before you both start putting holes in each other, we need to talk." She slumped her shoulders in a way that had both men stepping forward to reach for her.

"I think I know who our murderer is—and you're not going to like the answer."

―――――――――

"I'm sorry, but none of this explains what you're doing at my house or why you were skulking around the river like a pair of juvenile delinquents."

"Victor, you're not listening." Tess sat on a bizarrely floral couch in the middle of the living room, her legs pressed tightly together to avoid the careless, overly familiar manspreading of Jared, who was seated much closer to her than she cared for under the sheriff's watchful eye. "Peter *Oblonsky*. The award-winning author. One of my closest friends. A man who is currently sitting at my house with my teenaged daughter, teaching her everything he knows about dead bodies."

"I heard you just fine," he said irritably. Instead of sitting in the equally floral chair opposite them, he'd opted to tuck his hands under his arms and stand leaning against the mantel, his shoulders propped in a way that made it difficult to tell whether the wood beam was holding him up or the other way around. "And I don't believe you now any more than I did the first time you said it. If you'll recall, the last time there was a murderer in our midst, you were almost certain that Nicki was the culprit."

"Nicki?" Jared interposed loudly, his grin starting to dawn. Of all of them, he was the only one who found anything remotely amusing about this situation. "As in, Nicki-*Nicki*? Federal Agent Nicki?"

Frustration rose up in Tess's throat. "That's neither here nor there. The point is—"

"The point is," the sheriff interrupted with a drawl, "that you and Mr. Wilson were looking for a burial site on my property."

Tess's mouth fell open, and the sudden feeling that she'd been cheated added to her feeling of constriction. "How do you know that? Did you find it? You totally found it, didn't you?"

The sheriff's mouth formed a flat line. "I found it." "And?"

He glanced at the wall behind her. Tess had already made a note of the grandfather clock that stood there, a piece as overblown and fussy as all the rest of the furniture in this place. She'd never been inside the sheriff's house before, so to find that it was more like an antique shop run by an old Victorian maid than a bachelor's quarters was taking some getting used to. "And my team should be here any minute to start processing the scene. I doubt you two will want to be here when that starts."

"Wait. Then you know?" Tess was on her feet in an instant. "About the sand particles Sylvia found on the body? About how someone is trying to frame you?"

"Don't you mean, how Peter Oblonsky is trying to frame me?" the sheriff corrected her, but with so much sarcasm that Tess winced under the weight of it.

"It's not as far-fetched as you think," she protested. For some reason, knowing that Sheriff Boyd had called his team in to survey the burial site was making her feel even more frantic than before. It was exactly what she expected him to do—and not at all what Detective Gonzales would have done in the same situation—but that didn't make the facts any easier to swallow.

At some point, the evidence was going to be too overwhelming, even for a man of Victor's position. Especially if his team could prove that the body had been here. Especially if Jared was going to sit there, hopped up on false ideas of romance, while he absorbed the information. A federal agent with connections like his could ensure that the right pressure was brought to bear to make an example of Sheriff Boyd. And Nicki, who was as by the book as Sheriff Boyd in her own way, would have no choice but to support it.

"If you'd heard what Wingbat said, how easily he outlined the events that took place here and Peter's capability to carry them out, you wouldn't be so blasé about this," she accused.

Something in her tone must have reached

through the sheriff's shell. The line that had been growing steadily deeper between his brows suddenly halted its progress. "You really think this hacker friend of yours is telling the truth?" he asked. "That Peter Oblonsky—a well-known, well-established author with a successful career and no reason whatsoever to visit a small town in Washington State—killed these women over a period of three decades?"

"It's possible."

"And that he arrived here for the sole purpose of stealing two of their bodies to cover up his crime?"

"The timeline fits."

"And then he handed over a third one in the dead of night using an elaborate ruse involving my squad vehicle and a hackable lighting system? Because... he was getting bored?"

"Or because he wanted to pin the crime on you," she suggested. "Especially if the body's been buried on your property this whole time—or if he planted enough evidence to make it look that way. If anyone would have the knowledge to make a convincing crime scene out here, it's a forensic expert. Where is the spot? Is it by the river? On the other side, maybe? We looked for a footbridge, but—"

"Tess, are you even listening to yourself right now?" the sheriff demanded.

"I know it sounds far-fetched, but nothing else

makes sense," she said. "Especially once we start tying in the *Let Sleeping Dogs Lie* book. Peter's an author—and like you said, a well-known, well-established one. He'd know the ways and means of getting a book published without any ties leading back to him, *and* he wouldn't need to touch the advance. He has more money than God."

Jared coughed gently. It was the first time Tess had heard him do *anything* without barreling in like a bulldog. "Don't forget that he was the one who brought the book to your attention in the first place. You never would've remembered it if he hadn't reminded you."

Victor pushed himself off the mantel, something that was starting to look like capitulation squaring his shoulders. He even looked at Jared with burgeoning respect. "That's true. There's also the fact that you, specifically, were asked to blurb that book. You said the publisher was all over you for a quote, right? Per the author's request?"

Tess held herself perfectly rigid. She'd forgotten about that part, but it only hammered another nail in the coffin that would carry Peter out of this town and into the nearest prison. If he really was playing some kind of twisted serial killer game over the course of a lifetime, then there was no reason why he wouldn't want to rope her into it with him. If *she* were a serial killer, it was exactly the sort of thing she'd do.

"Our killer has to be old, right?" she asked, doing her best to corral her thoughts in a semblance of order.

"Old*er*, yes, considering the date of our first disappearance," the sheriff agreed. "But that's assuming all the murders were done by the same person—a thing we haven't confirmed beyond a doubt, and a thing we aren't likely to do unless those first two bodies are recovered."

Tess waved this off. *He* might need evidence to prove the murders were linked, but she didn't. Her imagination was ready and willing to provide what hard facts couldn't.

"Okay," Tess began, "So we're looking at someone in their midforties, at the very youngest—and likely a bit older than that. I have a hard time picturing a teenager taking down a twenty-three-year-old Annabelle Charles." Tess clasped her hands on top of her knees. It was the only way she could avoid fidgeting; she was too worked up, too ready to head out there and finish this thing. "There aren't that many people in town who've been around for all those deaths—or who could have stolen the bones from the morgue and then digitally covered their tracks. A lot of them—like my grandfather—have passed away. Others—like Herb and Edna—don't even know how to text properly."

"But Peter doesn't live here," the sheriff pointed out. "As far as I can tell, he's never even visited before. What possible motivation could he have for murdering three women over the span of three decades?"

Tess swallowed heavily. Her theory on motive was starting to take rapid—and convincing—shape, but she was having a hard time saying the words aloud. Of course, they had the motive in *Let Sleeping Dogs Lie* to fall back if they wanted to, but Tess had never liked those Agatha Christie vibes. There were plenty of people who'd wanted Annabelle Charles dead, but Lucretia's death was looking more and more like a crime of opportunity. And Yasmine Kope, well…there was no saying what had happened to her without first discovering what the killer wanted.

And that, Tess feared, was information. Firsthand, diabolical research.

There was no doubt in her mind that they were looking for someone intelligent. Someone meticulous. Someone who threw himself so wholeheartedly into his work that he was a bona fide expert in just about everything.

In other words, Peter Oblonsky.

"When Peter and I first met, he knew almost nothing about hacking," Tess said, her voice taking on a storyteller's lull. "Just like he knew very little about forensics before he started testing out his hatchet theories on dead cows. He's as old school as it gets when it comes to book research—like a Method actor, but taken to a whole new level."

She waited for either of the men to interrupt, but they were listening to her with an intensity that might, in a less confident woman, have stopped her narrative short.

"According to Wingbat, Peter threw himself just as wholeheartedly into his hacking research. No sooner had he sampled a taste of what the World Wide Web had to offer than he started experimenting on his own. And learning on his own. And growing on his own."

Tess paused, allowing her words to settle. A genius with an insatiable appetite for knowledge was a dangerous thing. Especially if he wrote horror novels on the side. Tess might be willing to tie herself to a chair in order to capture an element of realism in her thrillers, but Peter had always taken things one step further. In order to keep writing about such terrible subjects, he needed things to be dark. Dangerous.

Deadly.

"Forget the butchered cows, you guys," Tess said. "A man who wants to push things—*really* push things—wouldn't stop with long-dead farm animals. He'd seek out fresh terrors…and fresh victims."

And then he'd toy with the residents of a quaint

small town, pitting them against one another like a *Saw* movie, but set in Cabot Cove.

She paused, watching as her words settled in. She couldn't tell exactly when they landed, but the relief she felt once they did was immense. "Sheriff Boyd, what are the chances you can call a few of your deputies and have them pick up Gertie on the way?"

"Why?" Jared asked, his gaze sharp. "Do you think he might hurt her?"

The sheriff, however, was already halfway out the door. "Forget the deputies. If even half of what you're saying is true, I'm picking her up myself."

Chapter Twenty-Six

"SERIOUSLY, MOM? YOU'LL LET ME STAY HERE? And help them process the scene? And, like, test sand particles and look for dead body bits and stuff?"

It took all of Tess's self-control not to glance at Sheriff Boyd as Gertrude extolled the virtues of criminology and decaying human flesh. They'd decided that the less they told Gertrude—and by extension, Peter—about their real reason for keeping Gertrude under the sheriff's watchful eye, the better.

"Yes, but you have to promise to do what Sheriff Boyd tells you, no matter what. Remember, this isn't just his house. It's his crime scene."

"Ohmigod, Mom. As if I would. I'd never get in the way of a *real* investigation, and the sheriff knows it." She turned a pair of big, beseeching eyes his way. "Don't you? That's why you're letting me stay the night, right? Because you know I'll be a help?"

"I trust you to make good choices," the sheriff said, neatly sidestepping the question. "And to follow

Ivy's lead. Since I'm…implicated in this particular circumstance, I've recused myself from any further contamination of the scene."

"So I can go out there? Ivy knows you gave me permission?"

The sheriff relaxed into a fond smile. "Make sure you take notes for me, okay? I don't want to miss a thing."

"I'm on it, boss!" With an equally fond smile of her own, Gertrude dashed out the door and headed down toward the river. Tess watched her go with mingled feelings of pride and trepidation. The latter must have been more evident on her face because Victor lost no time in reassuring her.

"She'll be fine with Ivy. I didn't have a chance to brief her on all the details, but she knows enough. Peter won't be able to show his face around here without answering a lot of questions first."

Tess nodded and wrapped her arms tightly around her midsection. Since to discuss what was really on her mind—what on earth she was supposed to do with a murderous houseguest until such time as enough evidence was gathered to throw the book at him—she latched onto the second most important thing.

"I can't believe you weren't going to tell me that you found the burial site. You know how long I've been looking for those blasted bones."

Her words didn't, as she'd hoped, discomfit the sheriff in the slightest.

"If we're casting accusations around, what about the fact that you and Sylvia kept evidence from me in the first place? Or that you brought a federal agent onto my property in order to conduct an illegal search?"

Of those two, Tess had the feeling it was the second one that bothered him the most. "I didn't *bring* him. He followed me. It's different."

One of the sheriff's eyebrows rose to a supercilious degree. To her dismay, Tess found herself blushing.

"It's not what you think. He's always following me around. He's like a lost puppy without a home. What else am I supposed to do? Kick him?" She snorted at a sudden memory. "I tried that when I first met him, remember? He liked it."

The sheriff's stony countenance didn't crack. "Yes, Tess. I remember."

"Victor, it's not what you think. Am I flattered that a young, good-looking FBI agent has decided I'm some kind of rustic embodiment of all his romantic longings? Sure. Of course. Who wouldn't be?"

"Me," he said flatly. In an equally careful tone, he added, "Has it occurred to you that he's gotten himself awfully involved in your life awfully fast?"

Tess hesitated.

"He's working at your bookstore. He's helping you with your investigation. He's taking you on hikes and kissing you in alleyways. He's—"

"Wait. You know about the kissing?"

The look the sheriff leveled at her could have cut stone. In fact, that's exactly what it felt like, as though she was lying on a slab in Sylvia's morgue with all her parts on display.

"There's a murderer on the loose in my home-town. He's killed three women and could very easily swoop in to take another. My sister is still God-knows-where, and I'm rapidly losing hope of ever finding her. Yes, Tess. I know about the kissing. I know about *everything* that goes on around here."

There seemed to be little she could say to defend herself. True, she hadn't instigated the kiss, but she hadn't stopped it, either—nor, if she was being honest, had she altogether despised it. And there was no denying that the rest of what Victor said was true. Jared *had* inveigled himself into her life with alarming ease, and she *had* depended on him much more than she was accustomed to doing.

It was that realization, more than anything else, that caused her to lash out. She could withstand Victor's annoyance over her romantic entangle-ment, and even laugh at how silly she and Sylvia had been in thinking he wouldn't find out about the sand particles, but the fact that he knew Tess Harrow had willingly foisted her problems onto the broad, capable shoulders of a younger man was too much. She'd spent far too many years carrying her burdens on her own narrow, capable shoulders to take that blow easily.

"Jared can't possibly be involved in this case," she fired back. "He wasn't even *alive* when Annabelle Charles went missing. He's practically a child."

"I know that," the sheriff said with maddening calm. "The question is, do you?"

Tess threw up her hands, goaded to the absolute limit of her endurance. Clearly, any further discussion of their relationship was off the table for the foreseeable future—there was a good chance *both* of them would end up on Sylvia's slab otherwise.

"I give up," she said. "Talking to you is like talking to a rusted doorknob. What are we going to do about Peter?"

He accepted her truce with a sigh. "Watch. Wait. Let him make the next move. I don't have enough to bring him in for questioning, and even if I did, I'd be hesitant to show my cards this early in the search." His look was glowering enough to have Tess rethinking the wisdom of leaving the Jared question unanswered, but when he spoke, it was about the case. "I started rereading his research on hatchets and human bone. The similarities between his findings and these bodies are...worrisome."

Tess nodded gravely, but he wasn't done yet. He scrubbed a hand along his jaw and sighed again.

"I don't know what kind of monster uses literal murder as a way to help thousands of other forensic scientists solve crimes, but as far as motive goes, this one fits." He shook his head and prepared to go back inside his house. "I'll say this for you, Tess. Each of your crackpot criminal theories tends to be a little more outlandish than the last, but they almost always end up being right."

Chapter Twenty-Seven

SINCE NEITHER TESS NOR SHERIFF BOYD FELT particularly good about leaving her alone with a highly suspect old man—silver-tipped cane or not—Nicki volunteered to accompany Tess back to the cabin to spend the night.

"With the amount of time Jared and I are spending on this murder case, we should probably have the Bureau send Sheriff Boyd a bill," Nicki said as Tess pulled her Jeep in front of the house and put it in park. "Mason is over there, running logs up to Canada and coming back with dirty money, but are we stopping him? No. I'm stamping self-help books and collecting late fees while Jared practices writing his married name all over his notebook. Jared Michael Harrow, complete with a heart over the *i*."

Tess almost choked in protest. "Stop it. He doesn't do that."

"Well, no," Nicki admitted. She grinned. "But he must have been very distracted the last time he checked in with the field office, because they're already talking about finding a way to pull him from the case. I'll give you a free, all-access pass to the bookmobile after hours if you promise to keep flirting with him. Another week or two of you stringing the poor sap along, and I'll be rid of him for good."

"I'm not stringing him along," Tess protested, but the moment they walked in the door, it was to find Jared sitting in her living room with Peter, a withered bunch of daisies in his hand. Her heart sank. She'd seen those daisies sitting in the grocery store for the whole of the last week, getting reduced one hefty price tag at a time. "Oh. Jared. You're here."

"Don't worry. Jared and I had a nice little chat while we waited for you." Peter struggled to his feet. It took all of Tess's self-control not to run to his side to assist him. She had to firmly remind herself that those softly wisping white curls around his ears were deceptive; that his increasingly unsteady gait was nothing more than a ruse. This was a man who was using her for his own nefarious purposes—and who had been for quite some time.

She *really* needed to stop letting the men in her life do that.

"What did you talk about?" she asked, suspicious.

"His father, mostly. Reginald and I go way back."

"What?" Both Tess and Nicki shared a look of alarm. Tess was the first to recover—and to demand an explanation. "Why didn't you mention this before?"

Peter blinked at the vehemence in her voice but didn't take offense. "I didn't know it interested you. I've helped the intelligence community both here and back home to break several big cases. Reggie was just an up-and-coming new agent back then. I thought Jared here would enjoy hearing a few stories about those early days." He reached over and patted a kindly hand on Jared's. "We all have to start somewhere. Even a man as great as your father used to get up to a few larks every now and then."

Too late, it occurred to Tess that she'd never mentioned Jared's work as a federal agent to Peter. Sheriff Boyd knew, yes, and Nicki, but that was as far as the secret was supposed to have gone. In Peter's eyes, Jared should look like nothing more than a young, inappropriate fling Tess was using to get over her ex.

Since she was starting to get very tired of these two-faced games—particularly since she'd lost most of them—she decided to come out and ask about it.

"Who told you who Jared's father is?" she asked. "Or that he's part of the FBI?"

Instead of being thrown off by this direct attack, Peter chuckled in his most grandfatherly way. "He's the spitting image of his father, girl. I didn't need anyone to tell me what I can see with my very own eyes. Besides—the poor kid has federal agent written all over him." He glanced at Nicki with an apologetic grin. "You both do. Take it from one who's done his fair share of espionage; you can't throw your weight around the way you two do without drawing suspicion. None of this swaggering around, parking the bookmobile without fear of repercussion, or showing up here to stand over Tess like a dog guarding a bone. *Efface* yourself, that's the trick. Make yourself smaller— both physically and mentally. You both take up too much bloody space."

These words, which were uttered in a manner meant to rob them of any malice, made Tess's blood run cold. Effacing himself—making himself seem small and weakly—was exactly what Peter had done since the day she'd met him.

"I don't know what you're talking about," Nicki said coldly. "I'm a librarian."

"Sure you are." Peter patted that kindly hand on Nicki's shoulder this time. It looked about as comfortable as petting a rock. "And I'm spiritual adviser to the Dalai Lama."

Considering how many other things Peter seemed to have accomplished during his lengthy stay on earth, this didn't seem out of the realm of possibility, but Tess didn't dare say so.

"Sorry, Nicki," Jared said as he rose to his feet and belatedly held the flowers out for Tess. She took them, but only because she had to do something with her hands or risk throttling Peter with them. "He came right out and asked me about my dad. I didn't know how to lie my way out of that one."

"Do you know how to lie your way out of *any* one?" Nicki countered.

Jared rubbed the side of his nose, unoffended at this line of questioning. "I must be doing something right. Mason just offered me a job at his site."

"Too bad. Turn it down."

"What are you talking about? This is what we wanted—"

"What we wanted was someone discreet. Someone capable. You obviously don't know how to sneak up on a…"

Peter drew Tess aside as the two agents squared off to continue their argument. He winced as the sound of loud voices cut through the tense, almost malleable air. "I'm sorry. I didn't realize it would cause such a rift, or I wouldn't have said anything. Poor kid's got good intentions, but he couldn't lie his way out of a paper bag." He glanced down at the flowers in Tess's hand. "Seems to like *you* plenty, though. At least he's got good taste."

Tess suddenly felt very weary, very confused, and very old. She tossed the flowers aside, feeling even sorrier for herself when several of the petals fell off and scattered in defeat.

"Peter, you can't tell anyone about this. They're working on an important case that has nothing to do with the murders."

Peter made the motion of a zipper over his lips. "Who would I tell? I'm just a lonely old man with a lot of life stories and not much to show for them."

None of that was even a little bit true. Tess couldn't speak to the *lonely* part, and the *old* certainly fit, but he had a lot more than life stories. He had powerful friends and a powerful mind. Even more to the point—he had powerful allies. If Wingbat99 and Reginald Wilson were just a few examples of the people he carried in his back pocket, even a slam-dunk case with a fully signed confession might not be enough to convict this man.

"As soon as they're done arguing, I think I'll take Nicki out for a walk," Peter said with another of those smiles that seemed to indicate no harm.

Harm, however, was the one thing Tess knew she could count on. Especially when Peter glanced down at the flowers and laughed.

"You and that young man will have plenty to talk about without an audience."

"Tess, you don't understand. Remember when I told you that tailing people is the one thing I'm good at?"

Tess had to close her eyes and count to ten—not in an effort to compose herself, but because she needed to dim the wattage of Jared's earnestness. It wasn't going to do either of them any good to get sidetracked by something as disastrous as sentiment.

"I'm sure you're the best tracker the FBI has ever seen," she allowed as she opened her eyes to find that his expression hadn't changed in the slightest. "That doesn't change the fact that I can't allow you to continue like this. Do you have any idea what blowing your cover might cost the case?"

"Yes," he said. "That's what I'm trying to tell you."

Since she could hardly keep opening and closing her eyes for the duration of this conversation, she stepped into the kitchen and began rinsing the stack of dirty dishes in the sink. Only the direst of conditions would drive her to voluntarily do the dishes, which went to show how upset she was.

"I wish I could keep you on at the bookstore, I really do," Tess said, and meant it. "But I have to side with Nicki. You're too much of a liability to keep on, even as a favor to the FBI. Between what you confessed to Peter and your insistence on following me around everywhere I go—"

A pair of strong, heavy hands fell on her shoulders and whirled her around. Instead of his usual puppy-dog look, Jared wore that of a hungrier, more determined wolf. Despite her best intentions, Tess felt herself responding to it.

"You're a sweet kid, you really are, but—"

"I'm not sweet, and I'm not a kid, and one of these days, I'm going to prove it to you," he said, his fingers digging deep imprints into her shoulders. "But right now, I need you to listen. You know how I told you I've been keeping tabs on Adam?"

Tess nodded. "Yes, but you said he mostly just sits drinking at the bar. No offense, but that's not really tailing someone. He has to be moving around for it to count."

Jared shook his head, a lock of golden hair falling in a swoop across his forehead. "I know, which is why I paid close attention when his brother Zach started showing up to join him."

"So?" Tess said. "What does Zach have to do with anything? He's been largely MIA ever since he chickened out of turning on his brother. He's probably just drinking to numb the pain."

"Are you sure that's when he stopped hanging around town?" Jared asked. "Or was it when the bodies started showing up?"

"I—" Tess began, only to close her mouth with a snap. That kind of coincidence might not mean anything, but there was no denying that the Peabody brothers were a highly suspect trio. "I'm not sure. You'd have to ask Nicki."

"Fat lot of good that would do me," Jared muttered. "She doesn't tell me anything—not that I need her to in this case. I think I already figured it out. I was wrong. *Adam*'s not the one drinking at the bar all day. *Zach* is."

Tess blinked, unsure what he was getting at—or why. "I don't understand. Why would that make a difference, and what does that have to do with you stopping by here to bring me flowers?"

"I haven't figured out yet what they're up to, but the flowers are my cover," he said with a bitter laugh. When Tess could only goggle at him, he added, "What? You think I don't know that you and Nicki are using my feelings for you as an excuse to get me in with Mason? You think I can't tell that you're just stringing me along so I'll help with your case?"

Tess couldn't have been more shocked than if the floor opened up underneath her feet to reveal an entirely new treasure trove of bodies. She wasn't shocked at the accusations themselves, but that Jared knew enough to make them.

"I'm pretty sure Adam knows I'm watching him," Jared said, continuing as though he hadn't just knocked Tess sideways. "I'm not sure *how* he knows, but it has something to do with that day up the cabin. My working theory is that he's been going to the bar—and making a big deal out of me knowing about it—on purpose. He wants me to know he's there so he and Zach can switch places. So he can sneak out without anyone knowing about it."

There was no opportunity to say more, which was a shame for a lot of reasons—and not just because Tess wanted to find out more regarding the Peabody boys. There was no denying that she'd used Jared poorly—as the nodding, depleted heads of the daisies in a chipped mason jar could attest—but she wasn't as immune to his charms as she pretended. It was only fair to let him know that it wasn't all in his head; that the spark, if that's what you could call it, had been mutual, if not wholly welcome on her side.

Before any of that was more than a vague impression in her head, the door creaked open to reveal Nicki and Peter arm in arm, the former laughing uproariously at something Peter had said.

"I hope everyone's decent in here," Nicki called, still laughing as she popped into the kitchen. "Because Peter found some chanterelle mushrooms he *assures* me are perfectly safe to eat, along with some Conocybe he assures me are not. He's planning a feast as we speak. Apparently, he's a foraging and natural poison expert on top of everything else. Who'd have guessed it?"

Chapter Twenty-Eight

Not dying of Peter's mushroom feast was a surprise, but not nearly as much of a surprise as waking up to find Nicki's face about an inch from her own.

"Psst. Tess. Tess, wake up. Tess, why is it so hard to rouse you from sleep?"

"Go away," Tess grumbled, throwing her arm over her eyes to block out the bright morning sun. She didn't know if it was Nicki's librarian side or her federal agent one that was the early riser, but she didn't care for either one. Since Gertrude was safely spending the night at Sheriff Boyd's house, it was one of the few mornings where she could indulge herself. "I'm sleeping."

Nicki yanked the quilt ruthlessly from over the top of her. "No, you're not. You're coming with me on my rounds today. There's no way I'm leaving you alone in this house. Peter crept out at dawn, saying something about going bird-watching, so the sheriff asked me to get you safely away."

The last thing Tess wanted was to be jolted over the rutted roadways in the bookmobile, which was sorely lacking in the shocks department, but even in her sleep-bleary state, she could discern the wisdom in this. Nicki had done a good job of playing the role of lively, chatty librarian last night, keeping them all in stitches until Jared went home and Peter finally called it a night, but Tess wasn't sure she could maintain the farce on her own. Knowing what Peter was capable of, aware of how much danger she was in every time she turned her back on him, was no way to live a life.

Or write a book, which was a thing Tess seriously needed to start catching up on.

"Sheriff Boyd asked you to protect me?" she asked as she swung her legs out of bed and stretched. "That was nice of him."

Nicki thrust a travel coffee mug under Tess's nose. "Actually, what he said was, 'make sure she's not ruining my entire blasted investigation,' but I feel like the sentiment was the same." She grinned. "I think he's planning on sending Ivy over under the pretext of needing Peter to consult on some tricky bone question. That way she can keep an eye on him until I'm done with my shift."

Tess felt it to be pretty high-handed of Sheriff Boyd to order Ivy to watch Peter without asking her first, but she didn't bother pointing it out. As a rather high-handed officer of the law herself, Nicki wouldn't understand.

"Can't you at least call in sick today?" Tess complained as she got to her feet. "We could go to a spa instead. Or maybe sit at the bar and drink—"

"No way." Nicki grabbed some clothes and started tossing them at Tess. "You only want to go to the bar so you can watch Adam and Zach try to pull the wool over Jared's eyes."

"You think that's what they're doing?" she asked as she poked her head through a cashmere sweater. "They know he's following him, so they're just messing with him because they can?"

Nicki laughed. "Can you blame them? It's exactly what I'd do in that situation. Jared is such a dunce, he'd fall for anything."

———

It was difficult to say which of them noticed the cavalcade first.

Despite her intention to remain focused on the case and impervious to the charms of being an honorary bookmobile librarian for the day, Tess was enjoying herself. Not only was Nicki an entertaining companion, but visiting remote locations while bringing the gift of literacy was turning out to be pretty fun.

Okay, so she mostly enjoyed how everyone offered cookies, coffee, and gossip at every stop.

And it *might* have been fun to see people's eyes light up with recognition once they realized who she was.

But literacy. Literacy mattered, too.

"I could have sworn I just saw the sheriff's car whiz by," Nicki said as she pulled off the highway and turned in the direction of the Winthrop town center. Two more cars zoomed past, their familiar green and white exteriors denoting them members of the same force.

"And I think that was Ivy," Tess agreed as she peered over the dashboard to get a better look at where they were going. "A few more, and they'll have everyone out. You'd better step on it. They're going to want our help for this."

This wasn't even a little bit true, but that didn't stop Nicki from stepping on the gas and lurching the bookmobile into action. Designed more for education than a high-adrenaline car chase, the rattling truck took some time before it got up to speed, but they needn't have bothered. As soon as Tess realized they were heading in the direction of the county morgue, she knew where they were going.

"The missing bones," she said, so excited she started unclipping her seat belt before it was safe. "Nicki, pull over. I bet they found them. I bet they're back."

Nicki did as she asked, but with a frown that gave Tess pause.

"What?" she demanded. "This is a good thing. Without those bodies, the case would have been almost impossible to prosecute."

"I know," Nicki agreed as the truck crunched to a halt. She pointed out the window to where a cluster of activity was taking place. "But if it's just the bodies, why is every able-bodied officer on the scene? And why is Gertrude sobbing on the side of the road?"

It took several minutes to calm Gertrude down enough to get a coherent answer out of her.

Tess's initial fears, that the girl had been hurt in some way, were quickly laid to rest. No sooner had she run up to her daughter than the deputy in charge of watching over her heaved a relieved sigh and said, "Oh, good. Maybe you can talk some sense into her. It's not a tragedy…yet."

"What's not a tragedy?" Tess had demanded. "What are you talking about?"

The answer had come as nothing more than a wry grimace from the officer and a strangled sob out of Gertrude. It was taking the combined efforts of Tess, Nicki, and the soothing effects of a luke-warm soda to get the hiccuping hysteria down to a manageable level, but they were just about there.

"Gertie-pie, I can't help you if you don't talk to me. What happened, and why are you so upset over it? Did someone break into the morgue again?"

"She's...gone..." Gertrude's voice caught as she dashed the back of her hand across her eyes. "The...murderer...got...her..."

Tess met Nicki's eyes over the top of her daughter's head. Without a word, Nicki turned on her heel and made her way over to the line of police tape surrounding the building. Even though Nicki didn't have any jurisdiction in the case, Tess knew she'd get answers. Peter had been right about that; the federal agent in Nicki was too deeply ingrained to just disappear.

"The murderer is here? Who did he get? Not—"

"Ms. Sylvie," Gertie wailed. "She went missing early this morning, and they can't find her anywhere."

Tess had to fight against every part of her nature not to follow in Nicki's wake. Getting answers out of Gertrude in this state would be almost impossible, and answers were the one thing she wanted most.

Until, of course, she read the devastation in her daughter's eyes. Cutting open dead bodies and examining crime scenes was all fun and games until someone you knew and admired became involved. That was where scientific interest ended and pure, human emotion took over.

"Oh, honey." Tess pulled her daughter into her arms and held her there, the wracking of that ever-growing body shaking them both. "I'm sure it's not as bad as it seems. She's an adult woman, fully capable of taking care of herself. It's been really intense around here the past few weeks, and the morgue is under a lot of scrutiny over the security breach. Maybe she needed some time away. For all we know, she just took a little trip to clear her head."

Gertrude glanced sharply up, her tear-streaked faced grown suddenly pale. "Wait. How did you know that part?"

"Which part?"

Her daughter shook off the embrace and examined Tess's face as though reading it for clues. "That she was going on a trip? Did she talk to you about it? Did you know? You have to tell the sheriff right away. If she really *did* head to the train station, and that ticket wasn't just a clue—"

Tess didn't even know she'd released a groan until Gertrude cut herself off mid-sentence. And by then, it was too late to take it back.

"Oh. You didn't know."

No, she *hadn't* known, but it didn't take an investigative genius to figure out the next part.

"It happened again, didn't it?" Tess asked, struggling to keep her voice calm. A woman gone missing. Her disappearance made to look voluntary.

Few loved ones to demand answers in the messy aftermath.

Only this time, it wouldn't be so easy to sweep under the rug. Not now that they knew they were dealing with a serial killer. Not when every single police officer—and federal one—within a hundred-mile radius was on the case.

"Yeah." Gertrude's lower lip wobbled. "You should've seen Sheriff Boyd's face when he got the call. He looked…"

"Furious?" Tess suggested. "Outraged? Appalled?"

"No. Sad."

"But it doesn't make any sense," Tess said, unable to help herself. She knew Gertrude wasn't the person she should be having this conversation with, but she was short on options right now. "Why Sylvia? Why now?"

What she really meant, but didn't dare put into words, was, "Why Peter?" If his goal all along had been to use those murders as a way to enhance his understanding of death to use in a book, there was nothing to be gained by it now. All he was doing was showing off.

Either that, or Sylvia had discovered something that made her a target. The location of the missing bodies, perhaps, or a clue about who had broken into the morgue. They should have had her in protective custody.

Heck, what they should have done is have Peter in lockdown. Letting him walk around was doing a disservice to the whole community.

"That man was no more watching birds this morning than I was," Tess muttered, suddenly shaken with resolve. "Don't move, Gertie. I'm going to have Nicki drop you off at Tommy and Timmy's. You're not to leave their house for any reason—or with any person—unless you have my permission, got it?"

"Why? Mom, what are you going to do?"

Tess shook her head with grim determination. "I'm going to do what I should have done a long time ago. Fish and houseguests both start to stink after three days, and I, for one, am ready for a breath of fresh air."

Chapter Twenty-Nine

WHEN TESS WALKED INTO THE CABIN, IT WAS TO find Peter sitting with a pad of paper, a pen, and an open copy of *Let Sleeping Dogs Lie* in front of him. With his glasses perched on the end of his nose and his cane propped, as it always was, within easy reach, it was difficult to imagine he was a serial killer whose infamy spanned the decades.

"Ah, Tess," he said, pulling off the glasses as he smiled up to greet her. "I was hoping you'd be back soon. That young man was here again with an urgent message for you. I tried your cell, but you and Nicki must have been too far out of service…"

He trailed off as Tess reached up and grabbed the gleaming shotgun from above the door. It wasn't loaded, and she was a terrible shot, but Peter didn't know that.

At least, she didn't *think* he did.

"Oh dear." He raised his arms above his head, a slight tremor to his muscles as he extended them as far as they would go. Which, given his advanced age, wasn't far. "What's happened now?"

"You know what happened," Tess said as she held the gun steady. "Sylvia Nerudo is missing. Gone without a single trace…except for the train ticket pretending that she's skipped town."

"A train ticket to where?" he asked, blinking.

Tess gave a slight start. In all her haste to get Gertrude settled and hightail it up here to get Peter in custody, it hadn't occurred to her to ask where the ticket was supposed to have taken Sylvia.

Still. She took a deep breath and maintained her composure. "Does it matter? We all know she'll never reach her destination. Is she dead already, or do you have her hidden somewhere?"

"Tied up under the cabin where you and Gertie sleep?" Peter laughed softly. "After all my years as a horror writer, I like to think I could come up with a better plan than that."

"A better idea like terrorizing a whole town for three decades?" Tess scoffed. "Yeah. That'll do it. How much of what you did made it into your books? What other crimes have you committed in the name of 'research'?"

Peter grew so quiet that Tess was afraid he was having some sort of episode, but all he did was heave a sigh. "I knew it was a bad idea to introduce you to Wingbat," he said. "Is it okay if I put my arms down now? I don't think I can hold them up much longer. My strength isn't what it used to be."

If Peter was acting, he was doing a phenomenal job of it, his skin pale and his limbs shaking. When Tess nodded and allowed him to move them down, he gripped the edge of the table to steady himself.

"What are you going to do to me?" he asked.

"I don't know yet. Lock you inside the cabin? Haul you down to the sheriff's office? Torture you until you tell me what you did to Sylvia?"

"Those all sound like lovely options, but I think you should read the message from your federal agent friend first. He was a bit…chaotic when he was here."

Tess lowered the gun a fraction. "Chaotic how?"

Peter gestured down at his front coat pocket. "May I reach in and grab it for you? I think you should read it for yourself."

So far, this wasn't going even remotely the way Tess had planned. She'd had this gun pointed at her own head before, and her reaction had been a lot less sedate. She'd panicked and pleaded, and had ultimately ended up getting hit across the back of the head. Peter, with his decades of training and strange knowledge of the world, seemed to be doing none of those things.

"Yes, but do it slowly," she warned.

Peter took her at her word, his fingers creeping gently into his pocket before extracting a slip of yellow notepaper and extending it between forefinger and thumb. "He said you'd understand what it means."

Tess took the proffered slip and read it. The note wasn't very long or very legible, but she managed to grasp the contents in one quick glance.

Don't worry. I have Simone safe.

"Simone?" Tess demanded, her brows furrowed. "What does he mean, Simone? Simone Peaky? *The* Simone Peaky?"

"One would assume," Peter said, nothing but politeness in his clipped British voice.

"But you're Simone Peaky," Tess protested. She flipped the paper over, hoping for more clues, but there was nothing. It was just an ordinary scrap of notepaper—the kind you could buy anywhere, the kind she regularly scrawled plot points on. "What kind of cryptic nonsense is this?"

"I don't know, but are you going to explain why you're holding that gun on me?"

Tess reinforced her grip on the gun. "I told you already," she said, feeling irritable. The fun part about getting to this point of an investigation was not having to explain things anymore. This was where Peter was supposed to take over, outlining all his nefarious deeds so she could finally— *finally*—understand. "You're Simone. You wrote that book. You killed those women. You took Sylvia."

To her surprise, Peter laughed out loud. It was a hearty laugh, full of all the warmth she'd come to associate with this man, and it had a way of spreading. "Tess, love. You've really lost it this time. Why on earth would I have done all that?"

She had neither the time nor the patience to outline his motives to him. "What am I going to do?" she demanded. "I can't leave you here to keep murdering people, but Jared has obviously lost his mind. Do you think you'd fit in my cargo space?"

"No. I decidedly do not."

She narrowed her eyes. He *would* fit in the back of her Jeep, of that she was certain, but the trick would be getting him in there without causing irreparable harm. She'd been stuffed into a similarly sized trunk before. The muscle cramps were no joke.

"Put the gun down, sit next to me, and tell me what you think about this passage here," he said as he gestured at the book still lying open in front of him. He was no more afraid of Tess than he was of a gnat, which was a lowering reflection but not an inaccurate one. She could no more harm this man than she would her own father. "I'm not *certain* it's a clue, since it deals with the second victim rather than the third, but I think we need to reconsider whether the author knew about Yasmine Kope's disappearance."

Tess *did* put the gun down, but not of her own volition. It fell from her grasp like a dead weight, the heavy metal clunking against the wood floor with so much force that it startled her into a scream.

"For the love of Josefina, what now?" Peter demanded.

"Yasmine Kope," Tess said as she stepped over the now-useless gun and scrambled to the table. She snatched the pen up and flipped Jared's note over. After carefully writing down the letters of Yasmine's name, she did the same for Simone Peaky.

Y–A–S–M–I–N–E–K–O–P–E
S–I–M–O–N–E–P–E–A–K–Y

"Peter, why didn't you tell me?" she cried as soon as she realized what she'd done. With a little careful rearranging, the names were perfect anagrams of one another.

"I didn't realize," he breathed, leaning close. He cast a quick glance up at her. "I *should* have, but I never even thought to make the connection. What does it mean?"

Tess closed her eyes and willed her thoughts into a semblance of order. They were wild and clanging, so loud she could barely concentrate, but she hadn't written several novels in the waiting room of Gertrude's childhood dance classes for nothing.

"Simone Peaky and Yasmine Kope are the same person," she said before quickly shaking her head. "No, that can't be it, because Yasmine died decades ago. Simone Peaky took her name. Rearranged the letters. And then published a book in which Yasmine *didn't* die."

"Tess, maybe you should—"

"Shh." Tess flapped a hand at him without opening her eyes. She was so close she could practically feel the solution about to burst like a bubble on the tip of her tongue. "Instead of killing off Yasmine in the book, Simone killed off the sheriff's sister—a woman who went missing within days of Yasmine's death, and who hasn't been seen since. Why? What did she hope to accomplish?"

"Maybe it was a warning? A message?"

She popped her eyes open and swiveled to stare at Peter. "No. It was a clue. About where to find the bodies. About what happened to those missing women."

"If that's the case, then why haven't we found Kendra Boyd's body yet?" Peter asked, but with such a wide-eyed look that Tess knew he'd put the answer together the same time she had.

She also knew that she'd been wrong when she assumed that Peter was the one behind it all.

"Because Simone Peaky *is* Kendra Boyd," she said, her heart pounding so hard it was a wonder she didn't die on the spot. "She's alive. She's here. And unless I'm mistaken, I know exactly where Jared took her."

Chapter Thirty

THERE WASN'T ENOUGH TIME TO BRIEF SHERIFF Boyd on all the details, so Tess sent Peter ahead with an urgent message and an even more urgent plea: she needed backup, and she needed it stat.

She also needed it on top of a mountain that was only accessible via foot, which was why she declined the offer of Peter's company. She'd rather not hike up that trail with an old man riding piggy-back. Especially if the rest of her suspicions about the case were true.

Kendra is Simone. Simone is Kendra.

That twist alone was enough to provide fodder for a whole ten-book Detective Gonzales series, and it wasn't even the good part. Tess had been right all along when she'd said that Simone Peaky knew too much about the case to be an innocent bystander. She'd *definitely* been a bystander, but as for the innocence part...

Time and a jaunt up this mountain would tell that soon enough.

The gun proved a useful tool as she grunted and

heaved her way up the path. If it hadn't been useless before, it certainly was now, dirt compacted so far down the barrel that it would take Nicki and all her firearm expertise to get it clean it again.

Tess wished her librarian friend were with her now. She wished *anyone* was with her, but it hadn't been worth taking precious minutes to track someone down. If Jared had brought Kendra back to the shack, if he was sitting there twiddling his thumbs while Sylvia Nerudo was still missing, then he was a bigger clodpoll than she'd given him credit for.

"Like a couple of sitting ducks," Tess muttered as she clawed her way up a particularly steep overhang. "Just waiting for someone to burst in and murder them."

She knew she was on the right track when she took a short pause to catch her breath and saw a sudden flash of light at the top of the mountain. The shack wasn't so close that she could make out any of the details, but a light indicated life and movement. A light indicated that Jared and Kendra had already arrived.

Tess scrambled the rest of the way up in record time. At least, it *felt* like record time. Her shoes were starting to come apart at the soles, and her body was bathed in sweat, but it wasn't as if she was here to win a beauty contest.

Or to impress a man. She didn't care what Nicki

and Peter and Sheriff Boyd implied. There was no way she—

CLICK.

She felt rather than heard the sound of a gun being cocked and pointed at her. It was a sound she was coming to know all too well, and she immediately dropped her own rifle/walking stick at the sound of it.

"That's what I thought." A low, female chuckle sounded in her ear. "The next time you come running to the rescue, you might want to try sounding a little bit *less* like a middle-aged divorcée who hasn't exercised since the early 2000s. I heard you from a mile away."

Tess took instant exception to this. "How dare you. I'm not middle-aged. I'm in the prime of my life."

"Not for much longer." That low chuckle sounded again, this time accompanied by a jab of Sylvia's knee into her backside. "Get moving, and don't try anything funny. I'm not afraid to kill you where you stand."

Tess believed her. After all, she'd already killed at least three other women—a thing Tess would have realized a long time ago if she hadn't been so blinded by the thought of Peter as the culprit.

Peter Oblonsky wasn't the only forensic expert around here with a reputation to maintain. He also wasn't the only one with access to the morgue and city computers. Who better to hack in and wipe the records clean than the one woman who knew what needed to be erased? Who more desperate than a woman who needed to hide the exact evidence she was supposed to examine?

"What do you have planned for after you kill me?" Tess asked as she started moving toward the shack. "To hack me up and dissect me for parts? Write a paper on your findings only to have it rejected by every forensic journal worth being rejected by?"

She knew her theory was correct when she was suddenly and painfully smacked on the back of the head with the gun. The reverberation of it rattled her jaw and sent her sinking to her knees, nausea and blunt-force pain warring for supremacy.

"I know enough to be able to inflict a lot of pain without killing you. Unfortunately, that's not a topic anyone wants to publish academic research on."

"That's not true," Tess managed to say. "The CIA might be very interested in your findings."

Sylvia was startled into a laugh, but she cut it short before Tess could consider a stand-up routine as a way out of this mess. "This is your own fault, you know. Everything would have been fine if you hadn't told Sheriff Boyd your stupid theory about the murders being used as research."

Tess was exhausted, terrified, and suffering from what was likely a concussion, but even in that state, she still felt compelled to defend herself. "But it wasn't a stupid theory. I was right. I'm *always* right—not about the who, obviously, but about the what. It's my gift."

Sylvia snorted, but so quietly it didn't count. By this time, they'd reached the little clearing at the top of the mountain. The shack sat a few feet away, quiet but obviously inhabited.

"Who's going to be in there besides Kendra and that little boy toy of yours?" Sylvia hissed in her ear.

"I don't know."

The gun moved to her temple. "What do you mean, you don't know?"

"I mean, I'm unsure who they may have taken into their confidence. You're crediting me with a lot more advance knowledge about this whole thing than I have. I didn't realize Kendra was alive until about an hour ago." When Sylvia didn't do anything more than crouch in silence, her brow furrowed in thought, Tess felt emboldened to add, "But you knew, didn't you? You've always known."

"Of course I have," Sylvia muttered. "I'm the one who bought her bus ticket out of here."

This was enough new information to send Tess's senses into a whirl, but she wasn't given an opportunity to straighten them. With another of those knee nudges, Sylvia prodded her forward. Tess had to use all her concentration not to go sprawling on the ground. By the time she'd decided her best bet was to scream bloody murder and hope Jared would come rushing out with the ankle gun he always seemed to want to shoot at people, Sylvia was one step ahead of her.

"I've got your girlfriend out here, and I'm not afraid to splatter her head all over the ground." Sylvia placed her body behind Tess's, using her as a human shield. "Come out with your hands up, and I won't kill her...yet."

There were several rustling movements inside the cabin before Jared appeared in the doorway, his hands in the air and a look of deep concern marring the handsome features of his face. "Tess?" he called as he stepped out. When he caught sight of Sylvia holding a gun at her head, he released a low curse.

Tess winced. "Sorry. She ambushed me a little ways down the mountain. I think she was coming to murder Kendra before skipping town."

"Of course I was. It's what I should have done decades ago. Is she in there?" Sylvia motioned for Tess to precede her as she stepped closer to the cabin. "You might as well come out, Kendra. I know you're in there, and I know you broke your promise. I warned you what would happen if you did that."

Tess wasn't sure what she expected as a second person stepped out of the shack, but nothing could have prepared her for the sight of Victor's sister. Stately, defiant, and so much like him that it caused all the air to leave her lungs, Kendra was everything Tess expected her to be.

She was also alive…

For now.

Chapter Thirty-One

JARED HAD A SECRET.

That fact couldn't have been more obvious if he had a neon sign on his head and a sandwich board around his body, both loudly proclaiming *I have something to hide!* Tess knew it the moment she entered the tiny shack and was ordered to strip him of his weapons and tie him up using a set of weathered bungee cords.

"I know about the gun on his ankle, so don't even think about it," Sylvia commanded. "I've seen him flash that thing at least three times since he arrived in town."

As Tess sighed and reached down to remove the weapon in question, Jared winked at her. She jabbed him with the blunt end of the bungee cord in an attempt to get him to be less obvious, but it was no use. As soon as she closed her hand around the gun and handed it to Sylvia, who had her own weapon trained steadily at Kendra, Jared winked again.

Partly to cover up these clumsy attempts, and

partly because she was genuinely curious, Tess directed the attention back toward herself.

"How are you hoping to clean this whole mess up?" she asked as she finished securing Jared to the folding lawn chair. "You have to know that it's only a matter of time before someone comes looking for us. Then what? A hostage shoot-out? Death by cop? I hate to be picky, but that's not how I'd prefer to go."

Kendra, who had up until this point remained as uncommunicative as her brother, coughed gently. "Considering her past methods, I'm guessing she plans to set this up so I look like the guilty party."

Her voice was oddly soft-spoken—not at all the slow, confident drawl that Tess associated with Sheriff Boyd. Still, there was something arresting about the way she spoke, as if everyone in the room had no choice but to stop what they were doing and listen.

Which, considering they were all busy plotting ways to murder and/or not be murdered, was saying a lot.

A smile crossed Sylvia's face, moving so slow it was a like a slug leaving a trail of slime behind. "Bravo. That's exactly what I plan to do. Only this time, I'll be careful to make sure it actually works."

"*This* time?" Tess echoed, but there was no need. As soon as she asked the question, she heard the answer as clearly as if it had been spoken aloud. "The sheriff's car being used to drop the bones off at my store. The burial site on the sheriff's property. You did that on purpose. You were trying to frame him."

Instead of appearing proud of her work, the slug-smile faded from Sylvia's face. "I did it well enough to keep Kendra away from town all these years, but not well enough to make a convincing case for the authorities. Good thing I learn from my mistakes." As Jared chose that moment to set up a round of coughing that wouldn't have convinced a baby of his innocence, Sylvia turned her attention that way. "What's the matter with you? Why do you keep twitching?"

Tess had lots of follow-up questions, but she realized some issues were more pressing than Sylvia's twisted ways and means into a thirty-year murder spree. Especially when she caught Kendra's eye and realized she wasn't the only one who was finding Jared's lack of subtlety troubling.

Tess knew very little about Kendra Boyd except that the woman was smart enough to get a book published with complete anonymity, hide away from the world for several decades, and remain hidden even at the cost of breaking a beloved brother's heart.

It would have to be enough. With a quick nod

at the other woman, she positioned herself behind Jared and waited.

Kendra didn't leave her waiting long. With all the acting skills that Jared lacked, she forced Sylvia's attention over to herself.

"You brought this upon yourself, you know," Kendra said, still in that lulling, soft-spoken voice. "I held up my end of the bargain. I left town. I didn't tell anyone what you did. First Annabelle, then Yasmine... You *promised*, Sylvia. You swore you wouldn't do it again."

"And you swore you'd keep your mouth shut. I guess we're both liars."

"I *did* keep my mouth shut," Kendra said. "For over twenty-five years, my hands tied and a sword poised over my brother's head. How could I do anything else?"

Tess had her foot hooked underneath Jared's chair, ready to kick him over the moment she felt it was safe enough to do so, but at the mention of Sheriff Boyd, she stopped. If she'd had any doubts that Kendra was the author of *Let Sleeping Dogs Lie*, those overly poetic words would have convinced her. So would the story she was telling. It was the missing piece, the reason why she'd inserted her own death into the book instead of Yasmine Kope's.

"I left and kept your dirty secret. I lost my entire family to save my brother from your lies. I would have kept doing it, too, only you killed again. I knew it the second I read that news story about the missing hiker."

"You had no proof that was me," Sylvia snarled.

A genuine smile played about Kendra's mouth. "No, but I was right about where you buried her, wasn't I? It was only a guess, but I knew that burying Yasmine somewhere to frame my brother had to be killing you. You wanted the bodies to be just down the road—you wanted to visit them anytime you swung by the hardware store to pick up a screwdriver. Old Mr. Harrow and Herb were already using the place to sneak off and—" She cut herself off with a sideways look at Tess. "Never mind. It was a good place to hide things, that's all. And you knew it."

If Tess had any ability to be surprised left in her, she might have shown alarm at this revelation. As it was, she could only suppress a sigh. *Yet another thing I got wrong.* Edna St. Clair hadn't filmed her grandfather and Herb hiding bodies; unless Tess was very much mistaken, she'd stumbled on a love affair instead.

Poor Grandpa. Poor *Herb*.

"Tess," Jared whispered, his voice so loud it sounded almost like a gunshot. "Tess, you don't have to worry. I—"

Kendra interrupted with a loud laugh. "I knew

you'd killed Lucretia. I also knew it was high time I did something to stop you before you did it again. So I wrote a book, spilling every last one of your dirty secrets."

That was Tess's cue. Before Sylvia could react, she kicked Jared's chair so hard it toppled over. And then, even though it sickened her to do so, she kicked again—this time in the back of his head. The thud of her toe against his skull created both a sound and a sensation she would never forget, but it did the trick. Jared only had time to gasp and cry out before he fell unconscious.

"Oh, no!" Tess dropped to her knees and made a big show of worry for the younger man. Most of this wasn't feigned; she really hoped she hadn't done any lasting damage. He might not be much of an FBI agent, but she genuinely liked him. "I didn't mean to knock him over. I was so flustered and scared, and—"

"Get out of the way," Sylvia snarled as she bent down to check Jared's pulse and peek under his eyelids. Even though her specialty was dead people, her medical training was still better than Tess's. "He's fine. Just out cold. That's probably better. I don't need him to be awake for this next part. In fact, it's better if he's not."

Tess fought every urge to look to Kendra for assistance. She knew now that she and the sheriff's sister were on the same page, and that they had to stop Sylvia before she got away. She also knew that Kendra was smart—*scary* smart, and playing a much longer game than Tess could imagine.

"You." Sylvia pointed at Tess. "Get in the other chair. And you." This time, she pointed at Kendra. "Tie her to it."

"It'll never work," Kendra said. "Your finger-prints are all over this place. Even if you do put that gun in my hand and force me to pull the trigger, they'll know you were here. They'll know you were part of this."

"Of course they will," Sylvia said as Kendra began neatly and efficiently binding Tess to the chair. "That's why I'm burning the whole thing to the ground—with all three of you in it."

Chapter Thirty-Two

TESS TRIED NOT TO PANIC—SHE REALLY DID. SHE strove to have faith in the things she knew to be true, to trust that kicking their strongest, bravest, and most well-trained way out of here alive was the right approach.

It wasn't working.

"I thought Adam would be here by now," she said over the sound of crackling frames and the thick clog of smoke that was starting to overtake her lungs. "You said it with your eyes. I saw it in them. I *read* it."

"He will be," Kendra said with a heavy cough. "He was only supposed to be out gathering firewood."

"And Herb?" Tess asked.

Kendra was tied to the wall rather than a chair—an attempt, Tess was sure, to make a convincing crime scene after the fact—but she was still within Tess's line of vision. "You know about Herb?"

"Of course I do. It's why Herb had the map, and why he was so protective when I mentioned your name. He knew you came back the moment those bodies were found…and he wanted to help keep you hidden."

Kendra let out a low whistle, or as close to one as she could get while their mouths were rapidly drying out in the acrid air. "You *are* smart, aren't you? Now I understand what Victor sees in you."

There wasn't time for Tess to unpack this remark—or to ask any of the many questions that were burning on her tongue. She couldn't. Not when the rest of her was so close to *actually* burning. She started to saw her wrists against the chair, but if her experience underneath the hardware store had taught her anything, it was that she needed time to get through her bonds—and time was the one thing she didn't have.

Which was why she was so relieved when the door burst open to reveal Adam Peabody looking smug and disheveled, and with a streak of blood across his face.

"I hope that blood is Sylvia's," Kendra said just as Tess heaved a sigh and said, "Get Jared out of here first. I don't like how shallow his breathing is."

In the end, she didn't get her way. Jared was on the ground, which meant that he was breathing in a lot less of the noxious fumes than they were.

"Untie Ms. Harrow," Adam commanded a figure over his shoulder. Tess could make out the shape of another Peabody. "I'll get Kendra."

"And Sylvia?" Kendra demanded as Adam began expertly cutting the ropes that held her in place. "You got her?"

"We didn't." Zach slid a knife under Tess's bonds and gave one strong tug. "But the mountain did. She fell off the north face as soon as she spotted us."

It was on the tip of Tess's tongue to point out that the bloody streak on Adam's face gave lie to this statement, but Zach wordlessly handed Adam a handkerchief before hoisting Tess over his shoulder in what appeared to be a well-practiced fireman's hold.

"Volunteer fire brigade," he offered, sensing her incredulity. "Hold tight. You'll be fine once you're in the open air."

He was right. She *did* feel better once she filled her lungs with fresh, damp mountain air—and once both Kendra and Jared were deposited next to her. She was tempted to peek over the north face to see for herself what had happened to Sylvia, but she found that her legs were shaking too much to make the attempt.

"You're coming down from the adrenaline," Adam said as he handed her a water bottle. He waited until she drank some before grinning and adding, "I was on the volunteer fire brigade, too."

Tess wasn't sure what to say. She was grateful to both of the Peabodys for saving the day—and for being smart enough to stay hidden while Sylvia went her full length, but that didn't change the fact that they were both criminals—and that there was an unconscious federal agent next to her who was supposed to be investigating them. She had no idea how much they knew, or what she was supposed to do in this situation, but one thing was clear. Nicki wouldn't appreciate a blown cover just when it seemed the Peabodys were starting to soften.

As if aware of what was going on around him, Jared groaned groggily and rolled his head her direction, his mouth open as if to speak.

Tess wasn't about to make the same mistake again.

"Don't say anything, Jared," she commanded. "Everyone is alive, and you saved the day, but for the love of everything, don't try to speak."

Chapter Thirty-Three

MUCH TO HER DISMAY, TESS WASN'T PRESENT FOR the reunion of the siblings. By the time help arrived, the adrenaline had all but left her body, leaving her shaken, bruised, and suffering from smoke inhalation that made her head pound so sickeningly that it was all she could do to stay conscious.

She remembered riding down the mountain in a forest ranger's truck that bounced and jostled in ways that shook her very bones. She remembered vague discussions about bringing in a rescue helicopter to recover Sylvia's body from the bottom of the ravine where it lay. She also remembered Kendra slipping quietly away before anyone else arrived.

"Don't worry," Kendra said, her head bent close to Tess's as the sound of rescue approached. "I'm not leaving for long. It's just that I can't see him like this. Not yet. Will you explain it all for me?"

"I don't know it all—" Tess began, but she didn't bother finishing. What she didn't know, she could guess. And what she couldn't guess, she could easily fabricate.

After all, that was what she did. Wove stories out of thin air—unlike Kendra Boyd, whose only book had been written to provide a trail of bread crumbs to a crime that no one even knew was a crime.

Until, of course, Tess had uncovered the first of the bodies, and all the pieces had clicked into place.

She lay back in her hospital bed now, surrounded by flowers and friendly faces, feeling as though all was right with the world again. Or…almost right. One face entered looking anything but friendly, and the moment he crossed the threshold, everyone else fled.

"I think I'll head to the cafeteria to get a cup of tea," Peter announced before hobbling out the door.

"I could eat," Nicki agreed.

Ivy wasn't far behind. "I'm not hungry, but there's no way I'm sticking around for this."

"Fine," Gertrude grumbled, following at a much more sedate pace. "You guys are no fun."

"I don't look *that* bad," Sheriff Boyd said as soon as the last of them had made good their escape. He settled himself on a chair next to Tess's bed and ran a hand over the deep scruff of his jawline. "Do I?"

"You've looked better," Tess said, wincing. From the way he was holding himself, he probably hadn't slept in days. "Have you spoken to her yet?"

His mouth flattened into a hard line. "Yeah. I had to get her official statement."

Tess waited, her every nerve strained in an

attempt not to jump up and pull Sheriff Boyd into a hug. "And?"

"I'd rather hear your version, if you don't mind."

Tess sank into her pillow and closed her eyes, doing her best to downplay the way her heart was suddenly taking flight. She'd had plenty of time to think over the events of the past forty-eight hours; even more to wish that she'd been able to put it all together earlier. Everything had been there, but she'd been too distracted to realize it.

And that, unfortunately, was exactly what Sylvia had wanted.

There was no doubt in her mind that Kendra had been present at or witness to the first two murders. What her role in them might have been, Tess didn't know, but she was guessing Victor did. Sylvia knew, too, which was when everything had begun. Knowing she was vulnerable, that her entire future hung on Kendra's word, she'd found a way to shut Kendra up: either leave town and take the secret to her grave, or Victor Boyd—then just a boy of sixteen—would be the one to pay the price.

That was the part that hurt Tess the most. The murders were bad, obviously, and the fact that Sylvia had chosen her grandfather's hardware store as a final resting place for two of the bodies highly irritating, but Victor had only been a kid. So had Kendra, when it all came down to it.

Had Sylvia stopped then, quelled her murderous urges and strange, uncanny ambition to shine in the world of forensics, things might have ended there. But then a hiker had gone missing in the woods, and under such similar circumstances that Kendra, missing for over twenty-five years, had been forced to act. Only she had no way of being sure that her brother wouldn't be set up for the fall.

So she'd written a book. A halfway decent book, in which the details of the murders were close to the real thing, but not *so* close that Sylvia could take it out on an innocent man. Kendra had merely wanted to leave a few bread crumbs, a way to draw attention to the facts without bringing fire down upon her family's head. And the pen name—an anagram of the victim she herself portrayed—had been the key to link it all.

"Well?" Victor demanded.

Tess didn't have the heart to put any of that into words—not when Victor was obviously so raw. Instead, she opened an eye and examined him. "The thing I can't figure out," she said, and in a voice so drawling that not even Sheriff Boyd at his most upright could ignore her, "is why your sister was so adamant that *I* be the one to blurb her book."

He jerked up in his chair, looking more alert and—yes, okay—annoyed than she could have possibly hoped. "What are you talking about?"

Tess doubled down. "See, I think that's where I got thrown off."

"Not when you accused a sweet old man of murder?"

"The whole time, I kept thinking it had something to do with me."

"You think *everything* has to do with you."

"But that's just it. *I'm* not the one she was singling out."

"I changed my mind." The sheriff got abruptly to his feet. "I don't need to hear your version of events."

Tess shot out her hand and gripped Victor around the wrist. She didn't wait for him to react before sliding her palm down until her fingers were firmly twined with his. He stared down at their hands for a full thirty seconds before moving to Tess's face.

"She was singling *you* out," she said, so softly that Victor had to lean close to hear her. "Because she knew you were a fan of my work. She hoped you'd see that blurb and pick up the book based on my recommendation. She's been keeping close tabs on you all this time, hasn't she? Watched you grow up? Followed your career?"

His fingers flexed against hers so tightly that Tess had to fight a wince. "What does it matter? She never did the one thing that might have actually made a difference. She never told me the truth. Thirty years is a long time to go without a single word."

It was. It was also a more difficult situation than he realized. Risking the person you loved was a lot to ask of a woman.

"She was protecting you," Tess said. "No matter how hard I try, I can't find it in my heart to blame her for that. I hope she sticks around after all the dust settles. I'd really like to get to know her."

"I hope so, too," Victor said quietly.

The moment was interrupted by a soft knock at the door, followed by the entrance of a tall man with two black eyes and a bandage wound tight around his head. As soon as he caught sight of Tess and Victor holding hands, he halted. He would have back-tracked, but Victor took one look at him and sighed.

He also drew his hand out of Tess's and held it out to Jared instead.

"I haven't had a chance to express my gratitude for what you did up there on Ramsey Peak," he said, and without any of the rancor Tess expected. "Thank you for taking care of my sister. For pro-tecting her. I don't know what you said to Adam or Herb to get them to trust you with the truth, but I appreciate it more than you know."

Jared stared first at the sheriff's outstretched hand and then at Tess, a grin starting to dawn. Tess could see what was coming next, but from her position on the bed, she was powerless to stop it. If she was being perfectly honest, she was also hesitant to stop it. Curiosity was a thriller writer's besetting sin.

It was *this* thriller writer's besetting sin, at least.

"You're very welcome," Jared said as he extended his arms and pulled the sheriff into what could only be termed a bear hug. The sheriff bore it nobly but stiffly, his lithe form dwarfed by the younger man's. "I was in the right place at the right time, that's all. As soon as I finally figured out what Adam was doing, sneaking around like that, the rest of the pieces just fell into place. To be honest, I didn't believe it was your sister until I saw her with my own two eyes."

"Me, either," Sheriff Boyd admitted as he disentangled himself from the hug. His eyes flicked quickly to Tess's. "I'll just, ah, leave you two alone for now, shall I?"

"No, Victor, don't—" Tess began, but it was no use. She *might* have been able to turn Jared away if he'd sauntered in here expecting a hero's welcome, but he was bashful, battered, and absurdly boyish.

She sighed instead. "Tell your sister I said hello... and that she's welcome to stay at the cabin with me and Gertie, if she needs a roof over her head. It'll be tight quarters, but we'd be happy to have her."

"Thanks, but she's decided to stay with Herb for the

time being." Without another word, Victor nodded his head in a tight farewell and bore himself off.

To her surprise, Jared didn't speak right away. He watched the other man leave with an oddly wistful expression. "I'm sorry," he said after a brief pause. "I was interrupting something, wasn't I?"

"I'm not sure," Tess admitted. "Maybe."

Jared sat on the end of her bed, his body weight sinking into the mattress and pulling Tess down with it. "You might not be sure, but *I* am." He hesitated. "And so is the sheriff. I might not know much, but I can recognize a man in love."

Tess wasn't sure how to respond to this, so it was for the best that no reply was expected. Jared flashed her a rueful grin.

"Just…don't make a decision yet, would you?" he asked. "I have a way of growing on people."

"Jared…"

He pointed at his black eyes and grinned deeper. "It's the least you can do after kicking me hard enough for this pair of shiners. Seriously, Tess. Your MMA skills are off the hook. You have no idea how hot that is."

Even though the image of Sheriff Boyd's hand entangled with her own was still fresh in her memory, Tess flushed. "I could have really hurt you."

"With this thick skull? Nah." Jared dropped a hand on her ankle and squeezed once before letting go. "It was nice of you not to tell everyone why you had to put me out of commission. I was pretty close to blowing it back there, wasn't I?"

Tess held up her fingers in the approximation of an inch. "Jared, have you ever considered a different career? No offense, but you're the worst liar I've ever met."

He sighed. "I know. But I did tell you I was good at following people, remember? That's how I found out what Herb and Adam were up to. I thought that if I kept Kendra safe long enough for you to track down Sylvia—if I got just this one thing right—they might let me stay on the case here long enough to get to know you better. I never do, you know. By the time I start to make friends anywhere, I get posted somewhere else. Somewhere new. Somewhere I haven't screwed up yet."

"I'm sure Nicki will put in a good word for you," Tess said, her heart going out to the young man—in more ways than one.

Jared grimaced. "I'm not." He picked himself up from the bed and headed toward the door. Tess would have asked him to stay, but her lungs were starting to ache again. Jared might be able to bounce back from his smoke inhalation quickly, but Tess was older. And tired.

She felt those things even more when Jared paused and glanced back.

"But look at it this way—at least if I get fired from the Bureau, I can always stick around and finish fixing up your bookstore." He flashed her another of those boyish grins. "And don't forget—you'll need a part-time cashier once you're up and running. I can't remember the last time I read a book, but I hear *Let Sleeping Dogs Lie* is a good place to start."

"Don't you dare..." Tess warned, but it was no use.

"'A fast-paced, reckless tale that grabs you by the throat and doesn't let go,'" he quoted with a wink. "That sounds like the kind of story I can get behind."

Keep reading for a sneak peek of the third book in Tamara Berry's By the Book Mysteries series

Murder Off the Books

GERTRUDE'S CORPSE LAY AT AN UNNATURAL angle on the floor of The Paper Trail bookstore. Her pale skin glowed eerily under the lights, her deathly pallor made starker by the heavily winged eyeliner that circled her lids like a burlesque raccoon. No one in the store could discern the cause of her death, but it was obvious to any trained eye that—

"Ouch. I think there's a rock under my hip. Wait a sec."

The corpse wriggled, shifted, and dislodged a pebble from under the waistband of her torn black jeans.

"Never mind," she said as she popped the rock into her mouth. "It's just a jellybean."

"Gertie, don't eat that," Tess cried, but she was too late. Her teenaged daughter had already swallowed it. "And stop fidgeting so much. You're supposed to be dead."

"If she keeps eating pieces of candy she finds on the floor of the bookstore, she *will* be dead," murmured Nicki as she hoisted a box of books on her hip as easily as if lifting a baby. Tess couldn't help but be impressed. She knew from experience that a box of thirty hardback copies of her newest release,

Fury under the Floorboards, was no light burden. At a little over four hundred pages, it was her longest book yet.

It was also her most successful book yet, even though it didn't technically hit the shelves until tomorrow. According to her publisher, pre-sales were through the roof—or rather, through the floorboards. Ever since a cold case serial killer had been captured and arrested after decades-old bones had tumbled through this very floor and onto Tess's head, the entire world had been holding its breath in anticipation of her fictionalized version of events.

"Maybe we should conk Gertie over the head before the launch party tomorrow night," Tess mused as she watched her daughter's continued attempts to find a comfortable resting spot. "For authenticity's sake. If she's supposed to look like a corpse, she can't keep moving around."

Now that Tess was looking closer, she didn't think anyone had ever appeared less dead. Not even the veiny blue makeup along the side of Gertrude's temples could counteract the healthy, blooming glow of her. Ah, to be fifteen again. Before gravity had taken hold, back when skin cells regenerated themselves without the aid of hundred-dollar face cream, when she could pick up candy off the floor and suffer no more ill effects than—

"Gertie! Stop eating those." Tess nudged her daughter with her foot. "What's the matter with you?"

Gertrude sat up and popped another jellybean into her mouth. "I'm *hungry*, that's what's wrong with me. You promised me dinner at the hotel restaurant. How much longer is it going to take to get everything set up?"

Tess looked to Nicki for the answer. She'd wanted to hire an event planner for this—the grand opening of her new bookstore and launch party for the latest installment of her Detective Gonzales series—but Nicki had insisted she could handle it. The tall, willowy librarian not only ran a local bookmobile program, rambling along in a blue truck that covered every nook and cranny of this rural Washington county, but she also happened to be an undercover FBI agent investigating a money laundering scheme along the Canadian border. At this point, Tess was pretty sure the woman was superhuman.

"That depends…" Nicki consulted a clipboard on the top of the box. "Gertie, you have all the canapes prepped for the party tomorrow evening, right?"

Gertrude made a mock salute as she bounced up from the floor. "Aye, aye, captain. Most of it only has to be popped in the oven before it's ready to go. I still need to assemble the sushi, but we're having the tuna specially flown in tomorrow so it's fresh."

"And the fancy journalist you paid for is coming in on the same flight, right?"

Tess took instant umbrage at this. "I didn't *pay* for the journalist. He contacted me of his own volition. He wants to follow me for a week to get a good look at my writing process. It's for a feature."

Nicki leveled a look at Tess over the top of the box. "But he's staying with you?"

"He specifically requested it! He said it helps him get a personalized look at my life."

"The same week you're launching your latest book *and* opening a bookstore?"

"It was the only opening he had in his schedule!"

"When the town also happens to be teeming with fans, movie executives, readers, and every other living being who could feasibly be called a member of the Tess Harrow Fan Club?"

This was taking things too far. "It's not my fault I draw a crowd. I'm very popular these days. There's even a murder podcast about me."

"Ohmigod, Mom." Gertrude sighed as she finished scanning the bamboo floor for other signs of rogue candy. The floor was brand new, courtesy of the renovations that had transformed the old hardware store into a boutique bookshop, but Tess wouldn't have eaten anything off it. Especially since she couldn't remember buying jelly beans at any point in the past six months. "The podcast isn't *about* you. It's about solving murders that the police haven't been able to figure out."

"What are you talking about? They mention me all the time."

Nicki snorted. "Yeah, as the bestselling hack who hacks people up to get a story."

"One time. They called me that *one time* before my publisher shut them down." Tess grabbed her purse, her expert eye running over the bookstore one last time. After six months of hard work, a deadline to meet, and way more murder than any woman should have to encounter in her lifetime, it was finally done. She'd always said that giving birth to Gertrude had been the greatest accomplishment of her life, but getting The Paper Trail up and running was a close second. She had no idea how Nora Roberts made owning a bookstore look so easy. "Besides, that's what this party is all about, remember? We're making murder fun again."

Gertrude snorted. "Just don't hang that on a sign above the door, and I think we might get away with it."

Tess did her best to ignore the wave of anxiety this remark brought up. Throwing a murder-themed party as a way to entice customers into her store wasn't the most traditional way of going about things, but there was a lot more at stake than peddling a few books. Ever since she'd been pulled into not one but two recent criminal investigations, her writing career had taken off in ways she'd never anticipated.

The book sales and movie deals? *Fantastic.*

The staggering advances her publisher was dangling to keep her happy? *Keep 'em coming.*

The fact that she was starting to earn a reputation as someone who put her friends and family members in harm's way for the sake of a story? *Not exactly the look she was going for.*

One online journal had called her The Black Widow, despite the fact that her ex-husband was still very much alive and kicking. Murder Mary had been the term coined by another journal, this time in reference to Typhoid Mary, a person Tess didn't enjoy being compared to at all. She took public health seriously, thank you very much, and was doing her best to *avoid* causing additional deaths. But worst of all was the one who'd labeled her a less-than-charming Jessica Fletcher.

"Imagine if America's beloved *Murder, She Wrote* heroine had been cast as a frumpy soccer mom who wouldn't know a good subplot if it bit her on the a—"

Tess had stopped reading after that. She could handle being compared to serial killers, but her subplots were *amazing*, thank you very much. And Gertrude hadn't played team sports a day in her life.

In an effort to counteract the negative press—
and, okay, to show that she wasn't nearly as frumpy
as some of the Associated Press photos made her
look—she'd decided to throw a party so *charming*
that not even the hardest-hearted journalist could
resist. Tomorrow morning, the bookstore would
open its doors for the very first time. Tess would
spend all day signing books and peddling her
wares, after which everyone was invited to attend
a murder-themed party with cupcakes that oozed
fake blood and sushi made to look like grotesque
body parts. Everyone would eat and drink and be
merry, and all under the watchful eye of the journalist Tess had—okay, *fine*—paid to be here. The
plan was practically fool-proof. As long as everyone
avoided eating floor jelly beans, she was sure the
event would be a success.

It would be a new stage in her life—hers and
Gertrude's both. With the bookstore opening in
town, they were putting down real, lasting roots.
The kind that would outlive a few best-selling
novels, that would boost the local economy in ways
everyone would benefit from.

Not even Typhoid Mary could boast of having
such an impact.

"Relax, Mom," Gertrude said, as if sensing the
sudden trend of Tess's thoughts. She bumped her
mother lightly with her hip. "We've been planning

this thing for months. As long as you feed me before I pass out from malnutrition, we have nothing to worry about."

Tess could take a hint when it was pouting up at her. Carefully locking the bookstore behind them, Tess ushered her daughter and her best friend down the quaint, old-fashioned main street toward the hotel.

The town of Winthrop was nothing if not dedicated to its Wild West theme. Every other storefront boasted a false front and rustic wooden slats, and she'd designed The Paper Trail to match. Some people might think it strange to live and work in a tourist trap that boasted fewer than five hundred residents, but Tess wasn't one of them. There was fresh air, a decent school district, and all her favorite people in the world.

In fact, as long as mysterious bodies stopped cropping everywhere she turned, she might even call it perfect.

———

"Dahling, there you are!"

As soon as Tess walked into the restaurant attached to the hotel, every instinct she had warned her to flee. That voice was a herald of doom, the death-knell to all her hopes and dreams, the one thing—outside of a fresh corpse—that had the power to break her.

And if there'd been any mistaking who it belonged to, Gertrude's sudden shout of, "Grandma!" would have been sure to tip her off.

Tess felt as though she was watching the scene unfold from underwater—or, at the very least, through a thick plate of Plexiglass that held the water at bay. Either way, the imminent threat of drowning was present.

"How many times have I told you not to call me that? Call me Bee like everyone else. Grandma makes me feel so old." Despite the stricture, Bernadette Springer opened her arms to engulf her favorite—and only—grandchild into an enthusiastic hug. She met Tess's eyes over the top of Gertrude's head, her expression bland. "Well, dear? Aren't you going to tell me you're happy to see me? And introduce me to your friend?"

Tess could only find it in her to comply with the second request. No one—least of all her mother—would buy the first.

"Mom, this is my good friend Nicki," Tess said, gesturing at the woman next to her. "Nicki, in case you can't tell, this is my mother. Call her Bee like everyone else. Grandma makes her feel old."

"Very funny, Tess," her mother said as she accepted Nicki's handshake. After one glance at the librarian, who looked more like Iman stepping off a catwalk than a small-town bookmobile driver, she nodded her approval. "I don't know why any of you insist on living in this godforsaken town. When Dad died, I'd hoped I'd seen the last of it. It doesn't improve much with age, does it?"

"Neither do you," Tess muttered under her breath. Only Nicki heard her, so only Nicki choked on a laugh.

"I didn't know you were coming for a visit," Gertrude said as she tucked herself in the crook of her grandmother's arm, which was clad in a pink Chanel suit that Tess knew well. Her mother had been wearing that suit in some form or another since the sixties. Not the *literal* same suit, since even her mother's painstaking care couldn't make tweed last forever, but one of the replicas she kept on rotation. *As Jackie would've done.* "Mom never said anything about it."

"That's because your mom wanted it to be a surprise, my pet," Bee said as she nuzzled her granddaughter's head. This time, her eyes held a look of stern warning. Tess interpreted that warning as it was intended; namely, to pretend that she had any prior knowledge of her mother's descent upon the town. Bee had never been a communicative parent, especially regarding her whereabouts, but Tess was happy to play along. She had her mother had never seen eye-to-eye on anything except Gertrude.

According to Bernadette Springer, thrice-divorced attorney-at-law and general pain in Tess's backside, Tess had lousy taste in men and questionable fashion sense. Her career was a fluke, her personal life a shambles. Nothing she'd ever done had been good enough for the Springer family line… with the exception of bringing into it a child as intelligent and full of life as Gertrude.

"When I heard your mother was throwing a big gala in celebration of her new book, wild horses couldn't keep me away," Bee said with another of those stern looks. "She knows how much I love a gala."

"Gala is an awfully strong word," Tess said, her heart sinking. Since her mother sat on the boards of no fewer than three national charitable organizations, *gala* was a loaded term. Emphasis on the loaded. "I'd call it more of a light party."

Bee arched one of her eyebrows. They were thin and villainous, the inevitable outcome of the over-plucking trend of the 1990s, but the style had always suited her. If anyone looked like she planned to skin a pack of Dalmatians in the pursuit of high fashion, it was this woman. "You'll be wearing a dress?"

"Yes, but I draw the line at pantyhose, so don't even try."

Bee conveniently ignored this. "Food?"

"Of course. Gertie is doing most of the catering."

"Champagne?"

"Technically, it's more of a sparkling wine."

Not even this blow could quell her mother's fervor. "If it looks like a gala and tastes like a gala, then I'm calling it a gala. Now. Where are we having dinner tonight?"

Tess recognized this as the double-edged question it was. Most people would take one look at the scene around them, with wagon wheels arranged artfully on the walls and the mounted animal heads looking them over, and assume dinner would take the shape of a fifteen-ounce steak brought out on the end of a pitchfork. Which, incidentally, was what Tess had been looking forward to all day. Her mother's distastefully wrinkled nose broadcast what she thought of such a rustic offering.

Fortunately, Gertrude came to the rescue before any lines of battle could be drawn.

"We're eating here, of course," the girl said without a trace of irony. "They have the best burgers in town. You can get a regular burger, a buffalo burger, or, if you're really lucky, one of the chef's specials."

"This place has a *chef*?"

Gertrude giggled and began dragging her grandmother toward a booth near the back. It was located underneath the scraggly visage of an elk who'd long ago lost one of its glossy black eyes. "Well, he's more of an enthusiastic amateur, but it still counts.

If you guess which animal was ground up to make the special burger, you get it for free. I was super close last time. I said ostrich, but it was really yak."

The look that Bee cast over her shoulder at Tess was one that she planned to store up and protect in her heart for years to come. *Save me*, that look said. *This child of yours is an abomination against nature.* Tess only waggled her fingers playfully at her. If her mother was going to start popping up in town unannounced and sporting a haircut that looked like a shellacked helmet from a sixties time capsule, then she could eat an ostrich. Or a yak.

"Sorry about this," Tess said with an apologetic grimace at Nicki. "If you'd rather cry off for dinner, I'd totally understand. I don't know if you can tell, but my mother is a bit…much."

"Are you kidding?" Nicki led the way toward the table with a grin that boded ill for the meal to come. "The great Tess Harrow has a mother? Like *that*? I wouldn't miss this for anything."

"Don't say I didn't warn you." Tess loped after her, but her steps felt as heavy as her stomach. "The last time she visited us was when we lived in Seattle. We ended up having to entirely rebuild the west side of the house. That was her *Breakfast at Tiffany's* phase. She always forgot to check if her cigarette holder was extinguished before bed."

"And what phase is this?"

Tess set her mouth in a grim line. "Ask me again in an hour. From the look of things, we're going full Jackie-O."

———

Not for nothing was Tess Harrow a thriller writer who specialized in twisty murder mysteries. It didn't take her the full hour to uncover the clues and figure out her mother's newest obsession; it took twenty minutes.

"Oh, God. It's Elizabeth Taylor," she hissed in a low voice to Nicki, who'd been sitting with a grin splitting her features the entire time she'd been watching the three generations interact. "The size of her earrings, that helmet of hair, the way she keeps drawing out every syllable... I'll bet you a million dollars her luggage contains nothing but girdles and necklaces as big as your head."

"Since I know you actually have the bank account to back that bet up, there's no way I'm taking it," Nicki hissed back. "Besides—what's wrong with Elizabeth Taylor? I always thought she seemed like she'd be a lot of fun at parties."

Tess agreed, which was the exact problem. Having a silver screen goddess as a party guest was great; having one as a mother was an entirely different ordeal. Especially when the party in question was supposed to be providing Tess with an aura of respectability. Her mother putting on the airs of a famously impetuous, outspoken personality was about as far from respectable as you could get.

"I'm not sure this salad is agreeing with me," Bee said. She creaked back against the vinyl booth seat and lifted her napkin delicately to her lips. "There's something off about the dressing."

"Do you want to try some of my burger instead?" Gertrude offered as she held up a red, oozing piece of meat that even Tess shuddered to look at. "I've got it narrowed down to moose or kangaroo, but I'm leaning toward the second one. How hard do you think it is to import meat from Australia?"

"If you love me, Gertie, please don't ask me that right now."

Since Bee really did look green around the gills, Tess slid along the booth to let her mom out. "The bathroom's around the corner and through the swinging saloon doors," she said. "If you hit the spittoon statue, you've gone too far."

Her mother's look of leveled scorn said everything she felt about spittoons, no matter how artfully they'd been arranged. "This had better not be an attempt at poisoning me to get me out of the way for your party," she said. "I'm not as easy to kill off as one of the characters in your books."

"That's not a bad idea, actually," Tess mused as

she watched her mother's determined march in the direction of the bathroom. "There are several poisons that would knock her out for a few days without actually killing her. Strychnine is a definite no-go, and there's no way I'm playing around with cyanide. But something gentler…ipecac, maybe. Or eye drops in her coffee. I've always wanted to try that one."

"Mom! We're not poisoning Grandma."

Tess waved her hands like a magician showing off her trick. "Maybe I already have. Maybe you should be careful not to eat any of that dressing."

Nicki swept a pinkie finger through the white, gelatinous tub that sat on the edge of Bee's garden salad. Popping it into her mouth, she said, "There. Now if your mom dies, I'm going out with her." She paused and picked up the ramekin with a wince. "Actually, there's something seriously wrong with this ranch. I hope Cyrus didn't leave it out overnight again."

Discussing poisons and room-temperature mayo-based dressings went a long way in suppressing what remained of Tess's appetite, but Gertrude attacked her burger with renewed vigor.

"It's not sweet enough to be moose," she said, chewing thoughtfully. "And there's a bit of earthiness in the aftertaste. I'm officially going with kangaroo."

Since Gertrude had yet to successfully guess the mystery meat despite their weekly trip into town to make the attempt, Tess wasn't optimistic about her chances of a cheap meal. Not that it mattered when Gertrude bolted upright in her seat, the burger falling to her plate with a wet *thwap*.

"I think one of us should go check on Grandma," she said, her voice so thin and tight that it sounded as though it had been strung on a wire. "You won't believe who just walked in the door."

"Richard Burton?" Tess guessed, naming the most famous of Elizabeth Taylor's seven husbands.

Nicki snorted. "John Warner?"

"Eddie Fisher?"

"This is serious." Gertrude flapped her hand in a gesture Tess recognized as a request to borrow her phone. "I'm pretty sure that's Levi Parker."

"Who?" Tess asked. She handed Gertrude the phone and twisted to get a look at their mystery visitor, but her daughter kicked her under the table. With a howl of protest, Tess clutched at her injured shin. "There's no need to be so drastic, Gertie. I was going to be discreet."

Nicki laughed. "Tess, you haven't done a discreet thing a day of your life."

There was no time for Tess to defend herself before Gertrude dropped the phone in her lap and pretended to be busy playing with a straw wrapper.

"Wait—I can't google his photo yet. He's coming this way. Act natural."

"I *am* acting natural. You're the one who's suddenly all weird and fangirly over a random stranger. Is he one of those influencers you're obsessed with? Is that what this is about?"

"Mom! Levi Parker isn't on Instagram. He's—"

"A notorious murderer with a penchant for elderly widows," a smooth male voice said from behind them. "I'm flattered you recognized me so easily. What was it that gave me away? The glasses? The tie? The face?"

At that, Tess had no qualms about turning around and taking thorough stock of this Levi Parker character. His glasses were ordinary enough, if a little too round for his face, and his tie was one of those skinny black ones that always made men look like door-to-door salesmen, but the real draw was the face. Tess wasn't sure she'd ever seen such a symmetrical collection of features before. Gently wisping crow's feet and a touch of gray at his temples put him at around her own age—midforties and inching on up—but that was where all signs of aging stopped. His tawny skin was flawless, his eyebrows like a pair of perfectly groomed pipe cleaners. A thin mustache last pulled off by Clark Gable quivered on his upper lip, and his eyes sparkled a deep, golden color that seemed unnatural by the dim lights of the restaurant.

By this time, Gertrude managed to change her expression of surprise to one of belligerent challenge instead. Tess almost pitied the poor man who was about to be on the receiving end of it. That expression had once caused Tess to throw out her favorite pair of gladiator sandals—a five-hundred-dollar strappy masterpiece that had made her legs look incredible. *It's fine*, Gertie had said at the time. *Wear them. Just as long as you want everyone to know you peaked ten years ago.*

"It was your face," Gertrude said, staring sullenly up at the feature in question. "You're all over the murder podcast fan boards. So people know who to look out for when their grandmothers go missing."

"Wait. You're *that* Levi Parker?" Nicki asked. "I thought you were still in—" She cut herself off with a start, but it was too late. The man fell into a rich peal of laughter.

"Rikers?" He grinned. "Nah. A prison like that has enough overcrowding without holding onto an innocent man. I got out months ago. Did I hear you say your grandmother is missing?"

"She's not missing," Gertrude said with a set of her jaw. "She's indisposed at the moment. And if you go anywhere near her, I'll—"

"Levi, dahling! There you are." Bernadette came out of the bathroom looking none the worse for wear. In fact, the sight of the newcomer seemed to revitalize her. She practically threw herself into his arms, her squeal girlish as it curled up to meet him.

"I've been so lonely without you," Tess's mother cooed. "You should've called me when your flight got in."

"And ruin the surprise?" Levi lifted Bee's hand to his lips and left a wet, lingering kiss on the surface. "You know me…the mystery is half the fun. I like to keep my victims on their toes."

Mention of the word *victim* caused Gertrude to shoot up out of her seat, but Bernadette only dissolved further into his arms. "Oh, you naughty boy. My granddaughter is present."

"Not only is she present, but she's calling the police. Grandma, did you know that this man is wanted for the murder of two women in New York and one in Detroit? That doesn't even count the theory that he was in Sedona a few months ago when—"

"Oh, he was definitely in Sedona a few months ago," Bernadette said with a laugh. "We met on a healing retreat back in June. The crystals in those mountains have incredible powers. One night, we slept in an energy vortex so strong that—"

Levi squeezed Tess's mother hard enough to cause the older woman to squeak. "I wouldn't say we did much sleeping out there, Bee."

"No." Planting her feet, Gertrude crossed her arms and took what could only be called a literal *stand.* "Something's wrong. He belongs behind bars. They don't just let people walk out of prison like that."

"Actually, they do if they don't have reason enough to hold them," Nicki said with an apologetic shrug. "Sorry, Gertie."

To an outsider, Nicki was just a well-informed librarian sharing her knowledge of the world, but both Tess and Gertrude knew better. If Nicki said something fell within the bounds of justice system, it did.

"Oh, that." Bee scoffed. "It was nothing more than a misunderstanding. Levi was in the wrong place at the wrong time. You know all about that sort of thing, Tess."

It was true. She *did* know all about that. She also knew that being in a relationship with a dangerous man was no walk in the park—it was more of a walk in the deep, dark woods.

"Those podcasts of yours love to play him up as the villain, but it's nonsense," Bee added. "It's all just storytelling. Isn't that right, Levi?"

Levi's eyes met Tess's in a quick challenge. "I think everyone here knows the power of a compelling story."

Tess wasn't sure what to make of this. On the one hand, she wholeheartedly agreed. Stories had the power to change hearts and minds, to reveal terrors and truths that might otherwise be closed to the human heart.

On the other hand, she didn't particularly care for potential murderers who were dating her mother.

"Well, I'm not ready to call it a night yet," Bee said as though they were discussing a quiet family evening rather than a walking, talking serial killer in their midst. "What do you say we head into the bar for a nightcap, cookie?"

It took Tess a moment to realize the cookie in question wasn't her.

"That sounds perfect," Levi murmured. He lifted one eyebrow in a debonair move that Tess had only ever assumed existed in novels. "Would you ladies care to join us?"

"My mom doesn't socialize with killers, thanks," Gertrude answered for them. "And I'm a *kid*. I can't drink at a bar."

Instead of taking offense, Levi chuckled and titled his head in a question for Nicki. "Fair enough. What about you? The invitation's an open one."

It said a lot about Tess's friendship with Nicki that the other woman immediately agreed. She'd no more abandon Tess's mother to her fate than she would her own. "That sounds nice, actually," Nicki said. "I hope you don't mind, but I'm a big fan of your podcast. Or, er, the podcast about you. Gertie and I listen to it every week."

"Excellent," Levi said with a flash of his teeth. They were perfectly white and straight except for his eyeteeth, which were angled just enough to give him the look of a vampire. He crooked both his elbows, one for Bee and one for Nicki. Bee's expression flickered in annoyance at having a third wheel, but Tess didn't care. What kind of a woman brought her much-younger murderous lover on a visit to her family?

"Don't let him out of your sight, Nicki," Gertrude warned as she watched the trio prepare to depart. "And see if you can get him to leave you his glass when he's done. So you can get his saliva and fingerprints."

Levi chuckled again, this time with an infectious charm that even Tess felt herself warming up to. "Bless you, child. Those things have been on record since I was younger than you." He winked. "If it makes you feel any better, I promise to send your grandmother home before midnight. I wouldn't want my Cinderella turning into a pumpkin."

"That's not how the story works," Gertrude muttered, but Tess doubted anyone heard her—or that it mattered. As Levi led his prey away, the girl turned to Tess and set her jaw. "Mom, pay the bill and follow me. We're going to the sheriff's office. *Now.*"

About the Author

Tamara Berry is the author of the By the Book Mysteries series, the Eleanor Wilde cozy series and, under the pen name Lucy Gilmore, the Forever Home contemporary romance series. Also a freelance writer and editor, she has a bachelor's degree in English literature and a serious penchant for Nancy Drew novels. She lives in Bigfoot country (a.k.a. Eastern Washington) with her family and their menagerie of pets.

Find her online at tamaraberry.com
facebook.com/TamaraBerryAuthor
Twitter: @Tamara_Morgan
Instagram: @tamaratamaralucy